Bound by Oath and Honour

by

Debbie Peterson

Bound by Oath and Honour Series

Bound by Oath and Honour

Contact Information: info@thewildrosepress.com

Cover Art by *Debbie Taylor*

The Wild Rose Press, Inc.
PO Box 708
Adams Basin, NY 14410-0708
Visit us at www.thewildrosepress.com

Publishing History
First Fantasy Rose Edition, 2016
Print ISBN 978-1-5092-0633-9
Digital ISBN 978-1-5092-0634-6

Bound by Oath and Honour Series
Published in the United States of America

"I'm not leaving until you tell me whatever it is you don't want me to know." She set her heels, and placed a hand on her hip.

His anger flared. "Is that right? A little while ago you couldn't wait to leave this place."

Tala gave her head a snooty little toss. "A lot has changed since then, wouldn't you agree?"

He brushed the barb aside. "Then let me get you a pillow and blanket. You can make yourself comfortable on my sofa."

Indignation filled her lovely eyes. "That's it? That's all you're going to say? Really?"

Micah met her gaze without a flinch. "Really."

"Whatever." She gave him a curt nod and stormed toward the door.

He had fallen into the deep, dark abyss of the feminine *whatever*. Nonetheless, he stepped in front of the entryway blocking her path. "Where are you going, Tala?"

"Back inside the forest, not that it's any of your business."

"Why would you do something as foolish as that?"

"To find some answers, since you're unwilling to share what you know." She gritted her teeth. "Now, get out of my way."

He held his ground while disregarding the directive. "Just what do you expect to find out there?"

She shrugged away the question. "I'm not sure. However, I do know those creatures left tracks. I'm quite adept at finding and following them to wherever they might lead. Trust me."

"Regardless of the danger?"

"I can take care of myself."

Praise for Debbie Peterson's
COURT OF THE HAWK

"A lovely multi-layered tale that combines romance, myth and mystery in a gripping story that had me eagerly flipping pages in my Kindle. From the rich historical legends to the gorgeously-detailed settings and, especially, the enchanting characters who populate the worlds Ms. Peterson creates, this novel is beautifully beguiling."

~Author Mae Clair

~*~

"Such a great story that reads like a fairytale. Immerse yourself in this beautiful love story filled with magic, romance adventure and danger. No cliffhangers which is a nice bonus."

~Paranormal Romance and Authors That Rock

~*~

"There is so much to love in this book for me—ancient tales, mythology, Wales, soul mates, true love, flirty ghosts, spoiled princesses, dastardly deeds, you name it. What you get is a book that is as engrossing as it is interesting. You will turn each page and gasp at the wonder held within those words. This is storytelling as its best."

~Archaeolibrarian—I dig good books! blog

~*~

"Debbie is definitely one of my FAVORITE authors! I recommend ANYTHING she has written!"

~I love to Read and Review Books Blog

Dedication

To Michael and Betty,
for the laughter and the joy you bring to my heart!

Chapter One

In a dreadful turn of events, whomever she pursued into the murky forest now hunted her, and with determination bent on success. Why on earth did she chase someone off the property after dusk anyway? Her heart pounded from the exertion to escape the woodland, and her lungs burned for lack of air. Any moment they would surely burst inside her chest, and right now her legs weighed a ton. What's more, she didn't know if she sprinted toward Westbrook Manor and the safety it promised, or in another direction altogether.

Tala whipped her head from side to side and then shot a glance behind her shoulder in search of her pursuers. All the while, the need to outrun the danger nipped at her heels. Branches creaked and leaves moaned as they pitched back and forth. Did they sway from the cool autumn wind or from the relentless shadows that followed? She didn't know and right this minute it didn't matter as much as getting out of this eerie forest.

No more than thirty seconds passed before her exhausted body insisted she pause and catch her breath. She huddled behind a tree surrounded by thick vegetation. By the time she recovered enough to stand and resume her journey, the sound of approaching footsteps halted her escape. She froze mid-flight.

Multiple sets of footsteps advanced uncomfortably close to her inadequate shelter. Voices whispered. She strained to listen as she dropped to a knee. Yet, their guttural inflection made it impossible for her to understand a single thing they said.

They conducted their search for what seemed like hours instead of minutes. All the while she prayed they would pass on by. Then one of her pursuers approached and swatted at the branches mere inches from her face. After one intense moment, the snap of dry branches somewhere behind the ruffian caught his attention. He whipped around toward the sound. In so doing, he kicked up a cloud of dust that assailed her nostrils. Just as she covered her mouth to smother the cough she couldn't control, a hail of gunfire echoed through the forest. The rapid blasts caused a moment of sheer pandemonium for her as well as those who pursued her.

Amidst the panic, her stalkers scattered in every direction possible. She too, bounded to her feet and took off running. Self-preservation kicked in. "Flee the forest" shouted over and over inside her mind. Tala didn't assess the direction or the origin of the commotion. She just ran. Amidst the commotion, the thunderous footsteps necessitated the need to look over her shoulder.

Twice.

Bewildered at best, she took in a breath and held onto it. For all of the trees, she didn't know which way to go or how she would escape the forest. She gazed off to her right and then her left seeking any kind of opening or path.

****

Bizarre images swirled around inside her head.

Tala couldn't make sense of them. In fact, at this precise moment, she couldn't make sense of anything. However, she could hear someone speaking. She didn't recognize the voice of the man who spoke.

"Is she going to be all right?"

"Yes, I think so. She just took a bump on the head," said a second male voice, far richer in timbre than the first. "Albeit a nasty one."

"So it appears. That's quite a bruise she has there. What happened?"

"In paying more attention to the threat behind her, she didn't pay attention to the very large tree in front of her," he said.

His companion laughed. "So tell me, why did this very lovely lady venture into the forest all by herself, anyway?"

The man blew out a scornful snort. "So she could get into more trouble than what she could possibly get out of without assistance."

Trouble? What in the world did they prattle on about? Tala struggled for a memory and finally found one. She had arrived in England four weeks earlier. As a favor for a friend, she took some photos of the wild falcons that settled into a more remote area of her land. Once she completed the task, her father asked if she would take a couple of extra weeks and assess the condition of the old family estate in county Staffordshire. She began by taking detailed pictures of the sixteenth century manor house inside and out. The other structures on the property received the same attention as well. For all of the damage, the tedious chore took the entire afternoon. Then just as dusk dimmed the early evening sky, a series of strange noises

3

caught her attention. So did the feeling that someone watched every move she made.

She looked for the cause and found a man-sized shadow skulking near the carriage house. Without giving a whole lot of thought to the consequences— okay, she didn't give any thought whatsoever to the consequences—she rushed headlong toward the shadow. Although she couldn't see the person responsible for that shadow, she hollered out he trespassed on private property. She demanded he tell her his purpose. He didn't answer. The intruder simply tore off running. She followed him through the open gate. Big mistake. After she entered into the deepest parts of the forest, the shadows multiplied. So did the number of footsteps that converged in her direction. But then, just before they discovered her hiding place, someone shot off several rounds from a rifle. Did the gang of ruffians want her dead?

No. That couldn't be right. Those who pursued her took off when the blasts sounded off as well. When she turned around and looked for the cause, she could swear she saw—

"Well, I guess I'll go ahead and take my leave. I do have other duties to attend to as you might recall. I'm sure you don't want to keep me from them," said the first voice.

"Really, Josiah?" The tone of the second dripped with scorn.

Another chuckle. "Don't be so bitter, Micah. We've all had assignments we'd rather not have had. The ealdormen just gave you a turn at one, that's all. But look at it this way; it could have been so much worse—"

Assignment? Ealdormen? What in the world did he mean by all of that?

"I believe you said you had somewhere to go, didn't you? Please don't let me keep you from your errands, duties, or whatever it is makes you so hard-pressed for time."

The snide comment made the man named Josiah laugh. Tala opened her eyes just enough to peek through her lashes and take in what she could without moving her head. She didn't recognize the antiquated cottage with its massive oak ceiling beams and faded plaster walls all but void of decorations. That, coupled with the odor of stale, musty air made her wary. From what she could see of the tall, broad-shouldered man who gazed out of the window, she didn't know him, nor had she ever seen him before. She didn't see any evidence as to his companion within the small sitting room either. But, where did the other man go? She didn't hear a door open or close—or even footsteps for that matter. Something just didn't seem right.

"You needn't put such effort into holding so still, Miss Westbrook. I know you're awake. Rest assured I'm not here to hurt you. If I wanted to do that, the deed would already have been done," the brawny man said without turning around. He sounded bored and for some unknown reason, that irritated her.

Tala tossed the homespun quilt off to the side. She sat up and dropped her feet onto the floor. Her fingers dabbed at the tender lump on the left side of her forehead. "Who are you and how do you know my name?"

"The name is Micah Berrington and—at least when

5

you whack your head hard enough—you talk in your sleep."

She dropped her hand on top of her thigh and huffed out a breath. "You expect me to believe I said my name in my sleep?"

Finally, he turned around and faced her. The moment his dark brown eyes connected with hers, her heart spun in wild circles. A swarm of bothersome butterflies, buried deep within her belly, took flight.

Handsome. Dark. Mysterious.

The words swirled around inside her mind as the man, dressed in black from head to toe, took a couple of slow steps toward her. All the while, her insides churned in a simple response to his mere presence. In an irrational way she couldn't explain, that increased her level of irritation as well.

"Believe whatever you wish."

She ignored the comment. "If you don't mind my asking, just where am I?"

"Not all that far from Westbrook Manor."

"How very informative."

In a show of exasperation, he took in a deep breath. Then with a bit of force, he blew it out again. "You're sitting on my sofa, inside my home—or, at least you're inside the residence I use when I'm in the area." He sounded bored again.

She gave him a nod and then turned her gaze toward the door. "Good enough. If you'll point me in the proper direction, I'll get out of your way and leave you to what's left of your evening."

He raked his hand through the length of dark brown hair that fell several inches below his collar in attractive, feathery waves. "Don't be ridiculous. I'm not about to let you go out there all by yourself. By now your friends have regrouped. They're probably waiting for you to show up so they can have another go at you."

Tala narrowed her eyes. "You think you can hold me here against my will?"

Again the question annoyed him. She could see it in the firm set of his finely chiseled jaw.

"Perish the thought. I merely meant that I would make sure you made it safely to your vehicle, Miss Westbrook. From there, you can go anywhere you choose.

She rose from her seat on the sofa, more than a little annoyed herself. "I don't need or want an escort, *Mr. Berrington.* I'm quite capable of getting back to the estate without assistance from you or anyone else for that matter."

"But I insist. I would never forgive myself if you encountered someone or something that hindered your journey."

Some "thing?" Did he see that strange creature too? She could see it so clearly inside her mind. Yet she still couldn't make sense of the image. That—that huge, mangy, wolf-like beast *stood up* on his hind legs and *ran...*

"Something?" she repeated.

He advanced another step and shrugged. "You could encounter all sorts of peril on your way back to the property. We've had reports of wild dogs in the area. There exists an abundance of adder snakes and gnarly roots. Even the trunk from an ancient tree might impede your journey."

"Very funny." She swept past him. Yet, before she could grasp the door handle, he had it in his hand.

He shook his head ever so slightly. "I'm sorry. I didn't mean any offense with the remark."

By expression alone, she could see he didn't. The man simply sought a way to lessen the tension between them. That sudden perception made her feel a little foolish and a whole lot ungrateful. He did save her from a harrowing situation, after all. She dropped her gaze toward the floor, took in a breath, and let it go alongside her animosity. Once again, she gazed into his eyes. This time, she managed a bit of a smile. "No, I'm the one who should apologize. I haven't thanked you for coming to my rescue. So, if you'll indulge the whim, I'd like to begin again?"

Micah said nothing in return. He merely cocked his head to the side and waited for her to speak.

She assumed an expression of aristocratic refinement, and then dipped both head and knees in a playful curtsey. "Hello, my name is Tala Westbrook. I'm here conducting a bit of family business for and in behalf of my father, Curtis Westbrook, and you are?"

Just a trace of humor entered his eyes. He returned the gesture with a slight bow. "Micah Berrington, at your service, my lady."

She breathed out a laugh after his very old-fashioned, but gallant reply. "Really, Micah, I'm normally not this rude. With that being said, I'd like to thank you for your help this evening. I hate to think of what might've happened out there if you hadn't come along when you did."

"Think nothing of it." He stepped back, opened the door, and waited while she stepped over the threshold ahead of him. While she lingered on the porch, he retrieved his high-powered rifle propped next to the doorway. He then joined her outside. Though she eyed the weapon, she didn't ask him why he thought it necessary to bring it along. Why bother?

****

At the end of the cobblestone walkway, they turned left, opposite the woodland. For a moment, Tala looked back at the trees in the distance. As she returned her gaze to him, Micah detected a bit of confusion, mingled with curiosity in those compelling, violet blue depths. So she did see them then. Most unfortunate. Yet, at least this far, she hadn't asked him about the malevolent shifters that inhabited the area. He would rather avoid the topic and the presence of the Gehíwan rebels altogether if at all possible. Since her intended visit should only last a few more weeks, he just might achieve that goal if he could keep her out of the forest. If luck remained his ally, he could conclude this tiresome assignment the moment she boarded her return flight to the United States. That suited him fine.

"Do you visit your cottage often, then?"

Her words sliced into his thoughts. "Excuse me?"

"I believe you said you lived at the cottage only when you were in the area. I assume from the bare shelves and the thick coat of dust on your furniture you've only just arrived?"

"I can see where you might assume something like that." His response coincided with a distant howl. Another, much closer to their position, answered the call. Tala halted her steps. She whirled around again and faced the woodland.

"Wolves are extinct in England and have been for ages," she hissed amidst the sudden chorus that all but surrounded them.

9

"Yes, they are."

She aimed her thumb toward the forest as she gazed at him. "Then how do you explain that?"

"As I said before, we've had numerous reports of wild dogs in the area and we've had them for quite some time now."

She shot a glance at the trees and opened her mouth. Without saying a word, she shut it again.

"Come on," he said before she changed her mind. He didn't want her asking the questions he didn't have any desire to answer. "We're within a stone's throw of the estate. Let's get you safely to your car before they get any closer, shall we? A pack of wild dogs can pose a danger if they're hungry enough."

She gave her head a little shake as she resumed their journey. "I'm not going to my car, Micah. I'm staying at the manor while I'm here."

He strode ahead of her steps and then blocked her path as he turned around. "You can't be serious. After what happened out there just a short while ago?"

A lengthy pause followed his question. All the while she pinned her gaze to his. "Exactly what did happen out there this evening—from your perspective?"

That set him back on his heels. How could he respond without revealing what he would rather not reveal? "I'm not sure. The darkness prevented me from seeing much of anything. However, I did see you running. I clearly noted the uproar that followed. From all appearances, you had encountered a bit of trouble in the forest. Therefore, I thought you could use some help."

She considered his explanation far longer than he thought necessary. Somewhere along the way, she lifted her shoulders and assumed an expression of concession. "And you were right. How fortunate for me you just happened to have carried a gun during your evening stroll."

"Most of the residents in this area hunt deer on a regular basis. Encountering a man with a rifle this time of year isn't at all unusual, I assure you. But that's a little off the current subject, isn't it?"

"Off the subject?"

"We were discussing your choice of temporary residence. All things considered, don't you think the best course of action is to avoid handing those men another opportunity to cause you harm?"

"Well, in order to harm me, *if* that's their intention, they'd first have to have returned to the house. Secondly, they'd have to get through a secured gate. Third, they would then have to enter a house that's locked up tight. Wouldn't you agree?" Without waiting for a reply, she stepped to the side and headed for the manor without him.

With nothing to do but follow, he rolled his eyes heavenward and silently bemoaned his fate. Why did they assign him a woman and why this woman in particular? He'd never fared well with the opposite sex—and especially not with the obstinate, troublesome, sort. He sought a different tactic.

"Is the house even livable? From all reports, the place has been all but vacant for decades."

"We've had a tenant or two along the way. Therefore, it can't be all bad, I'm sure." She turned to face him as they arrived at their destination. "Look, you needn't worry about me. I'll be fine I promise. Again, I want to thank you for your timely assistance. If we ever

11

run into each other again, I hope it's under much better circumstances."

Though she meant to dismiss him with her little spiel, he gazed pointedly at the wide-open, black-iron gates. "You know, I think I'd feel better about leaving you alone if I checked the place out before I leave. As you just so clearly brought to my attention, your friends might've indeed, returned in your absence."

His resolve irritated her. He could see it in her eyes. Nonetheless, she invited him to enter with a wave of her hand, but refrained from speaking. All the better—he didn't have any patience for idle chitchat.

"Why don't we start with the house? If I find all well there, you can lock and bolt the doors as I leave. I'll secure the gate after I've made a thorough sweep of the property, all right?"

"Fine." She conveyed her agitation by flicking a wayward lock of her long, golden-brown hair behind her shoulder.

Micah took the lead. The presence of the Gehíwans this close to the manor, coupled with her refusal to leave the premises, complicated his task far beyond what he had first supposed. Still, he just had to get the woman through the next two weeks unscathed. He could then leave this place and await his next assignment. He strode up the steps. Once he arrived at the door, he spared her a glance as he extended his hand toward the latch.

"Actually, the front door *isn't* locked," she said. "I left in rather a hurry."

"Well—at least it saves them the trouble of breaking it down, then, doesn't it?"

In response to the jibe, she simply huffed out a

breath. She clamped down on her teeth, and refused to look at him as he entered the house. Despite her indignation, she remained but a single step behind him. Once inside, she flipped the switch that provided meager light to the musty entrance hall. From the foyer, they wandered into the drawing room. Dust covered the tables. The faded rose colored upholstery on the Victorian-styled sofas and chairs had seen far better days. Worn draperies filtered light through the windows. He well understood the reason the locals deemed the place haunted.

Micah checked all of the closets on his way to the dining room, kitchen, bathrooms, and library. He found nothing one wouldn't expect to see in an old deserted house. Yet, the moment he took hold of the stairway banister, the putrid aura of an undesirable presence assailed him. At least one shifter, and more likely two, awaited Tala's return at the top of the stairs in their animal persona of choice.

After he chambered a round in his rifle, he placed a finger against the trigger. He faced Tala with lifted hand and palm out. "Wait here while I check out the second floor."

She gazed at him for several moments as if he had quite lost his mind. "I think not. In case you have forgotten, this house belongs to *my* family, Micah, not yours."

"I will *not* debate the issue with you right now. Either you can wait here as directed, or I will throw you over my shoulder and carry you back to the cottage. I'll then lock you inside for the remainder of the night. The choice is yours."

She sucked in a breath while her mouth dropped

another notch. "You wouldn't—"

"Oh, but I would," he whispered as he leaned in close to her face.

In evidence of his staunch determination, she gritted her teeth. She turned her head to the side. Once again, she refused to meet his gaze. "Fine."

The dreaded "fine" escaped her lips for the second time in less than ten minutes. This one had a bit more oomph and resentment behind it than did the first. He ignored it. Instead, Micah turned his attention away from her little snit fit and focused on the task ahead. The anarchists didn't have the ability to hear his steps, or detect his presence. That gave him the advantage right now. He climbed the stairs and stopped at the landing. The hallway extended in both directions. The layout of the house provided the Gehíwan thugs a variety of rooms in which they could hide. Yet without doubt, they had secreted themselves in one of the rooms to his left. He moved down the hallway. With each step he took, the strength of their stench increased. The foul odor led him to the last door at the end of the hallway, right-hand side. Once the turn of the knob alerted them to his presence, they would attack. He knew from past experience the rebels had every intention of ripping out Tala's throat—or something far worse.

He raised his rifle shoulder-high and kicked open the door. A wolf lunged at him. A split second later, a large panther with teeth bared, leaped over the chair to his right. He downed the wolf with a blast of his gun. Just as he cocked the rifle, the extended claws of the cat raked down the length of his arm. The attempt to disarm him didn't work.

During the melee, Tala screamed his name. She

bounded up the stairs in the same instant his booted foot connected to the cat's chest. The powerful impact thrust the agitated panther against the wall. With a single shot, Micah dispatched the shifter through the gates of hell where he could reside alongside his despicable companion.

Tala grabbed hold of the doorjamb and halted her steps. Her eyes widened as she gazed at the carcasses sprawled out on the floor. The sight rendered her speechless. Excellent. He had only a matter of minutes before the animal personas disappeared and their human form returned. The woman didn't need to witness that.

"I'll just get the bodies out of here before they make a mess on your floor." He grabbed hold of the wolf and tossed him over his shoulder with the sure knowledge the remaining shifters weren't anywhere near the manor.

In less than five minutes, he had the house cleared of assassins. He then made ready to leave. All throughout the process, Tala remained silent. With a hand on the doorknob, he turned and faced her. "I'll secure the gate. Make sure you have all entry doors bolted and locked as well. You might want to check all of the windows before—"

"Micah," she gasped as her horrified gaze locked onto his arm. "You're hurt."

He glanced at the injury himself. "No, it's just a scratch. You needn't concern yourself."

She shook her head as she leaned forward and assessed the damage. "That's more than a scratch. Your skin is in shreds. You have blood all over what's left of your sleeve. Come into the kitchen and let me take a look at it. I think you'll need stitches. There's a medical kit in the pantry. I also have one in my car if the one inside doesn't have the—"

"That won't be necessary. The wound isn't as serious as it looks. I'll be just fine," he said as he stepped outside. "Stay indoors and don't forget to lock and bolt *all* of the doors, all right?"

He shut the door before she responded or argued the point. Right now, he didn't have time to listen to either.

Chapter Two

Tala stared at the door for heaven only knew how long before the hands of her internal clock resumed. Once rational thought returned, she went over the events of what had just transpired many times over. Nothing made sense. How could both a wolf and a panther—creatures that most assuredly would not roam together in the wild—get through two closed doors and end up in an upstairs bedroom? Had they escaped from someone who kept them as exotic pets? But even if that were so, how did they get into the house? Better yet, how did they trap themselves behind a bedroom door? Micah somehow knew they were there. But how did he know that?

Micah.

The very thought of that man, despite his inexplicable, powerful magnetism—which she clearly wanted nothing to do with—set her teeth on edge. Just exactly what gave him the right to treat her like a child? What made him think he could bark out orders he demanded she obey without question? Worse yet, he did it as a guest in her house. She seethed as she recalled his threat to toss her over his shoulder. The moment he uttered his obnoxious ultimatum, she didn't doubt he could—and would—carry it out without effort. That fact made her even angrier.

Yet, despite his lack of charm, that ultimatum just

might've saved her life at the risk of his own. By all indications, a risk he anticipated. Why did he do that? They were little more than strangers. Didn't that carry old-fashioned gallantry just a bit too far? More important, what did he hear or see inside the house she missed? She headed straight for the ornate hand-carved staircase since that's where she and Micah parted company. A thorough examination of the railings and balusters yielded nothing out of the ordinary. Not even a stray hair from the animals' coats attached itself to a wayward splinter along the way. If Micah caught sight of any paw prints on the stairway carpet, their own footsteps quite obliterated them.

Tala stepped onto the landing and glanced over her shoulder. She then turned left. Her footsteps slowed as she approached the shattered casing around the bedroom door; a door which now hung precariously on its hinges. She stood for a moment in the hallway before she ventured inside. The windows drew her attention first. She scrutinized each of them in turn. They were all closed and locked. The curtains didn't show any signs of disorder. The chair in front of the fireplace lay on its side. So did both the lamp and the table next to it. Only half the rumpled duvet remained on top of the bed. She looked for traces of blood on the rug and found very little that needed attention.

Micah's arm didn't fare as well. As she recalled the injury, guilt washed over her. Twice now he saved her from serious harm, and she hadn't acknowledged the second. She would remedy that right after she cleaned up the blood. At the same time, she would tend his arm whether he liked it or not, if for nothing else than to assuage her guilt. Tala tidied the room. She then headed straight for the kitchen pantry. Her search yielded a dusty bottle of hydrogen peroxide someone left behind. The solution would easily remove the stains on the rug. She located a cloth and then made her way to the stairs just as her cell phone rang.

Tala shifted the phone to her ear as she ascended the steps. "Hello?"

"Miss Westbrook?"

"Yes?"

"This is Oscar Whitting. I understand you're seeking a general contractor for home renovation?"

"Yes, I am."

"Could you tell me what your particular needs are concerning this project?"

"Well, I'm not sure. The house hasn't been lived in for quite some time now so I don't know how much damage the place has sustained over the years. I can tell you first hand both the electricity and plumbing will need updating. I'll want you to check the roof for leaks and repair any decay to the walls—you know—that sort of thing. Once you've assessed the damage, I'll need an itemized bid for the work so I can—"

"Have you opened up any of the walls yourself in the rooms or closets—to check for damage, I mean."

"No, I've only arrived just today. So far I've only made general assessments."

"You've done nothing but walk through the rooms, I take it."

"Yep, that's about it. I haven't had time for anything else."

The man paused long enough to make the silence uncomfortable. "For your own good, I strongly advise you to leave everything *exactly* the way it is right now.

Do you understand? Don't go poking into things that are not your concern."

"Excuse me?" Tala stared down at her phone. She didn't much care for the man's heavy-handed tone of voice or his brazen demands. Did *all* of the men in England behave this way?

"I didn't mean to offend you, Miss Westbrook. I'm just trying to protect you from the dangers an old house might present. Oftentimes such homes are on the verge of collapse. Should you remove a load bearing wall or rip out a rotting board, the place might fall down around your head. Do you understand what I'm saying?"

The man's attempt at appeasement failed miserably. Still, she needed a contractor whether he sounded like a sinister thug or not. She ignored his apology altogether. "Can you meet with me tomorrow?"

"I can give you one hour of my time at 6:30 in the morning. If that's inconvenient for you, I'm afraid we'll have to make our appointment later on in the week."

"No, 6:30 is fine. I'll see you then." The call reminded her of her reason for being here. She forwarded the pictures she had taken to her father as promised. Once she completed the task, she climbed the stairs to the second floor. Somewhere along the way she must've earned the disdain of the fates for them to have given her two exasperating men to deal with in the same day. Of course, she supposed she should be grateful they didn't give her three.

****

Micah tossed the bodies of the Gehíwan convicts into the forest. He made sure they were near their deceased comrades for easier collection and disposal. Perhaps the act would serve as a warning against further attacks. They could kill each other if they so desired and be welcome to it. But he would insist they leave Tala in peace and unmolested during her final, two-week stay in England. If not, they would suffer the same fate. He stood for several minutes in silent observation of the woodland with nothing more than his troubled thoughts for company.

Not a soul warned him about the close proximity of the shifters to the residence of his newest charge. Didn't they think that little piece of information important in regards to this assignment? An assignment that still rankled him? Despite his desire to be anywhere but here, Micah cut an inconspicuous path toward the cottage. He would need a change of shirt before he returned to the manor on the off chance he needed to show himself to Tala before the morning.

At forest's edge, the ealdorman in charge of assigning his duties made a sudden appearance and fell into step beside him.

"Might I remind you," said Edward, "you didn't wait around for the full account of your current duty?"

Micah couldn't argue with that. He did walk out the moment the man revealed the first sketchy details. "I assumed when you told me a grand*daughter* needed a nursemaid for a short time all I need do is show up and—"

"You should never assume, Micah, and I don't recall using the term 'nursemaid' in connection with your task."

"Duly noted, Edward. You now have my undivided attention."

"We gave you this assignment because Tala's visit to England and Westbrook Manor coincides with Adolphŭs Aŭsberon's return to this part of the world. This, of course, has not gone unnoticed by his kind."

The revelation surprised him. "Why would he risk a return? Surely he knows some of the Gehíwan convicts have never vacated British soil."

"We're not sure of his reasons. Perhaps it has something to do with the key. Possibly at long last, he has somehow contacted the Gehíwan officials. I have Levi and Nathaniel looking into the matter right now. If the need arises, perhaps we can assist him in some way should the latter prove accurate. Nonetheless, his mere presence puts Tala in harm's way. This much you have already witnessed for yourself."

"That I have." Micah took in a deep breath and then let it go before he spoke. "She got a good look at one of them inside the forest."

Edward gave him a sideways glance. "That is most unfortunate."

"In more ways than one," he muttered. The curiosity in her eyes didn't bode well. Her reckless and impulsive nature concerned him as well. Still, he just had to get her through fourteen more days without injury.

"Well, be that as it may, I'm confident you can accomplish your objective with the same aptitude as you have every other assignment we've given you. That being said, there is one other important detail you missed."

"I'm listening."

"Adolphŭs Aŭsberon resided at Westbrook Manor for about two years before the anarchists finally tracked him there. No one else has stayed for any length of time since he fled the place almost three decades ago. Over the years, the malefactors have managed to keep the house empty by making all other occupants believe the manor is haunted. This you have already discovered. They believe Adolphüs hid his personal key somewhere on or near the property. They've yet to find it or they wouldn't still be in this particular area in search of it."

"Ah." His current assignment made a lot more sense now. The revelation also meant Tala, while at the manor, remained in constant danger. "She refuses to leave the premises," he said more to himself than he did in speaking with Edward.

"Such is not unexpected given her temperament. You'll need to watch over her very closely while she's here. Keep in mind that should the shifters decide to follow her once she leaves the area, your assignment, by necessity, will continue."

Of all the things he *didn't* want to hear."You really think that will be an issue?"

Edward rubbed a hand against his mouth and shrugged. "Such is possible if they think she has stumbled across Dolph's key, is involved with it in any way, or has knowledge of its location."

He resigned himself to his task. With all the self-possession he could muster, he nodded. "Understood."

The moment the word left his mouth, Edward disappeared. The likely reason for that? Tala approached. He could feel her presence growing ever stronger. By all indications, he would have less than a minute to get inside the cottage and change his shirt before she arrived at his door. But why in the world would she leave the manor when he told her to stay put? Didn't she understand the danger she just put herself in, or did she toss the knowledge by the way side along with any common sense she might possess?

Her knock sounded just as he slid a button through the third buttonhole of his black placket shirt. He fastened the last two before he opened the door despite her persistent hammering.

"Tala, what are you doing here?" He retained his grip on the doorknob as she barged inside. She headed straight for the small kitchen table left of the door and then dropped her bag on top of it.

"I'm sorry, but I just can't let your wound sit there and fester, Micah. At the very least, it needs to be cleaned and bandaged before infection sets in. The sooner the better. Now please, come over here and let me tend it."

"I appreciate the gesture. Truly I do. But it isn't necessary. My arm is fine."

She peeked inside her bag. Sparing him a glance, she withdrew a bottle of antiseptic and some gauze. "Perhaps it will set your mind at ease if I tell you I'm a wildlife photographer by trade. As such, I've had quite a bit of experience tending injuries such as yours—*if* that's what you're afraid of. I'm thorough and I'm fast. You won't feel a thing, I promise."

"I've no doubt. If I needed the service, you'd be the first person I'd call. But again, it isn't necessary." He offered her his hand. "Come on. Let me take you back to the manor—and this time, stay put?"

She dropped her gaze, exhaled a breath of resignation, and made her way to his side. But then, in a most unexpected move, she took hold of his cuff. At once she shoved the sleeve up to his elbow and exposed his bare arm. She gasped as her widened eyes traveled upwards and connected with his. For several infinite seconds she simply stared at him.

"A wound, no matter how trivial, cannot simply heal itself in less than one hour." She lifted her chin in an "I dare you to refute that" attitude. "And without any hesitation whatsoever, I could've classified your wound as far from trivial."

Micah jerked his arm away from her grasp. He yanked the cuff down the length of his arm, and buttoned it. "Look, you needn't concern yourself over something you—"

"What kind of being *are* you? What's going on around here?" She narrowed her eyes and jabbed her finger at his chest. "I mean—you have an arm that miraculously heals within mere minutes and without leaving a trace of that injury behind. Wild animals that *shouldn't* be anywhere in the backwoods of the United Kingdom, much less a residential property, managed to get themselves through closed doors. They then *hide* in an upstairs bedroom. Somehow you knew right where they were. How did you know that?"

He shrugged off the questions. "I don't know what you expect me to say. I don't—"

"I'm not leaving until you tell me whatever it is you don't want me to know." She set her heels, and placed a hand on her hip.

His anger flared. "Is that right? A little while ago you couldn't wait to leave this place."

Tala gave her head a snooty little toss. "A lot has changed since then, wouldn't you agree?"

He brushed the barb aside. "Then let me get you a pillow and blanket. You can make yourself comfortable on my sofa."

Indignation filled her lovely eyes. "That's it? That's all you're going to say? Really?"

Micah met her gaze without a flinch. "Really."

"Whatever." She gave him a curt nod and stormed toward the door.

He had fallen into the deep, dark abyss of the feminine *whatever*. Nonetheless, he stepped in front of the entryway blocking her path. "Where are you going, Tala?"

"Back inside the forest, not that it's any of your business."

"Why would you do something as foolish as that?"

"To find some answers, since you're unwilling to share what you know." She gritted her teeth. "Now, get out of my way."

He held his ground while disregarding the directive. "Just what do you expect to find out there?"

She shrugged away the question. "I'm not sure. However, I do know those creatures left tracks. I'm quite adept at finding and following them to wherever they might lead. Trust me."

"Regardless of the danger?"

"I can take care of myself."

"By far you are the most obstinate woman I have ever had the displeasure of meeting," he ground out.

Her eyes narrowed yet again as she leaned toward him. "You're not a pack of laughs yourself."

"My purpose here is not to entertain you."

"Oh, now you have assigned yourself a purpose concerning my life that somehow gives you the right to withhold information I know you have? You think you can just order me around and I'll obey your every command without question? If you truly think that, then you can just think again, buster. Now, for the last time, get out of my way or-or—"

"Or what?" he cut in.

"Just get out of my way, Micah. Now!"

"Nope, I'm afraid I can't do that." He ignored her rising anger. "Look, the way I see it, you have one of two choices. You can spend the night here on my couch—by George, I'll even give you the bed upstairs—or you can spend it at the manor. Either way I will stand guard over you just to make sure you don't do anything I consider foolish."

Indignant heat colored her cheeks. "I will have you arrested."

"Go ahead and try that tactic if you think you'd have even the smallest measure of success. However, I think I should tell you no matter how hard you try, no matter what you do, you will go no further than this cottage—or the manor—until the morning comes."

"Well, we'll just see about that, won't we?" The fire in her eyes contradicted the deadly calm in her tone of voice.

A chilling chorus of wolves ended the argument. From the sound, the shifters were very near the cottage. In all likelihood, they searched for Tala. He took hold of the door handle with one hand and grabbed his rifle with the other. "Unless you want to be on the menu, I suggest you stay put."

Though he detected a bit of fear alongside her animosity, she said nothing as he closed the door behind him. He stood still for a moment. The cry of the wolves originated in front of the cottage and to his left. He stopped at the end of the walkway. The echo of

27

howls drew his attention toward the lush vegetation across the neighbor's hay field. Moonlight reflected in two pairs of eyes deep within that vegetation. The first warning shot he fired nicked the ear of the wolf to the left. His second shot grazed the shoulder of the wolf to his right. They both tore off running in the opposite direction. At the same time, a host of other shots were fired from somewhere in the distance. In less than a minute, all vocal evidence of the wolves had disappeared. Only then did Levi and Nathaniel emerge from the shadows with broad smiles on their faces. Their presence didn't surprise him.

He gave them a nod as they approached. "Thanks for the assistance."

"No problem," said Levi. "We were in the area looking for Dolph anyway."

"Yes, Edward mentioned that. Have you had any luck in locating him?" he asked.

"Not so far, but we haven't given up the hunt yet," Nathaniel said. "We're sure he's here somewhere."

Levi nodded in agreement. "The good news is the insurgents don't have any idea where he is either. Well, at least not yet anyway, so that's something that works to our favor."

"Yes it does, and if at all possible we need to keep it that way," he said. "In my opinion, keeping Dolph safe and alive is just as important as keeping Tala safe and out of trouble."

"Don't worry. We're very well aware of what's at stake here." Levi then turned toward Nathaniel for a moment and gave the man a conspiratorial wink. The grin he sought to hide came anyway. "Putting that aside for a moment, tell us, how are things going with *your* part of this mission?"

Micah shook his head. "Not as well as I would like. Miss Westbrook is the most maddening creature I've ever been assigned to work with. Unfortunately, she witnessed some things I would rather she hadn't. As a result, she just keeps digging and refuses to leave well enough alone. "

Nathaniel chuckled. "She's asking too many uncomfortable questions, is she?"

"You don't know the half of it," Micah replied.

"Why don't you just bed the girl and be done with it," said Levi. "A little bit of romance and sweet talk goes a long way when it comes to dealing with the women folk. I guarantee you afterward she won't give you any more trouble. She probably won't even ask any more questions. Trust me; I know from past experience. She could even become an enjoyable diversion after your mission ends."

"That might be how you conduct business with your various charges, Levi. However, I assure you I do not."

Levi returned a nonchalant shrug. "Your loss."

Nathaniel waved Levi's comments aside. "Then just answer her questions, Micah. There's no shame in letting her know what's going on when it's her life we're talking about—when it's her life at stake. All but a few of the guardians at one time or another has had to take that path and well you know it."

Micah leaned forward. "Yes, but I have not."

"There's a first time for everything, Micah. You know that. Again I'll remind you—sometimes the truth is the only honorable option we can take."

Micah didn't have time to answer. He turned his

gaze toward the cottage. "You need to leave now. Tala is about to leave the cottage and I need to go in there and put a stop to it."

Chapter Three

Micah burst through the cottage door and rushed up the stairs. Tala stood before the open window with a series of knotted sheets in her hands. As ridiculous as it seemed, the sheet tied securely at the bed post indicated she had every intention of climbing out the window. He released an irritated sigh as he strode toward her. In the same moment, she whirled around toward him. Her face registered both shock and dismay.

"Tala, what on earth are you doing? Don't you have even a shred of common sense about you?"

"You can't keep me here against my will," she spat.

He flicked a hand toward the window. "So you think your only means of escape is climbing out a two-story window with a rope made of bedding?"

She shrugged and then turned her face away in silent refusal to look at him or answer his question.

"A window on the second floor seems a bit extreme. Why didn't you just go out the back door?"

That grabbed her attention. Her eyes blazed as she clenched her teeth. "I did try. The deadbolt is locked and it takes a *key* to open it. Therefore, I didn't see any other option."

Try as he might, he couldn't halt the grin, though he hoped he masked it with a slight back and forth rub across his mouth. "You didn't think to use the front door?"

She narrowed her eyes. "This isn't funny, Micah!"

"No, I suppose it isn't." He shook his head "Look, despite what you might think, it's not my intention to hold you prisoner. However, I will keep you safe whether you like it or not. Going outside alone, where the danger is obviously present—even to you—is something I can't let you do."

She whisked past him then and headed for the stairway. With no other choice available, he followed her down the steps.

Once they returned to the sitting room, she whirled around and faced him. "The way I see it, *you* have one of two choices if you're so obsessed on keeping me safe. One, you can accompany me back inside that forest. Two, you can answer my questions so I don't have to make the trip. Your choice."

Had he somehow, or in some way, drawn the ire of the ealdormen and for punishment they assigned him this irritating, stubborn little vixen? He rubbed a hand across his brow. Never once had any of his charges forced his hand in this way. Yet, as Nathaniel just pointed out, most all of his compatriots within the Bewitan Fierd couldn't say the same thing. Now—with more reluctance than what he could possibly express—he would join their ranks. He didn't see any other viable choice on his short list of options.

Tala would indeed find her way back inside that forest unless he disregarded the Bewitan creed, hogtied her and then held her against her will for the final two weeks she remained on British soil. His superiors wouldn't look kindly on that solution. Therefore, they might foist even more of her ilk upon him. That particular scenario would make him wish for death like nothing else did. Still, after the assignment ended and they parted ways, the power he held could make her forget he, as well as the Gehíwan world, ever existed. A power he never once used. He had taken pride in that.

Micah took in a deep breath and gave it a slow release. He resolved then to answer only the questions she asked and offer nothing more. "All right, Tala, have a seat."

She eyed him with suspicion. "Does that mean you're going to answer my questions?"

"Yes."

"All of them?" she ventured further.

"All of them."

****

For some reason, Tala actually believed him. She returned to the sofa and sat down. The moment he sat in the chair opposite her, she leaned toward him.

"Tell me who you are."

Just as he opened his mouth to speak, she halted his words with a lift of her hand. "And by that, I don't mean just your name. That I already know, if you spoke the truth—which for whatever the reason, I trust you did. Right now, I want to know *what* you are."

His almost imperceptible grin followed the question. He dropped his hands onto his lap and clasped them loosely together. "Just *what* do you think I am?"

"I don't know. You're no mere mortal, though. That much is obvious since your ravaged arm now shows no sign of injury whatsoever. Are you an angel?"

He laughed outright. "Not quite."

"An immortal of some kind then?"

"Do you really believe such beings exist, Miss

33

Westbrook?"

"I'm beginning to." She pinned her gaze to his. "Now, answer the question, are you an immortal of some kind?"

"Of some kind?" He tilted his head from side to side as he repeated her words with slow deliberation. "I guess you could say that."

A shiver of apprehension raced down her spine. She gulped past the knot in her throat. Somehow she expected that reply. Yet at the same time, she didn't know if she truly believed his answer. Indeed, she didn't know if she *wanted* to believe it.

She lifted her chin a notch for nothing more than a presentation of bravado. "Explain—and I want the details. Don't make me drag them out of you one by one, or I give you my word, we'll be here all night long."

His eyes took on a faraway expression. For several long moments, he held his peace. She waited it out. "In the year 1691, midway through the month of July, my military regiment, under the command of William Stewart, stepped onto a battlefield in Aughrim, Ireland. History records this battle as one of the bloodiest battles ever fought on Irish soil with over seven thousand dead. If you choose to verify this yourself, all you need do is research the claim. I'll not burden you with the gory details of this event. However, I will testify of its truth. I'll also tell you death would've taken me that day, had it not been for a mist that suddenly sprang up from the ground and carried me off of the field."

"A mist?" That piqued her interest. Her professor had told a similar story in a college history class, when they studied the significant battles of World War I. As she recalled, a group of men from the Sandringham Company, which suffered heavy losses at Gallipoli, vanished from history without a trace. Witnesses said that, under heavy fire, the men under the command of Captain Frank Beck advanced into the wood as ordered. Once inside, a sudden formation of ground-level clouds swallowed them up. The men disappeared before their very eyes. The only artifact ever recovered after several exhaustive searches? The watch that belonged to Captain Beck.

He nodded. "A dark mist so thick, one couldn't see anything or anyone else within it. I also found I couldn't make my way out of it. Even as I searched, the sounds of the raging battle grew ever more faint and then ceased altogether. Just as I wondered if death had claimed me, the haze cleared. I found myself standing in a massive room with a multitude of magnificent pillars lining the walls on either side. Exquisite furnishings in hues of white and gold were scattered about the place where a woman, I'm sure, might expect them to be. Inside that lavish room, I could see small groups of men scattered about, deep in conversation with one another. None of them paid me any mind as I travelled the length of the marble floor. In that same moment, someone emerged from a large set of double doors at the end of the great hall. With a broad smile on his face, he approached me. He called me by name and extended his hand in welcome. I said something like, 'this can't be heaven, yet it sure doesn't look like the hell I expected either.' The man laughed and nodded in full agreement."

His voice trailed off. But Tala didn't want the story ending there. "Did he say where you were?"

"Do we really have to do this, Tala?" he asked.

The very look in his eyes begged her to stop digging, but she just couldn't. She had to know everything. "Yes we do. Now, did he tell you where you were?"

He dropped his gaze to the floor as he released a quiet breath. "All right. He told me I stood inside a central building known to us as the Frithgeard, in the realm of the Bewitan Fierd."

"The realm of the *what*?"

"The Bewitan Fierd or loosely translated, the realm of the guardian army. While talking with my host, he told me the realm is a dwelling place for each of the first-born sons of eight men and their descendants. In the presence of Pope Leo the Fourth in Rome, these men swore by blood and oath that in time of need, they and all the generations of *their* first-born sons would forever protect Alfred, son of Æthelwulf of Wessex. They also swore to protect all of *his* direct descendants in the same manner. They bound themselves to this duty until such time as the world no longer existed or—in such a case as his line ended and they had no one left to protect. So far, neither of those events has occurred."

"Pope Leo the…," she sputtered. "You aren't talking about Alfred the Great, are you?"

"Yes, I am."

She gave him a sideways glance. "You don't really expect me to believe all of this, do you?"

He shrugged away her skepticism with a look of indifference. "As I said before, you're free to believe whatever you wish."

"Well, even if your story proves true, which I doubt, I don't see what that has to do with me or—"

"Whether you know it or not, you are a direct line descendent of Alfred, Miss Westbrook, and until I am released from my present duty, I am sworn by binding oath to protect you. I will not abandon that duty just because you think it's inconvenient."

She drew her brows together as she gazed at him. "Protecting me from what?"

"From whatever dangers you might face."

That gave her pause. "Just how long have you had this assignment?"

He seemed loathed to answer the question. Nonetheless, he took in a breath as he met her gaze head on. "Since the day you arrived in England."

"Why?"

"Because the situation warranted it."

Yet, she didn't need his assistance until she entered the woodland, did she? Nothing untoward had happened while she visited with Susan and took the pictures of the falcons her friend had wanted. Unless— "Those creatures in the forest—you not only saw them, you know what they are, don't you?"

He hesitated before he answered with a reluctant nod.

"Care to enlighten me?"

"Not if I can help it."

"Micah—"

He held up a hand. "The less you know, the better off you are. Take my word for it. I am asking you to let it go. Let me handle this. Just go on about your business. Do whatever it is you need to do. Board that plane as planned, and go home. At that point, your life can return to normal without any further interference on my part. That should make you happy, shouldn't it?"

She shook her head. "No. That's contrary to my upbringing. According to the wisdom and teachings of my father—and Sir Francis Bacon, I might add—knowledge is power."

"I'm not so sure that applies in this particular situation."

"You promised to answer all of my questions, remember?"

He rose to his feet and approached the window. She waited for him to speak for what seemed an inordinate amount of time.

"Micah?"

"Please don't make me answer any more of your questions. You're better off not knowing, trust me."

She scrunched her shoulders together as she clasped her hands. "I'm sorry. I can see for some reason this is difficult for you, but I have to know."

"They are a race of shifters, known as the Gehíwans."

Her eyes widened as she sucked in a breath. "Shifters? As in…as in shape shifters?"

He turned around, gazed into her eyes, and nodded. "These particular beings can change their physical structure from their human persona to any animal of similar weight and size. But once they choose one, they must keep it for the rest of their life."

"Like a very large panther or an enormous wolf, for instance," she said, recalling their foul carcasses again.

"Yes, but I'll also tell you the grand majority of them have chosen a wolf persona."

She leaned toward him. "What were they doing at my father's house? What do they want from me?"

"We're not sure. Right now, all we have is speculation," he said.

"Still, I'd like to hear your thoughts on the matter."

"They're just thoughts, Tala."

"I want to hear them."

He clenched his fist. "You are by far, the most stubborn woman I've ever met. Do you know that?"

The comment brought a smile to her face. "Yes, I can be all of that. You might want to prepare yourself for it so that whatever I may say or do in the future doesn't come as quite a shock."

Micah blew out a heavy sigh as he shook his head. She didn't care. He could shake his head until his teeth rattled if it made him feel better. "As you were saying?"

"If you insist on this, let me begin with a bit of history so the story makes sense."

"That's fine by me. I happen to have a passion for history and therefore, you'll have my absolute attention."

"The Gehíwan denizens are not from this dimension of Earth."

A charming grin overtook his exasperation as he studied her with an intensity that made her feel a bit self-conscious. She wondered over her facial expression and sought to quash whatever embarrassing thing she presented.

"Does that fact surprise you?"

"Well, yes, I suppose it does, although I must admit, the theory is a frequent topic of conversation in many circles."

"Trust me, it's not a theory. There are many dimensions to this Earth, the realm of the Bewitans among them. Anyway, many, many centuries ago, insurgents sought to overthrow the democracy of the Gehíwan government. These insurgents had every intention of replacing it with an evil, tyrannical, all-supreme ruler that would surpass any born to this world. A civil war ensued that almost destroyed their entire world. In the end, the anarchists were defeated and their leaders brought to trial. They were found guilty of treason and they, as well as all those who refused allegiance to the lawful ministry, were banished to an impenetrable penal colony located here."

"Here? As in England—here?"

"No, here as in this dimension. They built their fortified prison in the most inaccessible parts of Romania, high in the mountains, and then shielded the fortress from human eyes. For over three centuries, they successfully incarcerated these prisoners as well as all those who followed for related crimes without incident. But then, with the assistance of a rogue guard named Beldūrq—who by design and cunning infiltrated the penal system—they escaped. I should probably stop here and tell you it takes four keys to gain entrance to the realm of the Gehíwans. Two are required on this side of the portal, and two on the other."

"I see, and is this portal you speak of in Romania as well?"

"Yes, it is."

"Are there any others?"

"None I am aware of."

"Then I don't understand why they're here in England if this portal is in Romania."

"Because once they escaped, the vastly out-numbered guards took their personal keys and scattered. They knew the insurgents desired a return to their realm so they could renew their efforts to overtake the government. The loyal Gehíwan wardens vowed to do all in their power to prevent that from ever happening. These guards managed to destroy or bury their keys in various places throughout the world before the insurgents tracked each of them down, one by one. Once found, they killed them for their refusal to disclose the location. Of course, even if they had given up the keys, their fate would've remained the same and they knew it."

Tala's hand traveled to her throat. "All of the guards are dead then?"

"All but one," he replied. "A man by the name of Adolphŭs Aŭsberon is still alive. Beldŭrq and his comrades hunt him, even now."

"They are looking for him here in the county of Staffordshire?"

He nodded. "And even as close as Westbrook Manor."

"Why are they looking for him at the manor?"

"There are a couple of reasons. First and foremost, several decades ago, Dolph leased the property from your grandfather and resided there for a couple of years. The possibility exists the man hid his key somewhere on or very near the premises. As a result, a number of shifters have never vacated the area in order to search for it. Two, for whatever reason, Dolph has returned to this area and the Gehíwan convicts know it."

"Why on earth would he come back, knowing they hunt him?"

"We don't know. We are trying to find out."

"I take it from everything you've told me, you've had experience with these shifters before."

"A time or two, yes."

"Is that why they assigned you to me?"

"They didn't give me a reason, but that one is a good possibility."

Tala took some time and considered everything he had just said. If not for the fact she had witnessed some very bizarre, mystifying things in her travels throughout the world, she would've thought him a lunatic. Her experiences in the field, alongside the instant repair of his badly injured arm, not to mention the wild animals inside the manor, said otherwise.

His tale of the shifters and their Romanian penal colony made a bit of sense as well. The abundance of strange myths and legends concerning werewolves in that area of the world could fill an entire library. While in central and southeastern Europe, she met credible, no-nonsense people who claimed to have seen them. Her personal witness of strange creatures lurking in the wild places of the world, including those that chased her inside the forest this evening, couldn't be ignored either. Now, a faction of those beings had focused their unyielding attention upon Westbrook Manor, and all for the need to recover a single key.

"Keys are so small, though," she murmured more to herself than she did him. "How could they ever hope to find one, especially if the guards buried them in some unknown place, deep in the earth?"

"This particular key is larger than what you think, Tala." He hesitated as he dropped his gaze downward for a moment. "Tell me, have you ever seen pictures of or read articles about the Nebra sky disk?"

"I have a hazy recollection of the name—I think it's some kind of bronze disk they found in Germany a few decades ago?"

"That's right. Have you ever seen pictures of it?"

She shook her head. "Not that I can recall."

"The piece is almost twelve inches in diameter, and weighs in at about five pounds. Inlaid in gold, is what scientists believe is a representation of a crescent moon, the sun, and a series of small, round circles depicting the stars. They discovered the relic in Nebra, Saxony-Anhalt. Contrary to popular belief, it's not a religious artifact, a calendar, or an astronomical instrument, though we are quite content to have everyone in this dimension believe so."

Her mouth dropped. "Are you telling me that disk is one of the keys?"

"Yes and no. In an attempt to create a duplicate, the rebels took the one they possessed apart and made a replica from the materials found here. However, since our materials react in a far different manner than their own, they could never get the copy to work. Therefore, they abandoned the piece inside the cave and resumed their search."

"Do you know how many keys are still in existence?"

"Not with exactness. But do keep in mind; they only need one more to open the door, and there's no telling what might happen on either side of the portal, should that occur."

"Are you telling me those who man the portal on the Gehíwan side don't know who it is that's waiting to enter from here?"

"No, but they do have several safeguards in place."

"How does the gateway work?"

"Once the keys are put in place on this side of the

portal, a series of lights appear on both sides of the gate. The Gehíwan officials then insert their keys. They enter a code, and the doorway opens. The procedure is the same if the officials want the wardens to open the door on this side of the portal."

"Then by their silence alone, they must know something dreadful has happened to the wardens, right?"

"That's a reasonable assumption, coupled with the fact their calls to open the door have gone unanswered."

She drew her brows together. "Wait just a minute. What you're saying doesn't make any real sense. I mean, you're talking centuries here. Are you telling me these beings truly have that long of a lifespan?"

"They are living proof that they have an incredibly long lifespan in comparison to your own. In addition, Miss Westbrook, their reckoning of time is far different. I would estimate a decade of time in their dimension is akin to a century in yours. In that regard, they pay no attention to the passing of it while in this dimension."

****

For several minutes, Tala didn't say anything. Micah had no idea as to the direction of her thoughts and didn't want to lead her in any, save one. "In light of tonight's events, except for those instances your presence is required at the manor, I think it best if you stay here at the cottage. You'll be far safer inside these walls than at—"

She interrupted with a shake of her head and abandoned her seat even before he completed the suggestion. "No, I can't do that. All of my things are already at the estate. As you might've noticed, I have groceries piled on top of the kitchen counter, and some of them need refrigeration or they will spoil. On top of that, I have appointments with a few contractors tomorrow and one of them very early in the morning."

"Do you really find it much of a problem to collect your belongings, bring them here, and rise a littler earlier than expected to meet your contractor?"

A heavy sigh followed the question, which once again denoted her irritation. He could return the sentiment but held himself in check.

"I just feel the need to stay at the manor and keep a close eye on things, Micah. So, that's what I'm going to do." She turned away from him then, and gathered her medicinal supplies from off of the table. "Since you feel it's your avowed duty to stand guard over me every single minute regardless of venue, what difference does it make where I sleep?"

Chapter Four

Micah didn't see any point engaging in a battle he wouldn't win. Instead, he snatched his rifle from the corner, grabbed his coat since he probably wouldn't return, and opened the door. Before they crossed over the threshold, both Levi and Nathaniel made a sudden and unexpected appearance at his doorstep.

"Going somewhere?" asked Nathaniel. He and Levi breezed by him and entered the sitting room without a backward glance.

"Doesn't look like it at the moment, now does it?" He swung the door shut with a bit more force than necessary and put both rifle and coat aside. Then, with a brisk wave of his hand, he invited a gaping Tala to join them. "Tala Westbrook, may I present Nathaniel Rockwell and Levi Blackford. They are…colleagues of mine."

Tala managed a slight nod. Both men jockeyed for first position as they gathered around her like ravenous predators. "Pleased to meet you both," she murmured.

"Likewise," said Nathaniel, who took her hand first and lingered over it far longer than necessary before relinquishing it to Levi.

In turn—at least in Micah's opinion—Levi also played the fool. Had neither of them seen a pretty face before? Tala shifted her wide-eyed gaze toward him, seeking direction. Again, with a sideways nod of his head, he directed her toward the sofa. Once she settled into the cushions, he sat down beside her. At the same time, his companions found chairs of their own.

Micah looked at each of the men in turn. "I assume you have news that couldn't wait for a better time?"

Levi raised a brow.

"You can speak freely," Micah said.

An irksome smirk appeared at the corner of Levi's mouth over the revelation. He ignored his unspoken taunt by giving Nathaniel his full attention. At least Nathaniel looked pleased, rather than smug.

"Well I must say, that's good news for all concerned," said Levi.

"How so?" he asked.

"We've located Dolph Aüsberon."

"Where?"

"Not far from here, actually." He tilted his head ever so slightly in Tala's direction.

Micah understood. Somewhere on or near the seven-acre property that comprised Westbrook Manor, the Gehíwan guard had taken refuge. Yet, somehow, he had eluded the notice of the convicts who hunted him. "How did he manage to slip past Beldūrq and his henchmen?"

"A couple of centuries worth of dedicated practice or so he says. Dolph tells me he's visited the area many times in the past without notice," said Nathaniel. "This time, however, the wind made a most unfortunate, unexpected shift in direction at the worst possible time—and revealed his presence."

"Yes, but the thing is," said Levi, "he wants to speak with Tala."

"Me?" She drew her brows together as she put a

hand to her heart. "He asked to speak with me?"

"Well, not by name, of course. You see, Dolph conducted a search of his own inside your carriage house earlier today. In the midst of the search, he caught sight of you as you entered the property with keys in one hand and bags in the other. He assumed a member of the Westbrook family had returned at long last, since you arrived without the current proprietor at your side. He's quite anxious to speak with you. Now that Micah has explained the circumstances surrounding you and our current state of affairs, we can accomplish the task far easier."

"What did he hope to find inside the carriage house and what does he want to speak to me about?" she asked.

"He didn't say, he just asked to meet with you as soon as possible."

Micah shook his head. "I don't think such a meeting is wise. Why don't you just ask him what he wants and you can deliver her response?"

"We suggested that very thing since we knew it would be your choice in the matter," said Levi. "Dolph said such an approach not only wasted precious time, it also increased the danger for everyone concerned should he require additional questions after her reply."

"I think he's right about that, Micah," Nathaniel added. "One visit is far better than the prospect of two or three."

In the exaggerated huff perfected by her species, Tala slung her bag over her shoulder and rose to her feet. "Since I'm quite capable of making decisions for myself, the question should be directed toward me, not Micah, don't you think Nathaniel? Now then, why don't you have him meet me at the house? We were just heading that way before you arrived."

Micah loosed a breath of exasperation as he vacated his seat alongside Nathaniel and Levi. "No, that isn't going to work. The shifters will surely keep the manor under surveillance in the hope he returns. If we must do this thing, then I think it's best if we take you to him."

"They could just as easily follow us to wherever it is he's hiding," she argued.

Micah offered her his hand. "Not if you connect yourself to me. As your personal protector, the contact will shield you from the eyes of the Gehíwans—and anyone else for that matter."

"That's a fact, Tala. So no matter what, hold on tight, and don't let go of that hand," Levi warned the moment she complied.

Nathaniel rubbed his hands together. "All right then, is everyone ready?"

****

Tala needed a minute. She needed it to make sense of what Nathaniel just said. Her heart's erratic response to the sheer power of Micah's hand also needed some normalcy before she could take a single step. Until now, she didn't know how much of the tale concerning her guardian's altered state of being she accepted. Yet, the instant he encased her hand within his, a fiery jolt coursed through her veins and left a searing trail of heat in its wake. In turn, the beat of her heart accelerated and produced some kind of upheaval deep inside her belly. Surely, no mere mortal could have produced such a sensation, could he?

No—wait a minute. Her gaze swung back and forth

49

between Levi and Nathaniel. Both men, as tall and powerfully built as Micah, were quite attractive in their own way. Did all of the guardians look like this or were these men outside the norm? Levi, with his long, almond-brown hair, green eyes and dark brown scruff had a boyish sort of charm that instantly captured one's attention. Nathaniel's deep blue eyes, complimented his dark brown hair, while the deep dimples on each side of his face made for a most captivating smile. Each of the men had taken hold of her hand without producing so much as a spark of heat in response. Once again, she dropped her gaze to the large hand that held her own. Perhaps because he'd been designated as her protector?

"Tala?"

The sound of her name startled her out of her reverie. She sucked in a breath as her gaze drifted from Micah's hand to his eyes. He didn't seem the least bit disturbed by the contact. "Hmm?"

"Are you all right?"

She bit down on her lip as she slowly nodded. "Y-yes."

He eyed her for a moment. "We don't have to do this right now if you'd rather not. Dolph can wait for a better time."

"No. I'm ready, really."

Micah drew her close to his side as they headed for the door. They trailed Nathaniel and Levi out of the cottage, down the walkway, and all the way to the boundaries of Westbrook Manor. The lush vegetation that surrounded them kept them well hidden in shadows. Not, she supposed, that they needed it. All the while her insides churned in response to her guardian's close proximity.

They turned just shy of the northern fence and followed its course to the end of the property. From there, they climbed down the steep, rocky incline, which led to the river. Levi then ushered them inside a dank, dark, rocky cavity hidden away by dense foliage smelling of stagnant water and damp earth. She couldn't see a thing, yet their guide seemed sure of his steps.

They walked deeper inside the narrow corridor that headed back in the direction of the manor. After a minute or two spent in total darkness, she spied a faint light up ahead. Within that light, she could see the silhouette of a man. He moseyed toward them as they approached. Only then did Micah let go of her hand and it maddened her, if given the choice, she would much rather have clung to him. At once she shook away the ridiculous thought and focused instead on her surroundings.

Tala didn't know what she expected to see. But the man who shifted his gaze away from Levi and settled it upon her, looked nothing like the vision her mind conjured. This clean-shaven, middle-aged man, average in stature, looked normal enough, except for perhaps the large, piercing gray eyes. A shiver coursed through her body as those eyes probed deep into her mind and left her a bit disconcerted.

"Dolph Aüsberon," said Nathaniel, "this is Tala Westbrook."

The man drew his clenched fists together and bowed his head. "Thank you for agreeing to meet with me, Miss Westbrook."

She met his gaze with directness. "Not a problem. Is there something I can do for you?"

"I hope you can tell me where your grandfather stored my personal possessions," he said.

The unexpected question caught her off guard. "Your-your possessions?"

He lifted both brows and shoulders in concert. "By necessity, I vacated the estate in rather a hurry. I took nothing with me. Upon my return, my belongings were gone. The new proprietor didn't know anything about them and unfortunately, his predecessor had passed away."

"But that happened ages ago. My grandfather died during my childhood. I have no idea what he did with your things."

Dolph's shoulders slumped forward. He heaved a sigh, and gazed at the ground. After a moment he took on a hopeful expression. "I don't suppose you have a way of finding out, do you? Perhaps he left a paper trail of his dealings behind, or a business journal of some sort?"

"Well, I don't know; I guess I can contact my father and see if he knows anything. But I'm sure by now, any clothing you might have had or—"

"I'm not looking for clothing, Miss Westbrook," he interrupted. "Specifically, I'm looking for my cane. Nothing else is important."

She drew her brows together. "Your cane?"

"Yes, the piece is quite unique. I cannot tell you how imperative it is I get it back. The sooner the better."

"Is that what you searched for while inside the carriage house earlier today?" she asked.

Dolph nodded. "I'm sorry I startled you, but you see, until today, the opportunity to thoroughly search the structure has eluded me for one reason or another. However, I'd have you know your timely interruption made my escape from the insurgents possible. For that, I must thank you."

Micah moved a half-step forward. "I assume this cane you speak of has something to do with your key?"

"Yes, a three-dimensional head of the phoenix adorns the tip of the cane. This emblem unlocks a small hidden chamber inside an ancient church in Romania. The chamber protects my key to this day and only that cane can open the door."

"Ah. We're a little less than two months away from a black moon," said Nathaniel. "I presume you hope you can return home during this event?"

"Yes, I am."

"You have another key then," stated Levi.

"Not in my possession," Dolph replied. "But I now know where one is."

Micah rubbed a hand across his mouth. "Are they close together?"

"Relatively speaking. They are within one hundred kilometers of each other."

"How do you hope to collect them both with the traitors hot on your trail?" asked Nathaniel.

A slight grin tugged at the corners of Dolph's mouth. "Using the right timing, my vast experience in eluding them, superior cunning, and a bit of luck."

"You've got to do better than that," Micah said. "Whether willing or not, giving them a key is not an option, Dolph."

"I'm aware of that, Micah. Nonetheless, the rebels are growing stronger each day in ways you can't even begin to comprehend. They not only pose a danger to my realm, but this one as well. If I don't leave now and return with an army, any hope we have of apprehending and confining them will be lost. In turn, they will overrun this world. They will enslave its people, just as they intend to enslave mine once they find a key. Now, I have a few advantages they remain unaware of and I will be very careful. However, that's a moot point if my cane is not located and returned."

Tala's heart raced over the chilling revelation, as well as the dire consequences if the man failed in his quest. "I'll do everything I can to find it. You have my word. I'll call my father right away and get back to you with an answer as soon as I can."

Dolph bowed his head. "I would appreciate that very much. Thank you, Miss Westbrook."

Tala paused for a moment. "How will I get in touch with you?"

"I'll stay right here. For now, this is the safest place for me to wait. Should that change, I'll let you know. Oh, and by the way, you should know the name under which I leased the house—Theodore Crosby."

"All right, I'll remember that." She turned toward Micah. "Are you ready to go then?"

In answer, he took hold of her hand—which, much to her dismay—produced the same sensation as before. Her guardian then focused his attention upon Dolph, and nodded. "We'll talk to you soon."

Just as they turned in the direction they had come, Dolph extended a hand in the opposite direction. "If you follow the path, the tunnel will lead you to a hidden door inside the cellar of Westbrook Manor. You'll get there in no time at all."

"Really?"

A broad smile emerged, which revealed canine teeth far sharper than any human should possess. The sight unnerved her. "Indeed. I used it many times during my stay."

Though Micah maintained eye contact with Dolph, he gripped her hand a little tighter and shook his head. "No, it would be unwise to enter the house that way. Your rebels know Tala left the premises and will watch for her return. If she just suddenly shows up inside the manor, they'll wonder how she got there and look for the unknown entrance. In all likelihood, and sooner rather than later, that would lead them to your sanctuary."

Dolph spared her a glance. "You're right, of course. I didn't think about that."

Micah cocked his head toward the hidden access even as he tugged her in the reverse direction. "We'll use the cellar door when we have the answer to your question."

"Then I'll seek for a bit of patience and look forward to your return."

****

No one uttered a word as they retraced their steps down the muggy corridor. Micah didn't expect them to. Somewhere along the way, Nathaniel and Levi took their leave. No surprise there either. As they left the tunnel behind, he and Tala walked alone. Several times, while they headed for the cottage, her gaze strayed away from the trail and settled upon him. Without doubt she had at least one question. Any moment now, she would blurt it out regardless of the consequences the knowledge might bring. He braced himself for the onslaught.

"Micah, why can't the shifters see me when I am physically connected to you?"

Not half as bad as he expected. In response to that fact he chuckled inward. "Because they can only see me if I want them to. Should I hold your hand, put my arm around your waist, your shoulder, or anywhere else on your body, you become an extension of me. Does that make sense to you?"

"I suppose if I try really hard I can force it to make some."

By expression alone, he could see the revelation perplexed her. "Why does such a thing trouble you anyway? After all, it's not the most difficult thing you've accepted today."

"Well, they obviously targeted you when they made their assault in the upstairs bedroom. The arm they ravaged is proof enough of that. So, if they can't detect your presence unless you allow it, how did they know you were there?"

He narrowed his eyes and clenched his jaw over the recalled memory. "Because I thought they should know just who dispatched them to the hell from whence they came. Therefore, I didn't conceal my presence from them during the melee."

She did a double take. "Then they know who and what you are?"

"Not with any degree of certainty."

"Exactly what do you mean by that?"

"They have encountered us a few times in the past. Those encounters revealed that we're different from the humans they prey upon, they just don't know how or why."

"I see."

While she thought on that, he studied her lovely face. Despite his disdain for his current task, the infuriating girl intrigued him far more than he cared to admit. Far more. The sudden knowledge of that fact bombarded his mind and he craved a speedy end to this assignment even more than he did before. He didn't need—or want—any complications to his life.

"I didn't understand Nathaniel's reference to the black moon. Does it hold some kind of power or significance?"

The question cut into his thoughts. "Not power in the way you mean. The keen senses of the Gehíwans are strongest during a full moon. Hence, the countless werewolf references that speak of the creature's response to it. In direct opposite, they are at their weakest point during the new. When a new moon happens twice in a month, they are weaker yet. Therefore, the night of the black moon is Dolph's best chance to slip through the portal undetected by his kind."

A look of determination settled over her features. "Then we shouldn't waste any time, should we now. Can I call my father now without the insurgents hearing me?"

He swung their coupled hands a bit forward and gave her hand a gentle press. "As long as you maintain contact with me, they can neither see you nor hear anything you say."

"That's a very good thing to know." Tala halted her steps just shy of the gate and scrolled to her father's name on her list of contacts. Once the call connected, they resumed their stroll. She gazed at him as she waited for her father to pick up his phone. The wait didn't take long.

"Well, hello there, princess, I didn't expect to hear from you quite this soon. How is everything going?"

In response to her father's chosen endearment, she developed a sudden interest in the bushes. She refused even so much as a glance in his direction. Yet, it would've given him a great deal of enjoyment if he could have captured her gaze at that moment. Still, other opportunities to bedevil her a bit would surely present themselves in the days ahead.

"Everything is going as well as expected. Did you take a look at the photographs I sent you?"

"Yes, I did. Seems I underestimated the damage," Curtis replied.

"Hopefully most of what you see is just cosmetic. I'll know more in the morning after I meet with the various contractors. However, the reason I called is because this evening I ran into a resident of the house from long ago by the name of Theodore Crosby. He had an emergency the day he left the house, leaving all of his belongings behind. That emergency delayed his return for quite some time. When he finally came back, he found all of his things missing and a new proprietor in charge of the manor. That man knew nothing about the removal of his possessions. Mr. Crosby hopes Grandpa put them in storage somewhere and he left a record of that fact in a journal or business ledger?"

A lengthy pause followed her inquiry. "None of that is ringing any bells, sweetheart. In addition, you're talking about something that must've happened a very long time ago. With the ridiculous reputation of the house scaring off potential renters, we've not had anyone living in the manor for more than a month or two at any given time for well over a decade. So tracking down something now might be impossible."

"I know, and he's also aware his chances are slim at best. But he has a very old cane that's not only dear to his heart; the piece is also quite valuable. This is the only thing he wants returned. He's a very sweet man. As a special favor, I would really like to track it down right away for him if we can. You see, his time here is very limited."

"Anything for you, you know that. I'll see what I can do. Just let him know that I can't make any promises."

"I will, and I'm sure he already knows. Thanks, Dad, I'll call you as soon as the contractors submit their bids, unless, of course, you call me with news first?"

"Okay, I'll get right to task. I'll talk to you soon." Tala returned the phone to her pocket as they approached the entrance. She would only give him her full attention after he opened the door and allowed her to step inside ahead of him. The lifted brow and stubborn set of her chin made it clear she hadn't changed her mind about spending the night at the cottage. So be it.

"Do you need to grab anything before we take our leave—toothbrush, pajamas, overnight bag—that high-powered rifle of yours?"

Her staunch refusal to stay put, alongside the not-so-subtle taunt, prompted a roguish grin. He leaned down toward her. "I don't require sleep, Miss Westbrook. Therefore, I don't have a need for *pajamas*, and even when I did sleep, I still had no use for such attire." His expression dared her to question him further.

A charming blush touched her cheeks the moment his underlying meaning hit home. Yet, he found it obvious she had no intention of getting caught in the snare she set herself. Indeed, she found it far more comfortable to turn tail and run.

In return, she merely sucked in a breath and hung onto it as she spoke. "Then are we ready to go?"

He let go of a chuckle as well as her hand, retrieved his coat and rifle, and cocked his head toward the door. "After you."

Chapter Five

Not a single word passed between them as they entered Westbrook Manor. The peaceful respite didn't hold though, for the moment he locked and bolted the door, she whirled around and faced him.

"Micah, what were the nature of your assignments when you encountered these shifters?"

"What?"

"The circumstances surrounding them, what did they entail? I'd really like to know."

He dismissed the unexpected question with the lift of a shoulder and a sideways swing of his head. "None of that is important."

She studied his face for several awkward moments. "Then why can't you tell me about them?"

"It's not that I can't. Again, the encounters just aren't all that important and they have nothing to do with what's going on here now," he said as he set his rifle in the corner, shrugged out of his coat, and hung it on her coat rack.

"If that's true, then I don't see where there's a problem in talking about them." She gave him a saucy smile and beckoned him into the sitting room. With a bit of reluctance, and no other option available, he followed. Once she made herself comfortable in the overstuffed chair near the fireplace, she gazed at him and waited.

His deliberate delay in forming a response didn't faze her. He gave up. "I expect you'll continue this endless badgering until you get your way?"

"Badgering, Micah?" She shook her head and tsked. "That certainly isn't my intention. Quite the contrary. After all, since it appears we'll be spending a great deal of time together, I can't think of a single reason we can't have a pleasant conversation or two, can you?"

"By speaking of topics better left alone?"

"No, by speaking of things that just might help prepare me for plausible situations in my immediate future. Situations I might not handle well and could've prevented otherwise if only I had a little more knowledge. You wouldn't want something like that on your conscience, would you?"

"Point well taken." He settled himself into the chair across from hers, propped a booted foot on top of his knee, and gazed pointedly at the mantel clock. "Will it satisfy you well enough if I give you the details of just one experience tonight? As you can see, it's getting rather late and you'll need some sleep before the dawn arrives, will you not?"

She glanced at the clock and then shrugged. "I suspect you're right. One story will do for now. So then why don't we begin with the last time you dealt with them?"

"All right, since you insist—the last time I encountered these mangy miscreants, newspaper articles concerning World War II made the headlines in every nation across the globe. In September of 1943, the Allies bombed the oil refineries and fields in Romania used by the Germans. As far as distance goes in the modern world, those fields were not that far from the Gehíwan penal colony. For the need of fuel the Axis powers fought back. At that particular time in history, the Romanians had thrown their lot in with the Nazis. However, unknown to the Nazis to this very day, the rogue shifters had filled many positions within the SS and Gestapo organizations."

Tala gaped at him. "You mean they actually fought in the war alongside humans?"

"That they did."

"Why on earth would they do that?"

"Not to benefit anyone in this realm, I assure you. The convicts simply decided the Nazis were the ideal ally because they had a firm conviction they would win the war. As you probably recall, history records Himmler as an avid occultist. The man went about searching for ancient artifacts and the power associated with them. Because of this, the malefactors infiltrated the SS, Nazi Party, and even the Gestapo so they could hasten their search for a key with a whole lot of human help."

"That makes sense." For the chill that had overtaken the room, Tala shivered. She wrapped her arms about her body seeking warmth and all the while disregarded the blanket on the sofa.

He shook his head. "Are you cold?"

"No, I'm all right." She dropped her hands into her lap in a ridiculous attempt to prove the claim. "Tell me, did they rise high enough in the ranks to choose the sites or did they just hope they'd stumble across a key while digging?"

"A little bit of both." He rose from his seat and approached the fireplace. Once he had built a roaring fire, he turned around and gazed into her eyes. "I should also tell you at that time, the Germans created the SS Volunteer Mountain Division, also known as the Prinz Eugen, in the area of Romania where a plethora of shifters resided. In turn, many of them enlisted in this infantry.

"An unknown part of this history is that the predominately Serbian Chetniks falsely presented themselves as Nazi sympathizers. Yet in truth, these particular Chetniks fought against the Germans. Unbeknownst to the Germans, they also engaged in violent aggression toward the Croats in Bosnia, meant to end in the complete and utter destruction of these people. They weren't the only ones that suffered the wrath of the Chetniks either."

Tala's hand traveled to her throat as her expression took on a mixture of horror and loathing. "That's terrible."

"Yes it is, but that's also the mentality of most wars regardless of realm. With that being said, credit must be given to these same Serbs for saving over five hundred American air crew members shot down during the air campaign in Romania. Among them, one Major James Seabright, an army intelligence and air defense specialist. He had accompanied a bomber aircrew with the mission to evaluate the defenses around Polesti, which is located in the foothills of the Southern Carpathian Mountains."

The moment he reclaimed his seat, Tala leaned toward him. "I take it this James Seabright is the one they assigned you to protect?"

"That's right. My assignment began the moment he and I boarded the plane."

"Did you allow him to see you?"

"In this situation, yes I did. I introduced myself to him and everyone else onboard, as a newly assigned member of the crew. Given the current state of the war at the time, not a soul questioned the claim."

"During your time together, did he ever find out you were more than just a mere, ordinary mortal?"

The question annoyed him. Did she think he just announced his state of being and purpose to whomever he protected? "No, he didn't. In fact, you're the only person I have ever protected who has made that discovery."

At his terse response, an almost undetectable smile curved a single corner of her mouth. "So, you boarded the plane and then what happened?"

"We took off knowing full well the risks of flying over Romania. Yet, I should also tell you at the time we didn't know a Gehíwan thug, known by the Germans as Major Beryx Cojor, headed the field intelligence at the Corp level of the Prinz Eugen Division."

"He worked intelligence? Really?"

"Yes, he did."

"These convicts are that smart?"

Micah shrugged. "Some of them are highly intelligent. Cojor happens to fall into that category. Unfortunately, he uses that intelligence for evil purposes. Anyway, once our enemies downed the bomber, Cojor discovered the craft carried Seabright. As a top priority, he hunted him down in the hope he survived. According to all reports, he wanted him in for his own special brand of interrogation—the gory details of which, I'll not get into. Yet this is another skill the shifters are especially good at performing."

Tala drew her brows together. "For what purpose? What did he want of the man? Did he carry secrets the Nazis wanted?"

"I'll never know for certain, because I never gave the fool the pleasure of capturing him. Perhaps, given Seabright's formidable reputation, Cojor simply wanted to see if he could break him."

"Now why doesn't that surprise me," she murmured more to herself than she did him. "So, after they blew your plane out of the sky, how did James and his companions escape horrific injury and death? I mean, with you onboard, everyone survived, didn't they?"

Her comment solicited a grin. "Your concern is only for James and the crewmen?"

She waved a hand in dismissal. "Oh, well, from what I have seen, falling out of an airplane shouldn't concern the great Bewitan warrior in the least."

Micah chuckled. "Perhaps, and to answer your question, yes they did. Anyway, we bailed out over the Serbia-Croatian-Romanian border alongside the members of the crew. Yet, as we touched down, we found ourselves separated from the others. Nonetheless, as it turned out, that made my job far easier."

"How so?"

"James Seabright is a noble man. If he considered it necessary, he would have sacrificed himself if it meant saving his companions. In that particular scenario, I would've had to run far more interference to ensure his survival. In turn, that would've raised a few eyebrows—even suspicion. After all, how many bullets can a man take and still remain standing?"

"You have a valid point there. So after you lost

track of the others, what happened next?"

"We were hunted by a twenty-man detail led by Cojor."

"Why didn't you just take hold of the man, hide him from their eyes, and disappear?"

"For several reasons I won't go into, that tactic wouldn't have worked in this situation."

"Oh. Well, had you ever encountered Cojor before?"

"No, I hadn't. However, once he got close enough to our position, I could sense the foul stench of his kind. Of all of the Gehíwan fugitives I've ever dealt with, none of them had the tenacity, single-mindedness, and disregard for life of any kind as Cojor had. Over the following days, we had a couple of intense skirmishes. Sixteen of Cojor's men died during the various melees, all of them German, save three."

She bit down on her lip as she scrutinized his face. "I would imagine you're responsible for the death of the three shifters on his team and probably most of the Germans, right?"

"I didn't stop to count."

"Did you kill Cojor?"

He firmed his jaw. "No, I didn't. I intended on ending his miserable existence the moment I took out the men shielding his foul body. Despite that intention, Seabright—a member of the army pistol team and a darn good shot I might add—put a couple of bullets in him before I had the opportunity myself. In the blink of an eye, Cojor's surviving cohorts removed him and themselves from the battle. From all reports, the maggot survived."

"If Seabright is such a good shot, how did he miss

his aim?"

"James didn't miss; he just didn't target the specific areas fatal to the Gehíwans."

"They are different than ours?"

"Somewhat."

Tala tilted her head to the side while her eyes probed his. "I think you liked this James Seabright."

"He earned my respect many times during the weeks we spent together. Anyway, we finally fought our way into the hands of the Chetniks. From there, with the aid of the Partisans, we made it to the coast. We ended up in the hands of the allies where we parted company. He stayed out of trouble after that and therefore, he no longer required our services."

****

Tala shifted her gaze toward the flames as she pondered the incredible story she hadn't quite expected. She wondered then if he thought of that assignment as business as usual, or did it run outside the norm? Right then, she wanted the answer more than she did anything else.

"What manner of assignment did you have last? Before me, I mean." The moment his 'that's something you aren't entitled to know' expression took hold of his face she lifted her hand with her palm outward. "If you expect any peace, you might as well tell me."

He rolled his eyes heavenward. "Did anyone ever tell you just how exasperating you are?"

"More times than I can count. So?"

"Protecting a Navy SEAL on special assignment."

"Up to his eyebrows in horrific danger, I assume?"

"Something like that."

"Have all of your previous assignments possessed

this element of extreme peril?"

"They wouldn't have needed me if they didn't."

"Then standing watch over me must seem pretty tame after all of that. I mean, in my case all you need do is keep the convicts away from my doorstep until they're satisfied I have no knowledge of—or possession of—their elusive key, right?" The humor that filled his eyes confirmed the statement. "Out of curiosity, how many other women have you protected since they swooped down and carried you off to the faraway land of the Bewitan Fierd?"

"There haven't been any others. You're my first."

Though she tried, she couldn't suppress the smile that followed the revelation. "Does that bother you?"

"Does *what* bother me?"

"Watching over a mere female who is not engaged in some kind of high-risk military conflict."

Micah lifted a brow. "Not in the least, Miss Westbrook. Now the midnight hour has already come and gone. As I recall, you have an early morning appointment. Why don't you get some sleep now?"

She turned her head and gave him a sideways glance. "And while I sleep what exactly will you be doing?"

"Making sure you stay safe, of course."

The 'how' of that duty made her instantly wary. "You don't think you're coming into my bedroom while you just sit there and watch me, do you?"

Micah shrugged away the question. "Not unless I think it's necessary."

That scenario didn't settle well at all. Tala already knew nothing she said would dissuade him from barging into the bedroom she selected upstairs should he hear the slightest sound. Worse yet, the thought of him staring at her while she slept seemed anything but pleasant. She eyed the sofa that appeared somewhat comfortable. The large living room would give him far more space than any one of the bedrooms upstairs. Perhaps he could find himself a book and read by the firelight. She gave him a nod. "Then to save you the trouble, I'll just go ahead and sleep on the sofa—at least for tonight. After all, you've already got a cozy fire going. I might as well use it."

Micah flashed a knowing grin as he rose to his feet. He headed for the chair in the corner and removed a blanket and sheet from the pile stacked high on top of it. He then took hold of a pillow from off of the window seat and placed it against the armrest of the sofa. "Would you like me to tuck you in?"

Her cheeks flamed with a curious mix of mortification and indignation over the mere suggestion. She could feel it. "No, thank you, Mr. Berrington. I am quite capable of making my own bed and settling myself into it without any help from you."

Despite her haughty response, once the lights went out and the shadows played eerily against the walls, Tala took a great deal of comfort in knowing her brawny guard stood watch over her. That comfort steadily increased as sinister, unfamiliar noises disturbed the otherwise quiet of the night and made sleep long in coming. While she waited for sleep to overtake her, she mulled over the events of the day. Mere hours really, that seemed almost like a lifetime.

She connected to Micah in a way she couldn't quite explain. A part of her detested the man and scoffed at the story he offered concerning parallel dimensions, strange keys, and rogue shifters. The other part of her said his story rang true. He couldn't possibly manufacture the events that had transpired. Why would Nathaniel, Levi, and Dolph go along with such a ridiculous hoax? Even if they did, for what purpose? The slight possibility of recovering a cane just didn't warrant such an elaborate ruse. Besides, he had done nothing but watch over her—just as he declared he would. Though she found him obnoxious, she also found him intriguing—and that probably scared her far more than accepting the truth of his tale.

Far more.

Chapter Six

Micah turned his gaze away from the window just as the clock chimed the three a.m. hour. The maggot that patrolled the grounds of the manor had grown weary of his duty and skulked into the shadows. The shifter took quite a risk in burrowing down for some sleep. His kind wouldn't think twice of killing him for the infraction—not that he expected anyone to check on him anytime soon. So much the better.

He stood by the sofa and gazed down upon Tala's lovely face. A deep, peaceful slumber had finally claimed her for the first time tonight. He hoped it would last until the morning. Despite her bravado, he found it obvious each aberrant noise, both in and outside the house, had kept her from sleeping too deeply before now. He couldn't fault her for that. Not after everything she had witnessed and the incredible revelations she grudgingly accepted as truth.

He took a moment then and looked back on the first four weeks of this duty. During those weeks he had witnessed her varying moods and scrutinized her character from every angle as he stood guard over her. He had enjoyed her laughter and interesting conversations. Each moment of inner reflection, he observed unhampered. He sensed the depth of her adventurous spirit. The girl's courage and tenacity surpassed every other female he had ever known.

72

Therefore, it didn't surprise him for the first time since becoming a member of the Bewitan Fierd, he found himself wandering into the dangerous 'if' territory. Yet, in spite of that danger—and the foolishness of the act— he allowed himself free rein.

If he and Tala had met while still in his mortality, would she have captured his interest in the same way she did now? *If* so, would he have pursued her regardless of any obstacle placed in his path? *If* he had prevailed in his quest, and *if* their relationship had flourished, would she have responded to his touch then the same way she did yesterday? Though he concealed it well enough, he could feel the burst of fiery heat that passed between them equally as well as she did. Just having her hand in his filled him with more pleasure and contentment than he thought possible for such a small simple thing. He had never experienced anything quite like it before while engaged in similar circumstances.

What are you doing, Micah, he silently berated. Entertaining things that might have been—and could never be—had never done anyone an ounce of good. He let go of a ragged breath and headed for the stairs. A doorway needed repair before the morning arrived. He wouldn't have the scheduled contractors wonder over and question the fresh damage.

Soon after he finished the task, the rumble of an engine drew his attention toward the drawing room window. A vehicle with a contractor's logo painted on the side pulled up in front of the house while the sound of grinded gears echoed all about the neighborhood. Seconds later, the derelict shifter assigned to patrol the property sprinted from his hideaway. He approached the truck. The man inside lowered the window and engaged the watcher in conversation. Countless times they directed their attention away from each other. They gazed at the house with an intensity that disturbed him. He found it obvious they either plotted Tala's immediate departure from the premises or her demise. In all likelihood they focused on the latter. As far as they were concerned her life bore no value of any kind. The early hour gave them ample opportunity to rid themselves of her without detection of any neighbor that might happen by. At the same time, they could remove the threat of renovation to a house they had claimed as their own.

Though loathed to wake her, Micah turned away from the window. He went to the sofa, and hunkered down beside her. "Tala, you need to wake up now," he whispered.

Despite the calm tone of voice he used and the gentle pressure on her shoulder, Tala bolted upright and gazed at him with widened eyes. "Is something wrong?"

"Not wrong, really—just not what you expected this morning. As it turns out, the contractor you're meeting with is a Gehíwan malefactor. He parked his stolen van outside your gate about twenty minutes ago. At this moment, he's deep in conversation with another of his ilk. The appointment is nothing more than a sham meant to get inside the house unhampered and see what—if anything—you might've disturbed."

"How can he pretend to be a contractor when he isn't one?"

"He could very well be connected with the building trade. The Gehíwans can be found in almost every occupation you can think of. In order to blend in they too must have a means of making a living. After all, they can't steal everything they need, now can they?"

"I suppose you're right." She raked her fingers through her tousled hair as she squinted at the clock. "He's here early, what shall I do?"

"I don't think he'll approach the door until it's time. Still, I think you should get up and get dressed just in case he finishes his discussion with his cohort and lets his impatience get the better of him."

Tala peeked down at her nightgown. "Do you think I should send him on his way—tell him I no longer have need for his services or something?"

"No, they're a suspicious lot. Dismissing him outright might make him believe you've somehow found the key, along with some kind of hidden hoard you don't want anyone to know about. I think it's best if you let him in so he can see you've done nothing to the house. Give him the grand tour and ask him the questions you've already prepared. Once you're finished, tell him you need his bid as soon as possible. Make him believe your time here is more limited than it really is."

"Why?"

"Just so they don't try and schedule any unnecessary visits," he said.

Her brows knit themselves together as she took in a shallow breath. "You're not leaving me alone with him, are you?"

****

Micah shook his head and as a slight grin emerged, he cupped her chin for several uncomfortable moments. All the while his thumb brushed back and forth along its length. That simple caress stirred the embers she thought she had quashed before sleep overtook her last night.

"Not even for a second. However, our shifter won't know that. You needn't look so worried, Tala. I'll not allow you any harm—least of all by the mewling, scurvy riffraff waiting outside your door."

"I know, really I do, it's just that—" She bit down on her lip as she dismissed the rest of her remark with a slight shake of her head. "I'll run upstairs and get dressed—it'll only take me a minute."

He nodded as she rose from her makeshift bed and then climbed up the stairs. While she dressed, the smell of freshly brewed coffee wafted into her room. She barely noticed. Her heart hammered inside her chest as the weight of the duty hit home. Could she make the malevolent convicts believe she had no knowledge as to who they were and what they wanted? Despite her uncertainty, she left the bedroom and headed for the stairway. The moment she took hold of the banister, she met Micah's gaze as he waited for her at the bottom of the stairs with rifle in hand. He didn't look the least bit concerned. That alone boosted her confidence.

He cocked his head toward the walkway. "They're on their way up now."

"They?" She stopped midway on the steps and peered out of the window to the right of the door. Through the cream-colored voile curtains, she caught sight of the men as they strode toward the porch.

"Apparently your man required a companion, but don't let that intimidate you in any way, all right? I'll be at your side throughout the entire meeting."

Tala squared her shoulders, and gathered her

courage. Once again she looked him in the eye. "You needn't fuss, Micah. I'm sure I can handle this little task just fine."

He flashed a cocky grin and winked. "I know you can, and just for the record, *princess*—I never fuss."

The knock at the door prevented her fiery retort. She waited where she stood for several seconds. When she thought enough time had passed, she descended the remaining steps. With all the calm she could muster, she opened the door. As they crossed the threshold, Micah raised his rifle to the height of his waist. His finger rested against the trigger. The shifters didn't even glance in his direction.

The man to her left stepped forward. "Miss Westbrook? I am Oscar Whitting. This man is my assistant, Theodore Crosby."

Tala feigned indifference to the name—or hoped she had—as she met Oscar's gaze head on. "Please, come in."

"Where would you like to begin?" asked Oscar as his eyes darted about the foyer.

"I thought we'd start with the kitchen—it's this way. I noticed a leak coming from the bottom of the faucet. That will need attention along with everything else we've discussed."

Despite the obvious impatience of the Gehíwan convicts, Tala took her time going through each of the rooms on the ground floor. She pointed out every flaw she could see. Then, as she led them toward the stairs, she remembered the damaged doorway. She sought a reasonable explanation. Yet, as they approached the bedroom, all evidence of the scuffle had disappeared. She spared Micah a glance as the men poked about. He looked bored now and that almost made her laugh. Finally, she escorted them back to the entrance way.

"Well, I can't think of anything else, so—" she said.

Oscar gave her a curt nod. "All right, Miss Westbrook. We'll get back to you."

"You might want to do that sooner rather than later. Because of other responsibilities and obligations I have, I'll only accept bids until the end of the week. After that, I'll no longer be in the United Kingdom. By necessity I'll already have awarded the contract to the company I think most reasonable as well as competent."

The men exchanged a glance as Oscar turned the handle of the door. "That doesn't give us much time, but I'll see what I can do."

"Thank you for fitting me into your busy schedule and coming on such short notice." Tala accompanied them onto the porch while Micah stood right at her side. They waited there until the shifters climbed inside their truck and drove away. She could hear the gears grind each time they shifted, all the way down the street. Once they returned to the drawing room, she turned around and gazed at him. "Do you think they'll return the vehicle or just abandon it?"

"I wouldn't put it past them to just keep it," Micah said as he leaned his rifle against the corner of the wall.

Tala merely nodded in response as she momentarily dropped her gaze. Her confession wouldn't come easy. At last she swallowed her pride. As she looked up, she found Micah gazing at her most intently. "Micah? I didn't expect them to test me. Do you think I gave myself away when they introduced the second man using Dolph's alias?"

A small grin accompanied the slight shake of his head. "I think you did just fine."

"That doesn't answer my question—" Her cell phone rang. She glanced down at the screen. "My father." She turned away as she lifted the phone to her ear. "Hello, Dad. Do you have news for me already?"

"Believe it or not, I do," Curtis replied sounding very pleased. "Do you have something to write with?"

"Just a minute." Tala made her way to the desk and opened her bag. She withdrew a pen and an old envelope she hadn't discarded. "All right, I'm ready whenever you are."

"After a bit of detective work, I discovered my father gave every item anyone ever left behind to his cousin for safekeeping. This man's name is Hiram Collier. He lives in the town of Rotherham, South Yorkshire. I've just finished talking to him. He's now awaiting your call. If you like, he can see you this afternoon."

As her father rattled off the phone number and address, she jotted them down. "All right, I've got it. I'll give him a call as soon as I hang up."

"Good, and just to let you know, Hiram is getting up there in age. He's a pleasant man, but a bit hard of hearing now. So, you might want to speak up," Curtis warned.

"I'll do that. Thanks Dad, I know Theodore will be grateful for the time you spent in his behalf. I'll talk to you later and let you know how it all turns out, okay?" Tala turned around and as she looked at Micah, she gave him a victorious smile. Once she entered the number, she again lifted the phone to her ear. "Here we go—keep your fingers crossed."

Just as Hiram answered, Micah turned his gaze to the side window and then strode toward it. An instant later, he whirled around. He hastened his steps as he grabbed his rifle from the corner. Without saying a word, he disappeared from the room.

Tala found it difficult to keep her mind on her conversation. She muddled through the pleasantries then somehow made an appointment for later in the day without sounding like a complete idiot. The instant she ended the call, she raced to the window and peeked outside. She didn't see Micah, nor did she see anything that warranted his attention, much less his rifle.

The moment she turned away, two shots rang out in close succession. Her heart pounded loud in her ears. She ran for the door, flung it open and gasped in horror.

No more than two feet from her door, the bodies of her Gehíwan visitors laid sprawled out across the porch. Each clung to a gruesome-looking knife as their now sightless eyes gazed upward at the morning sun.

As Micah rounded the corner, she flew into his arms without giving the instinctive impulse any forethought whatsoever. With one well-muscled arm, he held her close to his chest. He whispered words of comfort while a deluge of emotions encompassed her—relief, horror, revulsion, contempt, and gratitude. Her guardian had saved her from something vile and hideous a third time.

She swallowed past the lump in her throat. Just as she opened her mouth to speak, Levi and Nathaniel emerged from the shadow of the trees. They looked at the bodies with disgust as they approached them.

Levi cocked his head toward the door. "Micah,

why don't you take Tala back inside and we'll join you in a few minutes? In the meantime, we'll remove the vermin from the property."

Micah nodded and then, with his arm still about her waist, he took her inside the house. He led her into the drawing room and settled her into the chair nearest the fireplace.

"You've yet to have any breakfast. Would you like me to get you something to eat? I've got some coffee brewing, or perhaps you'd rather have a cup of tea?" While he asked the question, he held onto her hand.

She shook her head. "No. No, thank you. I really don't want anything right now."

"I don't imagine you would." He gave her hand a gentle press before he released it.

While he busied himself with adding additional wood to the dwindling fire, her mind replayed the morning's events over and over again. She envisioned herself opening that door a second time, only to be confronted by the shifters with those awful knives in their hands.

"Did your grandpa's cousin say whether or not he had Dolph's cane?" Micah asked.

She welcomed the question, it halted the frightening vision. "Well, he didn't really know. He said he never gave the inventoried items much attention even when he received them. However, we do have an appointment to see him later this evening. I thought we could leave right after lunch—" Tala stopped short in response to the grin he so obviously fought to contain. "Oh. I'm sorry, do you eat?"

"Quite regularly, but not out of hunger or need." Just as he finished the comment, Levi and Nathaniel entered the room. Micah settled his gaze upon Levi. "Are we all clear?"

"For now," said Levi. "However, I'm sure they'll be back and in greater numbers."

"You need to get Tala out of here now, Micah—and permanently," Nathaniel said.

"I intend to do just that. We have a lead on Dolph's cane that'll take us to Rotherham. In fact, we've just made plans to go. From there, I'll put her on a plane." Micah turned toward her. "Do you think you could bump up that appointment by an hour or two? If not, we could just wait out the time at one of the—"

"No." She shook her head. "I can't go anywhere right now. As you know, I have another contractor due to arrive in just a little over an hour. I can't leave until after I meet with him. Getting someone to renovate the house is the reason I'm here, Micah. My dad is counting on me to do that."

"We'll take care of the appointment for you as well as everything else that needs attention around here," Levi said as for a moment, he met Micah's gaze. "That way you're not at risk should your contractor be another malefactor. Should the company prove credible, we'll make sure your father gets the bid. Will that work to your satisfaction?"

"That's a very good idea," said Nathaniel. "We don't need a repeat of what happened this morning."

With the blatant reminder, Tala rose from her chair. They were right. She needed to rise above her stubbornness and leave England. After a deep breath, she turned toward Micah. "All right, I guess I can go along with that. Now, how do you purpose we accomplish all of this?"

Her all-powerful protector advanced a single step. "I'm not sure what you mean?"

"We have to let Dolph know what's going on so that—"

"We'll pay him a quick visit through the cellar entrance before we leave. If we find his cane we'll simply have him meet us at our next location."

"Okay, but if we just get in the car and go, won't the rebels follow us to each of our destinations?" she asked.

"More than likely," he said.

"So then, what do we do? I don't want Hiram or his household in any danger."

Micah shrugged away her concern. "You needn't worry, Tala. I can elude a shifter without any problem. You just have to do what I tell you to do."

****

Three hours later, Tala dropped her white linen napkin on top of her empty plate. She looked at her watch and then gazed pointedly at the companion who sat opposite her. "I need to get back to the manor. Now," she said using a firm tone of voice.

"As you can clearly see, I'm not finished with my beverage," Levi replied as he picked up his crystal wine glass and swirled its contents.

She clenched her teeth and narrowed her eyes. "I think you've had quite enough, don't you?"

Right on cue, Levi sneered. Without taking his gaze off her, he held his glass aloft. At once he caught the attention of their harried waiter. "Another one, my good man and make it snappy."

The man returned a subtle bow. "Right away, sir."

Levi lifted the glass to his lips. Then before he

consumed the remainder of his wine, he tilted the goblet toward her and raised a disdainful brow. "Just so you know—this has been a far more entertaining companion then what you have been today, my dear."

Tala vaulted to her feet and spun away from the table without saying a word. Micah remained a single step behind her as she weaved through the tables of the elegant restaurant while heading toward the ladies room. The moment she stepped through the door, she took in a breath and turned around to face him. He offered his hand in silent expectation. Though she anticipated it, and sought to quell it, her heart took flight the instant he laced his fingers through hers. He pulled her close to his side. For the look on his face, he knew very well how he affected her. At least he had the wisdom to feign ignorance as they vacated the room.

Micah led her out of the restaurant and into the parking lot through the kitchen exit. He scanned every inch of the parking lot before he opened her car door. She slid into the seat. At once she eased the key into the ignition and turned it over just as he climbed in beside her.

She adjusted the mirror and then turned the wheel in the direction of Hiram's estate. "Well, I'm grateful that little affair is finally over. The whole lunch thing put me on edge."

Micah chuckled. "You shouldn't have worried. After all, you handled it like a pro."

"Now that's high praise, coming from you. However, since no one leapt across the table with knife in hand, I assume either we weren't followed, or our malefactors didn't think it necessary to accompany us inside the restaurant?"

"No, they followed us inside. The shadow dogs entered the restaurant about two minutes after we did."

Tala gave her companion a brief glance. "They did?"

"Yes. They sat in the corner booth just to your left," he replied with an air of indifference. "The imbeciles will probably sit there and await your return for heaven only knows how long."

"Do you really think they'll do that?"

"If they adhere to the duty to which they were assigned. With only one public entrance I don't think it will occur to them you are no longer in the building until the place closes. Between now and then, they'll probably just assume you're in the ladies room, crying your eyes out."

"Levi isn't just going to sit there and wait with them, is he?"

"No. Levi is already gone, I'm sure. You needn't worry. He and Nathaniel will meet us at the scheduled time and place just as we planned."

They drove the final fifteen minutes to Hiram's house in silence. Once they arrived at the doorstep of the beautiful, eighteenth century English manor, she turned her gaze toward Micah. "You will let him see you, won't you?"

"If that's your wish."

She nodded as she pressed the doorbell. "I think I'd feel better if he knew you were here."

The door swung open just as she finished the comment. The middle-aged man greeting them lifted a brow as his eyes darted back and forth between them. "Miss Westbrook, I presume?"

"Yes, and this is Micah Berrington."

With a sweep of his hand, he invited them inside. "Mr. Collier is expecting you. He's in the study, so if you'll follow me?"

The moment they entered the room that smelled of cherry tobacco, Hiram rose from his antique desk and approached them. He held out his hand and welcomed them with a broad smile. Though he glanced at Micah, he gave her his full attention.

"You were just a child in the last photograph your grandfather sent me. I can see you have grown into the beautiful woman your grandfather predicted you'd become."

"You're very kind, Hiram. Thank you," Tala said as she took in the vast array of books filling the shelves on both sides and behind Hiram's desk. She then turned her gaze toward Micah. "This is my good friend, Micah Berrington. I hope you don't mind that I brought him along?"

Hiram gave Micah a friendly nod as he shook his hand. "Not at all. Nice to meet you, Micah. Now, please, sit down and make yourselves comfortable. I'll have Rudger bring in some refreshments. Would you prefer tea or coffee?"

Tala's hand went to her stomach. "Oh, you needn't bother with any of that, Hiram. We have just had lunch, but thank you for the offer anyway."

Despite her impatience, Hiram insisted they sit down. For awhile he held them captive as he recalled a host of memories. Any other time she might have enjoyed hearing stories about her grandfather. However, the elusive cane remained uppermost in her mind. When the conversation finally wound down, her distant cousin opened a desk drawer. He withdrew a single key, and pressed the buzzer on his desk.

"I know you've come to conduct a search for specific items. Therefore, I won't keep you any longer. However, I'm afraid I can't climb the attic stairs anymore. Rudger is more than happy to look after you in my place. There are several boxes originating from Westbrook Manor up there, so feel free to take all of the time you need in going through them, all right?"

The dim light bulb in the attic revealed layers of dust on top of the boxes that were stacked haphazardly against the wall opposite the door. Rudger extended a hand toward them. He apologized for the disarray with nothing more than a lift of his brows. "As you can see, it's been quite some time since anyone has visited the attic. Due to other obligations we had today, we simply didn't have time to clear away the clutter after you called."

"We wouldn't have expected you to, so don't give it another thought," Tala said.

"Would you like me to help you?" he asked. "I'm not sure what you're looking for, but if you need an extra hand I'd be happy to help."

Tala shook her head. "I appreciate the offer, but we'll be fine. Feel free to hang around and watch if you'd like. However if you have other things you'd rather do with your time, don't let us keep you away from them."

Rudger bowed his head. "Then I'll leave you to your task. If you need anything, just let me know."

Two hours later, Micah picked up the last box, and set it down on top of the table. He peeled off the tape and opened it. Tala took in a breath. Her excitement grew as she looked into Micah's dark-brown eyes.

Dolph's intricately carved cane, with its phoenix head handle, rested on top of several layers of old clothing. With the greatest of care, he extracted the piece from its nest. Together they examined the three dimensional crest of the mythological bird and found it just as Dolph described.

Chapter Seven

The tranquility inside the rustic hunting lodge, with its wooden furniture and multi-colored braided rugs, provided a bit of respite from the day's worries and stress. Although Tala had questions aplenty, for the time being she wouldn't disturb the hush. Here and now, from the comfort of the chair where she had snuggled, she watched her handsome bodyguard as he built a fire to ward off the early autumn chill.

As he turned away from the fireplace, her gaze lingered over every inch of his perfect form and then settled on his incredible dark brown eyes—eyes that never failed to take away her breath whenever he looked at her. This had nothing to do with his immortal status either. She had no doubt whatsoever he had the same effect on the women of his time. Probably every woman he had ever encountered vied for his attention despite his brusque, overbearing, and more often than not, arrogant manner. She couldn't help but wonder just how many of them captured it. No matter how badly she wanted the answer to that question, she wouldn't ask him.

"You're awfully quiet," Micah said as he brushed the dust away from his hands. "Are you all right?"

She sat up a little higher in her seat, straightened the crocheted doily on the arm of the chair, and nodded. "Just a little tired, I guess. You must admit it's been quite a day and it began far earlier than either of us expected."

He aimed a thumb toward the old wooden door at the back of the room. "You can use the bedroom if you wish. I'm sure the feather bed is far more comfortable than the chair."

"No, I'm not that tired. Besides, everyone will be here soon, won't they?"

"Any minute now, but none of them would begrudge you a little sleep before I whisk you off to the airport."

"I know, but I think I'll wait anyway."

"That's your choice, of course." He eased himself into the large oak rocking chair someone had surely crafted a century or two ago. He settled into a slow, rhythmic motion. The creaks from the sway of the chair added to the symphony of the crackling fire.

As they gazed at each other, she couldn't help but smile over her small triumph. "What? You're not going to insist on having your way this time?"

"Would it do any good if I did?" he countered.

"No, probably not."

"That's what I thought."

Tala's smile faded under the power of his gaze. Heat rose from her belly and touched her cheeks. She fervently prayed within the play of firelight and shadows, he didn't notice the blush. Then, in a bid for some kind of normalcy, she took in a breath and slowly released it. "Tell me, in light of all that's happened since the day I met you, does Dolph now fall under the protection of the Bewitan Fierd as well?"

"No, I'm afraid he doesn't. At best we can only give him information essential to his cause if we've discovered it. As I said before, just the direct descendents of Alfred fall under our protection and then only in time of need."

"I remember you saying that. The comment made me wonder just who determines the need?" For such a simple question, he hesitated far longer than necessary. Apparent from his expression alone, she had once again strayed into a place he didn't want her exploring. "Is the question that difficult to answer or is it top secret?"

A deep sigh accompanied the slight shake of his head. "Those who keep track of the descendents make that call. Let's leave the subject at that, all right?"

"I can do that for you, at least for now. In the meantime, can you tell me how Dolph will escape the tunnel and meet us here with all the insurgents swarming Westbrook Manor?"

"I didn't ask, nor did he provide the details."

She halted her "*that's so like you*" response in the same moment she realized she didn't know him well enough to say it. So why did it feel otherwise? The man walked into her life just days ago. Despite that fact, it felt like she'd known him all of her life. As she mulled over the reason for that, Nathaniel and Levi entered the lodge, with Dolph in tow.

Nathaniel wore a smile just as broad as Levi's. As Dolph strolled up beside them, Nathaniel spared the Gehíwan warden a glance. He then gazed pointedly at Micah. "You remember Dolph telling us about the advantage he has over the insurgents? The one they know nothing about?"

"That I do," said Micah.

"Since you'll never guess what it is, I'll just come right out and tell you," Nathaniel said.

He paused long enough for Micah to expel an irritated breath and shake his head. "Are you going to do that today, Nathaniel?"

Though his eyes twinkled with mirth, Nathaniel assumed a serious expression and sniffed. "He flies."

Micah turned his narrowed gaze toward Dolph. "You shift into a bird?"

Dolph bobbed his head from side to side. "Yes, and something from my world that bears a strong resemblance to your golden eagle, I'd say."

"Indeed, and you should see that wingspan of his, Micah," Levi said as he swung his arms outward from the height of his chest. "We're talking at least eleven, perhaps even twelve feet here."

"Is that right?" Micah gazed at Dolph for several seconds. "Am I wrong in thinking you're the first Gehíwan native that has ever taken on the persona of a bird?"

"That I wouldn't know with any degree of certainty. However, to my knowledge, no one else has ever considered it," he said.

Micah stopped the motion of his rocking chair and leaned a bit forward. "But then they wouldn't, would they?"

Tala looked back and forth between Dolph and Micah. "Why not?"

"Because," said Dolph, "most of my people are drawn to an animal persona associated with agility, power, and cunning. Wolves are most often chosen because they run in packs, thereby keeping their clan and like-minded people unified."

"Then what made you opt for something different?" she asked.

"I liked the idea of flight and the ability to see the smallest of details on the ground from the greatest of heights." Dolph lowered his gaze and pursed his lips as he paused for several seconds. He sighed heavily and then looked at each of them in turn. "However, I feel I must confess while in my realm, I did, in fact, choose the wolf like most everyone else. So, the wolf is the only persona my people have ever seen—the only one I want them to see. I've never revealed my ability to anyone before. Indeed, I wouldn't have revealed it today had it not been necessary upon leaving the tunnel. I trust you'll not share this information with anyone else? For my safety, you must keep this information to yourselves, please."

"Don't worry. Your secret is safe with us," said Micah. "Even so, it's quite an accomplishment, is it not?"

"I had to work very hard over the centuries to achieve it," Dolph replied. "With the insurgents hot on my trail at all times, I concluded the only chance I had to outwit them and survive was to transform into something they couldn't catch without a great deal of difficulty. I believe the will to survive finally produced the desired results."

"Well, I for one salute you for it," said Nathaniel.

Micah nodded in agreement. "I think you're wise in keeping both the accomplishment and the persona a secret, for it's something no one in your realm would ever suspect."

"Very wise," Levi said. "In most cases, once a secret is revealed, it has a way of becoming common knowledge."

"You're right about that." Micah took on a

thoughtful expression. "I take it you used the eagle to locate the second key?"

"Not the precise location, which I still must find, but only the ruins of the castle that keeps it hidden," Dolph replied. "Without the eyes of an eagle, I don't think I ever would've found it."

"What do you mean?" asked Tala. "Shouldn't castle ruins not only be obvious but very well documented in both books and photographs?"

"These ruins have been lost to your history for quite some time now. What's left of the structure has been overtaken by the surrounding mountain vegetation. Therefore, the ruins are very difficult for anyone to see outright, or visit, without a great deal of experience in such matters I should think," Dolph replied. "One of the guards, a close friend of mine by the name of Chêzin, told me about the castle just days after the insurgents found him, tortured him, and then left him for dead. As you can imagine, the details he gave me as to its location were vague at best and it took me almost five years to find it."

"You said earlier these ruins are about one hundred kilometers away from your church, correct?" asked Micah.

Dolph nodded. "Yes—as the bird flies, anyway."

"How far away from the church is your portal?" asked Levi.

"Oh, no more than one hundred twenty kilometers at best," Dolph said.

Micah mulled that over for a moment. "How do you propose to bring them together? I'm quite sure the weight of two keys combined is more than your bird persona can carry over such a distance."

"You're right. Carrying both would be a struggle and quite obvious to anyone who might witness it. Therefore, I thought I'd recover the key belonging to Chêzin first, as it might take some days to find the exact place it's hidden. Once I have it in my possession, I'll bring it somewhere near the portal and bury it. Then just prior to the rising of the black moon, I'll travel to the church and fetch my key."

Levi huffed out a derisive breath. "You're taking quite a chance in doing that, Dolph. The rebels in the surrounding area could sense your presence and discover what you're about. If they stumble across the newly disturbed dirt and examine it—your quest ends and theirs begins anew."

"That's a risk I'll have to take, Levi," Dolph replied. "I'm afraid there's no other option."

Tala shook her head as she rose to her feet and approached him. "No, Dolph, that isn't the only option available. Levi's right. They sensed your presence at Westbrook Manor simply because the wind made an unexpected shift in direction. Since you've no idea where the key is amidst the ruins, they could do so again when you consider the length of time it might take you to find it. Your mission is too important to screw it up at the last minute. You need some help."

"There's no one else, Miss Westbrook. The insurgents have killed every nationalist on this side of the portal except for me. I'm on my own and have been for several years now."

"No, you don't understand. I'm quite willing and able to help you. Just give me the location of this castle. I promise you—upon my word of honor—I *will* find the key. On the night of the black moon we'll meet at the portal at whatever time you choose. Once we're there, you can slip through without—"

"You would do that for me?" Dolph cut in as a mixture of surprise and gratitude lit up his eyes.

"I wouldn't have offered if I didn't mean it," Tala replied.

"No! Absolutely not," Micah ground out as he leapt to his feet. "Are you out of your mind, Tala? Do you know what the insurgents would do to you if they captured you?"

Dolph, his discomfort obvious, shifted his stance and glanced at the door. "I think I'll—uh—just step outside for a breath of fresh air. I'll return shortly. Then if you should still desire, we'll discuss the location of the ruins and all of the details you'll need then, all right?"

Dolph didn't wait for a reply. Once the Gehíwan guard vacated the lodge, Tala turned her gaze toward Micah. "And do you know what will happen if they capture Dolph and his key instead? How many direct descendents of Alfred will be in peril when a rabid army of anarchists plow through the portal unhampered, Micah? Would you have enough guardians to protect them all during such a calamity?"

Micah firmed his jaw as he gave his head a vigorous shake. "No. We'll not even discuss this. You have a reservation on a plane bound for Maine, a plane scheduled to leave in less than six hours, I might add. For your own safety, you need to be on that plane. Should it become necessary, *we* can fetch the key for Dolph—"

"No, you can't." Tala folded her arms and anchored them against her body as she boldly met the fury shining in Micah's eyes. "You said you weren't allowed to help the man, remember? In addition, you know I can cloak my presence from animals in the wild. I can hide from people just as well. I have no doubt whatsoever that I can find that key and get it to the portal on time without any trouble whatsoever."

Micah rolled his eyes heavenward. "Tala, you're not being reasonable—"

"Look, with or without your permission, I'm going to do this, Micah. Nothing you can say or do will change my mind. Do you understand?" The prolonged silence that followed her tirade was deafening, even to her. Nonetheless, she refused to back down from her stance. She couldn't.

Finally, Nathaniel stepped forward. He put a light hand on top of her shoulder and gave it a gentle squeeze.

"I hate to say it, Micah," he said as he met her guardian's gaze, "but Tala does have a valid point. Dolph would take a huge risk if he followed the plan he's set forth. Could he pull it off? Perhaps. *But*, if he is found out, all hell will break loose in this dimension as well as his own. Tala is the perfect person to fetch that key. She already knows the circumstances as well as the importance that surrounds this task. In addition, she has a great deal of experience in the field. To top it all off, she has you to protect her. I've no doubt you can get her through this without incident."

"You've done this kind of thing before and under far worse conditions, Micah," Levi reminded him. "I'm sure even the ealdormen would agree given the circumstances, Tala's plan is the course we should take."

Micah put a hand to his hip and expelled a ragged breath. He closed his eyes against the barrage of reason and logic. When he opened them again, he looked at Levi. "You'll do me the favor?"

"Of course. We'll be back before you know it." He turned toward Nathaniel and cocked his head toward the door. "Are you ready?"

The words no more than left his mouth when the two men vanished from sight.

Tala gazed at Micah. "What favor? Where did they go?"

"To let those in my realm know of this change in plans. They'll also check the flights heading for Romania that still have empty seats we can commandeer," he said.

Tala fused her gaze to his and slowly approached him. As she halted her steps just inches away from where he stood, she placed a gentle hand against his chest.

"I'm sorry for all of the turmoil that's caused you so much distress, Micah. But this is just something I feel I have to do. You don't have to come with me if you don't want to." She swallowed hard. "I don't know how things work in the realm of the Bewitan Fierd, but maybe if you ask, they'll let you bow out?"

Micah took her hand and caressed the top of it with his thumb. "Such a thought would never cross my mind, Miss Westbrook. I'm afraid you're stuck with me until such time as my services are no longer required."

She gave him an enchanting smile—one that touched all the way through to his soul. "That's good. I'm kind of attached to my bodyguard. I must confess that at this point, I really don't want to break in anyone else. You were difficult enough for me to handle."

Despite her feeble attempt to lighten his mood, he gripped her hand a little tighter. "Do you have any idea what you're getting yourself into, Tala?" he whispered.

A soft breath of laughter accompanied her downward glance. She shook her head before she again lifted her eyes to meet with his. "No, not even remotely—and that's probably a very good thing, don't you think?"

"Perhaps." He paused for a moment. "I know this goes against the grain, but if you can, I need a promise from you. Do you think you can do that?"

"I don't know. You'll have to tell me what that promise is first."

"The course you've chosen is a difficult one. Far more difficult than you might imagine. Things don't always happen the way you think they will. There are far more Gehíwan convicts in Eastern Europe than there are here. By now, they may even know who you are. Therefore, you must listen to me at all times and in all places. Do as I ask. If I ask you for silence, or to hold perfectly still, or any number of things, you must do it immediately and without question. Explanations can and will come later. Will you promise me you'll do that?"

Her head dropped and she shook it a little. "You're right. That does go against the grain." She then lifted her gaze to meet his and smiled. "Nonetheless, I'll see what I can do, okay?"

Micah shook his head. "That's not even close to what I asked for. Would you like to try again?"

She drew in a deep breath and then gave it a slow release. "I promise—absolutely and without condition—I'll make every effort to do as you ask, Micah. You know I don't want to die. I don't want to be captured and tortured by ruthless Gehíwan convicts either. Truly I don't. However, I do want Dolph to make it home in one piece so he can gather his army. I then want them to take care of the mess his people created with their security breach, once and for all."

"No more so than I," he said. "So let's go get this done and do it without loss of life or limb, all right?"

"That sounds good to me."

Just as the words left her mouth, the trio returned with Levi ahead of the others. The man's gaze darted back and forth between him and Tala. "We were able to block the sale of two seats on a plane bound for Bucharest one week from today if you want to take it. All of the flights between now and then are booked, so I'm afraid we couldn't finagle anything earlier."

"The days in between shouldn't be a complete loss," said Nathaniel as he approached them. "Tala can use the time to square away things concerning the house with her father. She can let him know she'll be taking a little trip so he won't worry about her whereabouts."

"That'll work," said Micah as he moved toward the small table to the right of the fireplace. "All right Dolph, come over here please, and point out the precise location of the castle ruins. We'll begin with the mountain range and then move inward, all right?"

As the map emerged and hovered just above the table, Tala gasped. "Is that a hologram?"

"Something along those lines, yes." With an arm extended, Micah called her over for a closer look. In an instant she stood at his side.

Dolph extended a finger. "Right here, Micah. There's a river flowing downward from the mountains in this area. Follow its course about halfway up the peak. There you'll find a rather large tributary moving eastward."

Once Micah zoomed in on the region he selected, Dolph drew a small, imaginary circle on the right side of the chart. "I'll give you a detailed map before you go, but the ruins are located just about here. They're not easy to see for the thick vegetation that has consumed them, so you must pay close attention to the landmarks I give you."

"Are any of the walls still standing?" asked Tala.

"At the time of my visit, I could see the deteriorated remains of what I believe are the outer walls," Dolph replied. "However, just so you know, I haven't explored them. I didn't want anything disturbed in this area until the last possible moment for apparent reasons. In addition, I didn't think it even necessary until I found my cane and had it in my possession once again."

"Oh—with everything else going on I'd almost forgotten about your cane." Tala went to the fireplace mantel, retrieved the cane, and handed it off to Dolph.

"At long last." The Gehíwan guard bowed his head as he clutched the cane to his chest. He smiled his gratitude. "I cannot thank you enough, Miss Westbrook. I am forever in your debt."

"You're welcome," she replied. "Now, let's get those keys and get you safely home, all right?"

Long after the discussion ended, and the three men had left, Tala sat in the chair, gazing at the fire. Though Micah faced the window, he could see her reflection in the glass easily enough. He didn't see the concern or anxiety he expected to see. Rather she appeared serene as she contemplated her thoughts. He counted that a good thing. She deserved whatever peace and contentment she could find. The time she'd face unknown dangers would come soon enough.

His gaze wandered over her lovely face and form. Part of him rejoiced that the time of their parting had been postponed. Yet, his rational side bemoaned the fact. Every minute, every hour he spent in her company, would make their final separation far more difficult to endure.

"I guess I'd better go through my things, decide what I need to take along on this adventure and get them packed," she said.

Her comment ended his thoughts. He turned around and directly met her gaze. "You'll have plenty of time for that in the days ahead. Perhaps it would serve you better if you caught up on some sleep."

She abandoned her chair and looked over the luggage stacked neatly near the bedroom door. "My sleep will be more restful if I have everything separated into various piles tonight. You did say my photography equipment will be safe here, right?"

"Yes, but if it makes you feel better, we can have the lot of it sent to your father's home."

"No, he'll worry over the reason and wonder what I'm about. I'll just go ahead and leave it here with the rest of my stuff." Tala turned a slow circle as her gaze roamed over every nook and cranny of the antiquated lodge. She gazed at him with her lovely eyes and drew her brows together. "If you don't mind my asking, just where is 'here' anyway?"

"Just outside of London."

"Really? This entire area just seems far too remote and uninhabited to be near London—not to mention the fact that this old hunting lodge would fit far better on a movie set somewhere."

Micah wavered for only a moment. He couldn't see any reason to withhold information from her now. Once they parted ways, she wouldn't remember anything, anyway. "Not the London of the past."

A whole lot of confusion and a touch of fear filled her eyes. "What exactly do you mean by that?"

"Most of the shelters used by the Bewitan Fierd when in this dimension are dwellings that once existed, but are no more. This place, as well as some of the homes we'll be using during our expedition, is available for our use by way of a time-slip—sort of—if you can follow that." The expression on her face almost made him laugh, yet he stopped short of a grin. "Well, I suppose that's a bit much for you to accept this late in the evening. Maybe you ought to just go ahead and get packed if that's what you'd rather do. We can discuss it later if you wish."

For several seconds she said nothing. During the silence they simply gazed at each other while she came to terms with what he said. Finally, she turned and took a step toward her luggage. Then for whatever reason, she thought better of it. She whirled around and faced him with a hand on her hip. The humor shining within her eyes belied her serious expression. She lifted her chin a notch.

"Upon my arrival to these shores my feet were planted firmly on the ground, Micah Berrington, do you realize that? And then you brazenly walked into my life and turned my whole world upside down with your outlandish tales." She rubbed her lips together in a failed attempt to hide her smile. "I hope you're happy."

Chapter Eight

Tala had never blatantly bypassed airport security before. She had never boarded a plane without a ticket. Cutting to the head of the line never occurred to her and most certainly not while standing beside a man holding a rifle. She never invited herself to sit in first class either. Yet, as the jet taxied down the runway on its way to Bucharest, she could now say she had experienced them all.

She turned toward her accomplice who didn't appear the least bit remorseful for his scandalous actions. If anything he looked bored. She nibbled at a nail and hoped it hid her amusement well enough. "So let me guess. If not for me, you would've already arrived in Romania, and at the precise location Dolph pointed out on the map, thereby avoiding the drudge of physically crossing the miles between London and those hidden ruins deep within the Romanian mountains?"

For a moment, Micah dropped his gaze to their clasped hands. His thumb drew a path along the length of her finger. "Could you please tell me what possible good it would do me to be there without you?"

A quiet breath of laughter accompanied the slight shake of her head.

"Now what do you find so funny about that?" he asked.

"Nothing, really, just your aversion to answer any of my questions," she replied.

He huffed out a breath as he knit his brows together. "I don't have an aversion to answering your questions."

"Oh, but you do," she insisted. "You either answer my questions with a question, or you give me the 'that's not any of your business, missy, and I would thank you to remember that' look."

"No, I don't, nor do I even have such a look."

"Yes you do. What's more, every single answer I get has to be pried out of your mouth using no less than the strength of Hercules."

A touch of humor filled his eyes even as he assumed an expression of consternation. "You should know your excessive exaggeration doesn't become an Alfred descendent, Miss Westbrook. I must tell you I've never before seen the like."

"Is that right? Well, if I'm so wrong, then just answer the question."

"What question?"

Tala burst out laughing. She couldn't help it. At once she smothered the sound with her hand. Her gaze darted about the plane.

Micah chuckled as he gave her hand a little press. "No one can hear you, Tala. You're safe with me."

No doubt about that, she mused. Micah had made her feel safe from the moment she met him. Now that she thought about it, she should've had some degree of fear when she woke up in a strange house, with a man she'd never met hovering over her, but she didn't. A nod accompanied her barely visible smile. "I know."

Resigned to the three hour flight, she settled back

into her seat and turned her gaze toward the view the small window offered. Several times during the crossing, Micah filched beverages and snacks from the flight attendant's food cart for them to share. Despite the woman's growing confusion over her dwindling fare, his antics made her laugh and conquered the tedium of the flight. Then, once the plane landed Micah waited until after the last of the passengers disembarked before escorting her toward the exit. Although the people couldn't see them, they could feel something tangible if they inadvertently bumped into an arm or shoulder.

Just as they passed by the agitated attendant, the woman leaned toward one of her associates. Her eyes, filled now with horror, swept slowly over the plane's interior. She lowered her voice to a whisper. "Terri, I think this plane is haunted. Someone must have died in first class—"

Mouth agape, Terri stared at her for several seconds. "Don't be ridiculous, Beverly. What would make you say such an insane thing anyway?"

Beverly closed her eyes as a shudder overtook her entire body. "Things disappeared from my food cart more times than I care to recall… and they disappeared right before my eyes! Then, if you can believe this, empty bottles, cups, and food wrappers somehow found their way back on top of it each time I walked up and down the aisle."

Tala exchanged a glance with Micah. Even though she fought off the giggle that threatened escape, she couldn't hold back her smile. As she lifted a brow, she waved a finger in Beverly's direction. "That poor woman will need years of therapy. You know that, don't you?"

"Ah, she'll get over it," he said.

She drew in a sharp breath and feigned astonishment over his blithe reply. "Don't you feel even the least bit contrite?"

"Not even a smidgeon." He tucked her hand in the crook of his arm and winked. "Now come along, we have some ground to cover before we settle in for the night."

"We're not staying in Bucharest?"

"No, we'll head to an area a little more remote and closer to our destination. Levi should already have a car waiting for us for the first leg of our journey."

"Now that you've brought up Levi and the fact he's the one that got us a car, I have a question about your companions I've been dying to ask."

"Now why doesn't *that* surprise me any?" he asked.

She rolled her eyes heavenward. Despite the barb, she forged ahead. "If I have this right, you are my one and only guardian, protector, bodyguard, or whatever you want to call yourself, correct?"

"That's right."

"So then what role do Levi and Nathaniel play in all of this? I mean, they never seem to wander far from your side, so—"

"As your guardian, I am charged with straying no farther away from you than—for lack of a better explanation—what I can *feel* and then instantly respond to in regards to your well-being and preservation. Yet, at times the circumstances surrounding those we protect require things that can't be attained within that proximity. Things such as the gathering of important information, reconnaissance, supplies, or even acquiring a car. Does that make sense to you?"

"About as much sense as anything else, I suppose."

The car in question turned out to be a Jaguar that Micah drove far faster than what she thought safe or even possible for that matter. Still, his skill as well as that speed got them to their destination in half the time it might've taken otherwise and every minute counted. When he pulled up in front of the quaint little lodge, surrounded by nothing but forest trees and lush vegetation, she turned her gaze toward him. "Another one of your time-slip hideouts?"

He merely grinned as he vacated the car, came around and opened her door. After she exited, he took her bag and retrieved his rifle. "Lest you think I'm loathed to answer your question yet again, the answer is yes. This is another one of those places."

"What would happen if you walked into the place and found it filled with people?" she asked as he opened the entryway door and allowed her entrance into the darkened room.

"Then I'd shoot everyone inside, of course—men, women, children, dogs, cats, rats, or any of God's creatures that might enter the premises while I use it. After all, we certainly can't leave any witnesses after we break into the place and make ourselves at home, now can we?" No more than a two second pause separated the response from his laughter. As he gazed into her eyes, he traced along the length of her nose with his finger and winked. "I'm just kidding, Tala. You needn't look so horrified. Now, let me provide you with a bit of light and some warmth in here. Then if you want, I'll explain how all of this works, all right?"

"That would be great." She headed for the nineteenth century styled sofa, while Micah stooped down by the fireplace and picked up some kindling.

Once he had the fire built and the final lantern lit, he sat down in the sturdy leather chair across from her and looked her over. "Are you warm enough? If you aren't, I suspect we could find a blanket or two around here."

"No, that isn't necessary. I'm fine, thank you." She drew her legs up onto the sofa and reclined a little more against the soft arm pillow. "Since you refer solely to me when it comes to light and warmth, I assume on top of never getting hungry or needing sleep, you don't get cold or need light to guide your way in dark places either?"

The mirthful eyes, which accompanied a very charming grin, caused quite a commotion deep inside her stomach. "Makes me sound very mystical, doesn't it?"

"Or just plain creepy," she countered. "But since that's the case, why bother with a coat?" Not that she complained about the black, form-fitting duster he wore—quite the contrary, actually.

"Just to avoid attention and blend in more with the crowd when wearing a coat is expected."

"You? Blend in with the crowd? That's a laugh. Even so, we'll let it go for now, because I believe you were about to tell me all about those peculiar time-slips once you completed your list of self-appointed chores."

"Ah, yes," he said as he scratched at the corner of his mouth. "The phenomenon isn't unheard of, you know. Valid accounts of such an event have occurred quite regularly over the centuries. Even while in my mortality I personally witnessed a bevy of hysterical women swear up and down they had stopped at a quaint little town in northern England. They were on their way home from wherever they had gone off to, and spent the night at a very interesting inn. They said the proprietor, as well as his entire staff, seemed "very odd" and in turn that made them "very uncomfortable." So much so they rose early and bolted out of the door without their breakfast. Yet, no more than five minutes had passed before one of them discovered she had quite forgotten her parasol. Well, they just had to go back for this very essential item, right? Once they gathered their courage and returned, they discovered—to their horror—the entire village had simply disappeared, save the inn's fireplace and the chimney connected to it. Not a soul believed them at the time, me included. The townsfolk and even their husbands accused them of having indulged in the liberal consumption of spirits. A charge they denied with all the vigor they possessed, I might add."

A slight smile curved the corner of her lips despite all attempts to stop it. "Are you telling me, rather than being tipsy, they experienced one of your time-slips then?"

"Yes, they did. I know this because I have visited and used that very inn myself many times over the years. Just as there are various dimensions to this earth, there are also any number of time periods one can visit. They are not that hard to access if one knows how to use the gates and not just fall into one by mere happenstance as the ladies did in the story. Now, there are times, in order to keep those we protect safe, we need a shelter away from the dangers they face at the time. Since this is the case more often than you might think, we have located a number of accommodations in various areas throughout the world. Those assigned to this duty in my realm discover the time of abandonment or extended absence by the property owner. Then when necessary, we make use of them shortly after either one of those events occurred."

"Then depending on where we stay during this little sojourn of ours, we could be visiting a variety of different time periods, do I have that right?"

"You do."

"And as long as I am with you, we simply waltz in and out of them without any problem whatsoever."

"I don't know about the waltzing, but I guess that's a fair enough statement otherwise."

"Is is possible for someone to get stuck in a time he or she doesn't belong in?" she asked.

"Such a thing is possible of course, but it's a possibility *you* don't have to worry about—at least not while you're with me. Does that ease your mind a bit?"

"No, not really."

Micah chuckled.

A shiver traveled down her spine as she turned toward the fire. Getting trapped somewhere in history seemed a terrifying prospect. Yet, the more she thought about the subject, the more ridiculous it seemed. Except—here she sat—in another antiquated house that didn't look all that old. "You know, before we finish this quest I suspect you'll have me believing in leprechauns and elves, Mr. Berrington. What's more, I don't think you'll feel the least bit bad about that—not even when my family or friends have me committed to some horrid, sadistic psychiatric hospital somewhere while the doctors gleefully perform a lobotomy."

A grin accompanied the shake of his head. "No, I wouldn't go so far as to have you believe in the wee folk. Besides, you don't really have anything to worry about. I'm sure the minute you return to your lovely home in the United States you won't even remember I—the Bewitan Fierd or anyone connected to the Gehíwan dimension—ever existed."

"You want to lay a little bet on that one?" she challenged.

His grin slowly faded as the intensity of his gaze all but penetrated her soul. "I don't see where that would be a fair bet. Should I win the wager, you wouldn't remember you even owed the debt."

She snuggled a little deeper into the cushions and turned her sleepy gaze toward the flames. "I can guarantee you nothing on this earth could possibly make me forget you, Micah. Nothing."

Besides, how could she forget when she didn't want to forget? She wanted to help Dolph—truly she did. Yet, if someone asked for the underlying reason as to why she offered her assistance in the first place, she would admit that she just couldn't say goodbye to Micah right now. She enjoyed his company far too much. A day for goodbyes would surely come. She knew that. Nonetheless, as absurd as it seemed, she found a bit of contentment in knowing she wouldn't face their final farewell today.

****

Long after Tala had fallen into a deep, restful sleep, Micah added a few more logs to the fire. He then stepped outside for a breath of fresh air. Even though he looked up at the brilliant stars, his thoughts were far from them. Much to his personal detriment, he found himself thinking more often than not about Tala. What's more, those thoughts had nothing to do with his present obligations concerning her protection. For the first time since leaving that battlefield in Ireland, he wished for mortality, or that he could find an honorable way to explore the attraction he had for this woman. Then again, if wishes could truly be granted, perhaps the wisest wish would be to never have been given this assignment at all. Not that he could back out of it now. The time for that—if such a thing had ever existed— had already come and gone.

"I trust everything went according to plan?" asked Edward, who appeared suddenly near the entrance to the walkway.

"Not even so much as a single heart-stopping moment hindered our journey." He replied. "Is there a reason you're here rather than Nathaniel or Levi?"

"Well, for one, I thought I'd let you know the horses have arrived. You'll also find all of the supplies you'll need for the next portion of your journey inside the barn."

"That's good to know Edward, but Nathaniel or Levi could've told me that. That is their present duty, after all."

Edward shrugged away the comment. "I also thought I'd let you know the recent aggression by the Russians have made the Romanian government more than a little worried. They now feel it's in their best national interest to beef up their defenses."

"That doesn't surprise me at all, but again, what would that have to do with your visit?"

The slight shake of his head accompanied a

chuckle. "You're always in such a rush to get to the heart of the matter, Micah."

Without shifting his stance, he turned and gazed at the cottage door. "Perhaps that's because there isn't time for idle chitchat?"

"All right, I'll cut right to the chase. As we speak, the Romanians have made plans to build a secret missile air defense base for the protection of their country. Although they have several under consideration, one of the sites they'll explore is about two miles away from the Gehíwan prison. Right now, we don't know which site the twenty-four man team will scout out first. If they choose the location next to the penal colony, then you'll more than likely run into them as you and Tala head for the portal."

"The convicts won't tolerate anyone that close to their base," Micah said, more to himself than he did Edward. "Once the Romanian scouts arrive, a bloody carnage will surely follow."

"That it will. If such should be the case, then extra precautions will be necessary as you travel toward your destination."

Micah nodded. "Do you have any idea how soon the decision will be made?"

"If not already, then within the next twenty-four hours. I not only have Levi and Nathaniel looking into the matter, I also have Jeremiah shadowing one of the main officials in charge of the project. One of them will get in touch with you just as soon as the Romanians make their choice."

"All right."

"There is one more thing I wanted to say before I leave, Micah. In truth, it's the only reason I'm here right now."

"You have my attention, Edward."

"Just so you know, we are all in agreement this is the right course for Tala to take. I know this has been a difficult assignment for you, and for more reasons than you might care to admit. Nonetheless, Tala needs to find that key and get it to the portal before the insurgents find a second key themselves. Should the Gehíwan convicts succeed in their quest; this world could easily become a dark place with the chances of recovery slim at best, even with the help of the guardians. In light of that fact, we feel there is no one more capable than you in getting her through this danger no worse for the wear. Tala still has some important things she must accomplish in this life."

"I'm aware of that Edward. As with all those we protect, she wouldn't need us if she didn't."

Just as Edward opened his mouth to speak, Nathaniel stepped through the gateway. He gave Edward a nod before he turned his gaze toward Micah. "I take it Edward has filled you in on everything that's going on within the Romanian government?"

"Yes he has," said Micah. "Do you have an update for me?"

Nathaniel nodded. "I'm afraid the Romanians have just decided the site near the Gehíwan prison is the most advantageous place to put their missile base. Unless they change their mind, it'll be the first site they explore in the hope they won't have to scout out any of the others."

"Do you know how soon they'll head out?" he asked.

"Right now they're scheduled to leave at the end of

the month, perhaps a few days earlier if they can get the supplies and equipment they need together." Nathaniel paused for a moment. "Given that time frame, you'll run right into them, Micah, no doubt about it."

Micah's thoughts raced ahead as he pondered every possible scenario and consequence. "Perhaps that might work to our advantage, though. If the Gehíwans focus their attention on the Romanians, Tala and I just might be able to slip by without notice."

"That's possible," said Nathaniel. "But Dolph is a consideration in all of this as well. He too will have to pass by the malefactors without detection or harm."

Levi arrived just as Nathaniel made his comment. "I've just left Dolph. I told him all about this new development as well. He said with the exception of a windstorm that would give him away, he believes the added chaos caused by the Romanians will actually help us in our cause."

"I take it then Dolph has arrived at his destination without incident?" asked Edward.

"That he did," said Levi. "At this moment he's tucked away inside his lofty mountain cave, snug as a bug in a rug. I've no doubt he'll remain that way for the time being since it's impossible for the insurgents to climb up the vertical wall."

"Good. That's one less worry—"

The click of the door latch interrupted the conversation that had all but concluded anyway. His companions disappeared the same moment Tala stepped outside. She looked all about the area as she sauntered toward him.

"Were you just talking to someone?" she asked. "I thought I heard voices."

"You did. Levi and Nathaniel were just here, but they've gone on now."

"I wonder if I'll ever get used to all of your abrupt comings and goings."

"You just might if you're around us long enough," he replied.

"Maybe. Did they have a reason for their visit or did they just want to drop by and say hello? I mean—you all do nothing more than say hello from time to time, don't you? If for nothing more than to be social?"

"Oh, every now and then we might do something like that—if we have the time and are in the vicinity, of course."

Tala tilted her head to the side as she pointed a finger at him. "I think you're holding something back again. Is something wrong and you don't think I can handle all of the scary stuff?"

"Not at all, Levi simply stopped by to let us know Dolph has safely made his way to the wilds of the Ukraine as planned. Oh, and we now have horses in the place of the car." He paused for a moment. "You do ride, don't you?"

"Often." She glanced in the direction of the now missing vehicle. "So, when do we leave?"

"How about we let the sun rise all the way above the mountains? While we wait for that event, you can get something to eat."

"All right, I can do that," she said. "Is there food in that cottage or do you have to go out and hunt for our breakfast?"

He shrugged away the question with feigned indifference. "Since I haven't checked the kitchen larder, I'm not sure. However, if it's necessary I suppose I could rustle up a bit of game for you to cook. Of course, you'd have to gut and clean it first. That could delay our departure by a couple of hours though and right now, time is kind of important."

Her eyes widened and her mouth dropped. For several seconds she just stared at him. "You are kidding, right?" she finally asked.

He laughed at the squeamish expression on her face then brushed his fingers along the length of her jaw and nodded. "Yes, I'm just kidding. We have plenty of provisions in the barn."

She stepped back, placed a hand on her hip and shook her head. "You know—you can be such a brute at times, Micah."

His grin broadened. He winked as he bowed his head. "Guilty as charged, Miss Westbrook. However, I must confess I'm somewhat bewildered. Surely a wildlife photographer has experience in such things?"

Tala's eyes filled with sudden amusement as she lifted her nose a tad. She assumed an indignant expression and sniffed. "I only shoot animals with a camera, Mr. Berrington. I never eat what I can't find neatly packaged at the market. In the future, I'll expect you to keep that in mind."

Chapter Nine

"So, out of curiosity, are we still here?" Tala turned to the side in her saddle. She gazed all around the woodland, darkened now by the shadows of gray cloudy skies.

A look of confusion settled over Micah's face. "Sorry—still here?"

"Still here as in prancing through the mountainside somewhere in the past as if we didn't have a care in the world," she clarified.

"Now why would such a thought even cross your mind?"

"Oh, I don't know. Probably because we've been riding several hours now and the scenery doesn't look any different than it did when we left our secret hideout."

"That's because when we left our secret hideout, we returned to the present."

The unexpected reply both surprised and perplexed her. "The moment we stepped through the door?"

He shook his head ever so slightly. "Not quite, but shortly thereafter."

She gazed at him for several seconds as she came to terms with that. "You know, I think somewhere in the back of my mind I thought I'd see a flash of lightning. Maybe hear the serenade of angelic voices, rolling thunder, or at the very least, see some sort of brilliant light as we pass back and forth through your time portals. Yet, to date, I haven't noticed anything out of the ordinary."

Micah chuckled. "I think you're confusing a near-death experience with a visit in time."

"That very well may be," she replied. "But then again, don't you think the safest way for us to travel toward our destination is following the path somewhere in the past? Surely we could avoid the Gehíwan insurgents if we did that."

"We'd have to go back pretty far historically in order to accomplish that feat, and we aren't dressed for the occasion. I can tell you firsthand the local citizenry of differing time periods don't look kindly on things they don't understand—like a woman dressed in a black scooped-neck sweater and a pair of form-fitting jeans for instance."

Tala glanced down at her clothes. "What? Are you trying to tell me that my invincible protector doesn't carry a bevy of historical costumes in his magic "Mary Poppins" satchel—or in your case, a backpack—for such occasions?"

"Nope, I'm afraid I'm fresh out of those; both costumes and magic backpack."

"Nothing hidden away in your personal closet inside the mysterious realm of the Bewitan Fierd either?"

"I don't even have so much as a leftover waistcoat, cravat, chemise, petticoat, or corset to offer anyone, in or out of the realm."

She gave him a sideways glance. "So, what then—when you're all at home, do you just run around in white robes and nothing else?"

The question made him laugh out right. "Now I think you're confusing heaven with an ordinary dimension filled with a bunch of gritty, uncivilized, ill-tempered men."

The off-handed comment made her smile. "Tell me about it."

"About what?"

"Your realm, dimension, whatever you want to call your home base," she said. "What's it like there?"

"You should probably be a little more specific lest I bore you with mundane details you have no interest in."

"Okay. To begin with, do you each have your own house or do you all live in one big-gigantic commune of some kind?"

"We all have our own homes. Mine isn't very fancy by a woman's standards I'm sure. Nonetheless, it has all of the furnishings and comforts I could ever want or need."

"Do you have anything that resembles a mansion?" she asked.

"We have a fair number of those as well," he said.

"Well, does one earn a more extravagant home because of the honorable way one lived one's mortality, their current status, or something like that?"

"No, none of that has anything to do with where we live—it's simply the freedom to choose what we want. Those who govern our realm respect every individual's free agency and personal choices."

She drew her brows together as she shook her head. "I'm not sure I know what you mean by personal choices in this regard."

"All right, let me explain it this way—" He paused

as a reflective look entered his eyes. "Upon our arrival, we're greeted by the ealdorman charged with overseeing our duties."

"What's an ealdorman?" she asked.

"They are the ancient ones who govern our realm."

After a moment's consideration understanding dawned. "Ancient ones as in the eight men who first swore allegiance to dear old Alfred?"

A glimmer of amusement appeared in his eyes. "Yes. Are you all right with that one?"

"Yes, I think so."

"Good."

"So, after the ealdormen greet you, what happens next?"

"They tell us who we are, where we are, and why we find ourselves suddenly standing in a hall we've never seen before, surrounded by men we've never met. After they've answered all of our questions—and believe me, we have plenty of them—we're given several choices."

"Like what for instance?" she prodded.

"The first and most important choice we make is whether or not we'll honor the oath as pledged by our direct ancestor and stay. If not, we're returned to our exact time and place of departure without recollection of what transpired in the realm of the Bewitan Fierd. The intended fate at that moment takes over—and to answer the question I see you have—yes, some of them have chosen to return and take whatever comes. If we stay, we choose the location of the home we'll build, draw up a set of plans, and begin construction. We then oversee it down to the smallest detail. During that time, we're given in-depth instruction and training as to our obligations and the various types of assignments we'll face in the days ahead."

"Does the entire realm look all the same as in regards to environment or do you have the same variety we find here?"

"There's just as much diversity as one finds here. We have deserts, rolling hills, mountains, and valleys—streams, rivers, lakes, and oceans."

"So, where did you choose to build your cozy, ivy-covered cottage then?"

"What makes you think my home is covered in ivy?"

"Oh, I don't know, just the vision that popped inside my mind, I guess. I see marbled gray-and-white stones covering all of the outer walls. The house has large, diamond-paned windows that allow an abundance of light to fill the rooms. There's a wood-shingled, high-pitched roof and lovely gingerbread gables. Do I have any of that right?"

He dipped his head from side to side. "Quite a bit, actually. To answer your question, my home is nestled on the outer edges of a wooded mountain that overlooks an ocean. In my opinion, that's the best of all possible places."

The vision that popped into her mind filled her with delight. How she wished she could see it. She needed to know one more thing. "Do you have a ton of neighbors that surround your home, or are you out there all by yourself?"

"I have neighbors within a mile or two, but none of them are any closer than that."

"Well, I could see where that type of home and setting would suit you. After all, you seem quite comfortable in the remote cottages we've visited so far."

"I've never been one for opulence or overly crowded cities," he said.

"Do you want to know something that might surprise you, Micah?" she asked.

"If you'd like to share it."

"Despite what you might think, given the circumstances and wealth surrounding my birth, neither have I. In fact, I prefer small and simple myself, both in homes and place of residence."

By mere expression alone, she could see he didn't expect her to say that. "Is that right?"

She nodded. "Sometimes I think the bigger the house and city, the colder and emptier they feel. Maybe that's why I chose wildlife photography as my profession."

A flash of lightning, followed by a deafening clap of booming thunder swallowed his reply. A scant moment later, torrential rain pounded against the earth while a fierce wind whipped all around them. He grabbed hold of her reins, halted her skittish mount, and leaned in close to her ear. "There's a cave just up ahead. We can take shelter there until the storm passes."

"All right." She held tight to the reins as he led the horses up the muddy hill. They maneuvered around a rocky incline that snaked up the mountain and through a gaping fissure. The narrow passage opened into a cavity large enough to give them and the horses a safe haven with room to spare. Once Micah got the horses settled in, he piled the saddle blankets against the cave wall. The stack provided a comfortable seat. With a wave of his hand, he invited her to use it.

Once she took him up on the offer, he rummaged through their food pack. He handed her a bag of trail mix, some fruit, and a bottle of water before he sat down beside her. All throughout the process, lightning lit up the cave while the low rumble of thunder echoed all around them. The heady smell of rain and damp earth permeated all throughout the chamber.

"How long do you think the storm will last?" she asked.

"Hard to say," he replied. "This time of year it might pass in an hour or two, or it could rain all night long. If that turns out to be the case, I hope you won't be too uncomfortable in here."

She looked all about the cavity and shrugged. "Believe it or not, when it comes to shelter, I've endured far worse."

A slight grin turned a single corner of his mouth. "Have you now?"

"Yep. I remember a time when the high winds of a winter storm destroyed my tent while on a photo shoot in the wilds of Alaska. That wind then carried off the tattered remains to parts unknown to this day. I spent the hours between dusk and dawn huddled deep inside my Arctic sleeping bag. All the while I hoped I wouldn't die of hypothermia."

"I trust that come the morning, you—" Micah paused mid-sentence and then directed his complete attention toward the fissure. Without taking his gaze off the entrance, he rocked up onto a knee. With a sense of urgency, he beckoned her closer. "I need you to loop your arms around my neck."

As she opened her mouth to speak he drew his

brows together and clenched his teeth in irritation. "Just do it. Now!"

For the tone of his voice, Tala did as he asked without further delay. Yet rather than gathering her into his arms as she expected, he held his hands at the height of his chest with palms facing outward. A split second later five men entered the cave. She sucked in a breath as they traipsed toward them.

The dirty, scraggly-looking men stopped just short of where they sat. From what she could determine, they couldn't see them or go any farther. After a very brief discussion, the men sat down in various places inside the chamber. They leaned their backs against the rocky wall while their head and shoulders moved about in search of some kind of comfort. Once settled they closed their eyes and drifted toward sleep. When she thought enough time had passed, she turned her gaze toward Micah. She didn't ask the questions she wanted to ask for fear of disturbing their unwanted companions.

A slight grin grew ever broader as he settled one arm loosely about her waist. He dropped the other on top of his knee. "We're connected, Tala. They can't see or hear us."

Tala ignored his mirth as she turned her gaze toward their guests. "Who are those men?"

He shrugged as if the answer held no great importance. "Part of the Gehíwan rebel forces—doing nothing more than seeking refuge from the storm just as we did. You needn't worry about them right now."

"You can understand their language?"

"Yes, I can."

"They weren't tracking us then?"

"No, I don't think so."

"That's good." She again spared them a glance. "Did you create some kind of a barrier between them and us?"

"Yes I did. I didn't want them tripping over us or knocking into the horses." He gazed at her for a moment and then let go of a sigh.

That sigh made her feel like an errant child.

"Next time I ask you to do something, Tala, you need to respond a little more quickly than you did this time around. As you might've noticed, we didn't have any time to spare. Another second and they might have caught sight of you. That would've complicated things—not only now, but in the days ahead as we search for the key."

"I know." She drew her shoulders together in silent apology. "You just caught me off guard. I won't let it happen again. I promise."

Just then she realized she still had her arms looped around his shoulders and all but sat in his lap. The intimate contact flustered her more than she cared to admit. Heat rose to her face and exited her cheeks as proof of that fact. She didn't know if she should let go or stay put.

****

Micah somehow managed to quash a grin over Tala's uncertainty. For the pleasure of having her in his arms, he let her squirm another minute or two before he rescued her from discomfort. He let her slide off his lap before he dropped an arm around her shoulders and nestled her body next to his. "You might be more comfortable if you rest against me—at least until our friends take their leave, all right? Just maintain some kind of physical connection and you'll be fine."

Her relief obvious, she merely nodded and closed her eyes. She let go of a deep sigh as she settled her cheek against his chest. For a time nothing disturbed the silence, save the sound of the rain and the thunder. Just when he thought sleep had overtaken her, she stirred. "Micah?"

He lowered his gaze to her lovely face. "Hmm?"

"Are there any women in the realm of the Bewitan Fierd?"

"No, I'm afraid not. Why do you ask?"

"Just curious, I guess." After a pause, she drew back just enough to meet his gaze. "Is there a reason for that?"

"The answer should be obvious, shouldn't it? As I've already said, only the first-born sons are destined to become guardians. Our ancestors never included their daughters in that oath."

"Yes, and I understand that. But what does that have to do with the women the guardians may have loved and left behind? They did exist, didn't they?"

"Of course they did."

"And more than a few, I should think?" she pressed.

"First-born sons wouldn't exist in the numbers they do if the lion's share of our men didn't have wives and families, Tala," he said.

"Did you?"

"No, I didn't."

"Did you ever come close?"

"No."

She tilted her head to the side as she regarded him. "Well then?"

"Well then, *what*?" he asked.

She huffed out a breath of exasperation. "Is there a reason women are excluded from your realm?"

"I'm sorry. Your thought process is a little difficult for me to keep up with, so you'll have to have a bit more patience with me while I try to muddle through it. However, the only way I can think to answer your question is for you to compare the guardians with an army of your own Special Forces. Think of our realm as our permanent headquarters. Then, when we're called to duty, we march out and fulfill our given orders just as your soldiers do here. That being the case, and as far as I know, including women has never even been discussed."

"Well, it should be. The men I know wouldn't want to live in a world without the women they loved, so why would the guardians? I mean, how pleasant could a world filled with nothing but *gritty, uncivilized, ill-tempered* men, really be?"

How to explain what he would rather not? "We're kept pretty busy, Tala. Our assignments can last from several months to a couple of years or more, especially during time of war. Upon our return, we're given very little personal time before we're handed another mission. Therefore, don't you think it unfair to ask a woman, no matter how beloved, to while away the hours all alone while the man she loves is about his duty for long stretches of time?"

"Not if that's the life she chooses to live. Besides, in a place such as the Bewitan Fierd, is time even counted?"

"You're confusing my world with heaven again. Time in my realm coincides with your own. The sun rises and sets, just as it does here."

"But you said you didn't sleep, so I just thought—"

"I said we didn't need it, I didn't say we couldn't do it if we so choose."

"Oh. Well, do you then?"

"Do what? Sleep?"

"Yes, if even for nothing more than a bit of respite."

"Every now and then if the mood strikes," he said.

"Do you dream?"

"Sometimes."

She fell silent then. For the look on her face it seemed her thoughts once again carried her in a thousand different directions before bringing her back full circle. After the slow release of a deep breath, she again rested her head against his chest and closed her weary eyes.

"Well, if you want my opinion, I think the realm of the Bewitan Fierd should consider the needs of their guardians and make a few changes where women are concerned—particularly when it comes to those they loved and had to leave behind. I mean, it's not like the women would hurt anything being there," she murmured.

Micah said nothing in response to the comment. He would be lying if he agreed because concessions in regards to women *were* made. The guardians could dally with mortal women if they so chose. They had but one rule they had to follow: all such encounters had to be immediately removed from the woman's memory even if during their mortality they were married or betrothed to guardians. Though certainly not encouraged, the ealdormen even tolerated liaisons with women the guardians protected. His own personal ethics and code of honor didn't allow such an attachment. In his mind, that took an unfair advantage over the woman in question. Yet, right now, as he held Tala in his arms, he could feel his resolve weakening, especially since at the end of their journey together, he would remove all recollection surrounding this quest anyway.

But really, what good would it do other than satisfy his selfish desires for the here and now? At the end of the day, he would still leave her. He didn't want that day any harder than what it already portended to be.

The sudden appearance of another shifter at the mouth of the cave interrupted his thoughts. The man strode toward his companions. He kicked the foot of the one closest to him. As the startled rebel leapt to his feet, he spouted off a string of foul curses directed at the perpetrator. In turn, the commotion awoke the others. The new arrival waited until he had the full attention of each man before he spoke.

"Cojor wants all of us back at the base right now. He said Beldūrq has made an unexpected appearance, and he's arrived with almost his entire garrison in tow. He left but a small handful of men in England in the event that—"

"Do you know why they have come?" interrupted the insurgent to his right.

"Because they are almost sure Aūsberon has fled the United Kingdom. They also believe he's headed in this direction."

"Why would he do something as stupid as that?"

"That's obvious, isn't it? Beldūrq thinks he's retrieved his key. The only possible reason he would do that is so he can return home. That also means he has a second key in his possession as well."

The shifter laughed and slapped him on the back. "So, you're telling me the all powerful, omnipotent Beldürq let at least one of the keys slip right through his fingers, even when he had the man in his sights?"

"So it seems." Though raucous barbs and laughter followed the comment, the new arrival held up his hand in a request for silence. "There is a complication that just might go along with that."

"And that would be?" asked the convict to his left.

"There's a possibility Aüsberon entrusted a human woman with one of the keys. The why of that is what devils him most. Now come on, we've got to go before Cojor demands our blood in exchange for our tardiness. Without a doubt, we'll get all of the details once we arrive."

Micah watched the men as they exited the cave and all the while, he considered what they said. Although he expected Beldürq's return to this part of the world, he didn't expect Cojor to be in command of the insurgents here in Romania. Did Anton die or did Cojor displace him? Not that it mattered. Anton and Cojor were very much alike in their disregard for human life as well as the lives of their own people. He had already assumed Beldürq believed Dolph enlisted Tala's aid, so that didn't change anything regarding his strategy. Still, now that the shifters had confirmed the worst case scenario, his greatest challenge would come in keeping a tight rein on Tala's impulsiveness.

The Gehíwans had just handed him another valuable piece of information as well. If Cojor called all of his men to their base of operations, he and Tala could reach the ruins without having to maneuver through a whole garrison of insurgents. That also meant they could take a more direct path. His gaze then turned toward his charge. Her even breathing told him she slept peacefully. Nonetheless, he adjusted her position so she could rest a little more comfortably against his chest until the storm abated.

As fate would have it, the rain didn't end until the early hours of the morning, not that he complained over the delay. He loved the feel of her in his arms.

The shrouded light of dawn slowly roused Tala from her slumber. As she arrived at full awareness, she opened her eyes and turned her sleepy gaze toward the fissure.

"They've gone," he said in response to her unspoken question.

"I can see that now." She hid a yawn behind the palm of her hand as she sat up. At the same time, she didn't put any distance between them. "How long have they been gone?"

"A while."

Again she searched the entrance to the cave before returning her gaze to his. "How long have I been asleep?"

He fought off a grin. "A while longer."

A breath of quiet laughter accompanied the slight shake of her head. She raised a hand to the side of his face and allowed her fingers to slowly trace the length of his jaw and back again. All the while, her lovely eyes followed the chosen path. At the end of the journey, she again gazed into his eyes. For an immeasurable amount of time, they simply looked at each other. The beat of her heart accelerated. She took in a shallow breath and hung on to it.

"Micah—" she whispered his name even as she tilted her chin upward and connected her lips to his. The moment she broke away from the kiss, he could see absolute shock intertwined with a touch of trepidation over having given in to the spontaneous desire. He wouldn't allow it.

In that small measure of time, he had the overwhelming need to wipe out the uncertainty. He would remove any misgiving she might feel. Right now, nothing mattered more than the feelings she had for him and those he had for her. The will to control his desire disappeared. With slow deliberation he cradled her closer to his chest and gently lowered his mouth to hers. For a moment he explored the softness of her lips for the pleasure it gave him to do so. Without thought to duty or honor, he deepened his kiss as he took full possession of her mouth. Fiery passion took hold of them both as one kiss led to another, and then another still before he ignored the number as well as the reasons he should stop—

Somewhere then, in the back of his mind he became cognizant of a single gunshot that only he would hear. At once the signal doused the flames on his rising ardor. With more reluctance than he thought possible, he ended the kiss and put a bit of space between them. Reason returned alongside the knowledge either Nathaniel or Levi were in the area searching for them. Before he responded to that gunshot he had to deal with his abominable moment of weakness. He released a ragged breath as he gathered his strength and harnessed his emotions.

"I'm so sorry, Tala, I shouldn't have done that."

Debbie Peterson

Micah took hold of her hands, rose to his feet and drew her up beside him. He shook his head as he held onto her gaze. "I promise you I won't let it happen again."

136

Chapter Ten

A multitude of thoughts swarmed Tala's mind as she looked into his eyes. He meant what he said. She could see the staunch determination in his gaze, his rigid stance, and the firm set of his jaw. At the same time, she could also detect things he couldn't hide. Traces of the incredible passion they had just shared lingered in his gaze—as did the hidden longing beneath his resolve. In that instant she knew, whether he admitted it or not, the power of the feelings he had for her—whatever they may be—equaled those she had for him. Therefore, her charming guardian would have to sort out those feelings in the days ahead, just as she would. Without doubt, they would be difficult, if not impossible, for either of them to ignore—especially when she didn't want them ignored.

You won't let so wondrous a thing happen again, Micah? Well, we'll just see about that, won't we now, she silently taunted.

She took a half-step back. As she slowly withdrew her hands from his, she made sure the tips of her fingers caressed the length of his palms with the lightest possible touch. The small smile she fought to contain over his outward response made an appearance anyway.

She shrugged. "Well, all things considered, I think that's a very good decision, Micah. After all, I haven't decided if I even *like* you yet."

A most attractive grin, slow in coming, accompanied the slight shake of his head. Obvious by the look on his face, he hadn't expected that reply.

"Is that right?"

Tala lifted a brow, but said nothing in return.

He chuckled as he took hold of his gun and chambered a round. "Wait here for a minute."

"Why? Is something wrong?"

"No, there's nothing wrong. I just want you to stay out of sight."

"Well, may I at least ask where you're going?"

"Not far, I'm simply letting Levi, Nathaniel, or perhaps even both of them, know we're up here. Right now they're somewhere in the vicinity looking for us. If I had to guess, I'd say they're a bit concerned since we didn't make it to our destination last night."

"Really? How do you know all of that?"

"They signaled."

"Oh." She stood on her tiptoes and peeked past his shoulder as she scoured what she could see of the mountainside. She didn't hear anything, did she?

He merely grinned as he turned toward the fissure. The moment he stepped out in the open, he aimed the barrel of his rifle skyward and pulled the trigger. Within minutes, Levi and Nathaniel made their sudden appearance at the mouth of the cave. They looked very pleased to see them.

"With the forest crawling with insurgents, we're surprised you made it this far up the trail," Nathaniel said as he and Levi followed Micah into the alcove.

"We arrived just ahead of the pack, actually," Micah replied. "To our great misfortune, some of them found their way inside the cave after the storm began.

For a short while we endured their stench."

Levi wrinkled his nose. "How revolting."

"Indeed, that couldn't have been pleasant for either one of you, but what made them leave so soon? The rain didn't let up until just an hour or so ago," said Nathaniel.

"I know, but Beldürq's unexpected arrival to this neck of the woods compelled their hasty retreat as so ordered by Cojor."

"Then you already know why Beldürq's here," said Levi.

"Yes, I think so. The lackey Cojor sent to round up all of the rebels didn't have a problem blurting out that little piece of information once he made it inside the cave."

"You know in addition to Dolph, they'll also be on the lookout for Tala, then, right?" asked Levi.

"They mentioned her."

Nathaniel hesitated as his gaze darted toward her. "Did they also mention Beldürq brought along a small sample of her scent?"

The look in Micah's eyes at that moment sent a shiver down her spine. She had never before seen him look so fierce.

Levi held up a hand. "Now, slow it down, Micah. They didn't get it at the house, I assure you. The company Josiah employed didn't miss a thing when they cleaned and sanitized the manor. We made sure of it."

"Then where did they get her scent?" he asked in a tone far too calm for her liking.

"As their only saving grace for having lost sight of her, they had the presence of mind and the opportunity

Debbie Peterson

to filch the napkin she used at the restaurant. Those were the words of the insurgent who made the report, not mine. As you recall the establishment had countless patrons that day. Because of that fact, it took some time for the employees to clear the table we used," Levi replied.

Tala gazed at each of the men in turn as she bit down on her lip. "I assume by the look on everyone's face, this is a bad thing?"

Micah turned toward her. As he gazed into her eyes, he shook his head. "No, it simply means we'll take a few extra precautions, that's all."

"Precautions? Like what?"

"You'll stay a little bit closer to me than what you have, at all times. You must be far more diligent in complying with everything I ask you to do and in the moment I ask you to do it. You needn't worry, Tala. If you do that, you'll stay safe enough," Micah said.

"I'm not at all worried. As you might recall, I've already given you my word I'll do as you ask." And without hesitation or complaint, she silently added. In fact, the directive to stick a little closer to her guardian filled her with a smug sense of satisfaction.

"So, under the current circumstances," said Levi, "are you heading to Costin's house for a day or two as we first planned, or will you head for Velica's villa instead?"

"Velica's," Micah replied. "Not only do we need to take advantage of the fact most all of the shifters have cleared the area, we should make up for the time we lost yesterday. Tala's a good rider. She can handle the extra miles in the more direct path just fine."

Levi nodded. "All right, we'll make sure the

supplies you need are waiting for you there then."

Micah put a hand on Levi's shoulder. "Would you mind adding my hooded cloak to that list of supplies? The black one at the back of my closet."

"No problem. I'll fetch it right away. Once we drop everything off at the house, we'll go hang around the penal colony for awhile and see if we can find out anything else that will assist you in your grand adventure."

"All right. Weather permitting, Tala and I will leave Velica's tomorrow morning. From there we'll follow Dolph's map to the letter as we head straight for the castle ruins."

"Sounds good." Levi turned his gaze toward Nathaniel and gave him a nod. "Are you ready to go then, my friend?"

The moment the men disappeared from the cave, Micah picked up their pack and then offered it to her. "Why don't you see if you can find something agreeable for your breakfast while I get the horses saddled and bridled? We've got a lot of ground to cover before the sun sets this evening."

Tala released the straps and peeked inside the bag. "All right. Would you like some breakfast as well? There's more than enough for the two of us in here. In fact, there's enough for an entire army."

"No, I'm fine. Just get something for yourself."

She laughed. "What? Do you doubt my culinary skills, Mr. Berrington?"

Micah gave her a sideways glance. "Should I?"

"There's only one way for you to find out, isn't that right?" she quipped.

"I guess you have me there, Miss Westbrook. Still,

we'll just have to wait for another time before we can solve that little mystery."

She tilted her head as she lifted her chin. "Coward."

Amusement filled his eyes as he turned and faced her full on. "Careful, now. Where I come from those are fighting words with some serious consequences."

"Ooh, the guardian proposes a wrestling contest. Sounds interesting. I wonder if I'll win this round."

A quiet chuckle followed the remark. "You're a saucy woman, Tala. You know that, don't you?"

She shrugged. "You're cocky. You also happen to be one of the bossiest men I've ever met. So, does that make us evenly matched?"

Micah took on an expression of indignation. "I'm not cocky nor am I bossy."

"Oh, I beg to differ, sir."

Far sooner than she desired, their playful banter ended. They abandoned the cave and headed for one of the "lesser" homes that, from what Micah said, the affluent Velica family built in the early twentieth century as a family retreat. True to his word, they rode in the most direct path possible.

With caution uppermost in their minds, they didn't speak until they were safely tucked inside the vacant, but beautiful villa. From what she could see as they entered, the Velica family had filled the home with the most opulent furnishings available to them at the time of construction. Rich wood tones used in both crown moldings and base boards complimented the Chippendale furniture. Cream-colored draperies graced the windows that sparkled in the late afternoon sun. A plush cream-colored area rug with an ivy themed border in vivid hues of green and brown centered the living room. A portrait of a mother, father, and three children hung above the fire-place. The Velica family perhaps? The house made one feel welcome.

Micah propped his rifle against the corner by the door and then slung her backpack over his shoulder. "I'll just put this in one of the bedrooms for you."

"Okay, thanks." She turned her gaze toward the window facing west, and for a moment enjoyed the glorious colors created by sun and clouds. Then just as the sun dipped below the mountain, her guardian returned to the room.

"Your things are in the first bedroom left of the main hall. The bed in there looks pretty comfortable."

"Does it?" she asked as she faced him.

"Well, let's just say you'll get better sleep in there than what you probably got inside the cave." He gazed about the room as the evening shadows settled in. "It'll get cold in here now the sun has gone down. I think I'll go ahead and get a fire started."

"That sounds good, and while you take care of all of that, I think I'll make us some dinner. I don't know about you, but I'm starving."

As Micah turned his attention toward building a fire, she headed straight for the kitchen. At her insistence, they didn't stop for lunch during their journey and right now her stomach lamented the fact.

As she inspected the cupboards and pantry, she discovered Nathaniel and Levi had supplied them with an impressive variety of food. Within the hour she had put together a fairly decent version of her 'out on the trail ranch-style chili,' served alongside honey butter cornbread. She topped it off with a fresh fruit cobbler.

143

Not only did Micah praise the meal, he shooed her out of the kitchen once they finished eating it.

"You cooked, so I'll clean up," he said.

"That isn't at all necessary, Micah. I made the mess, so I can help clear it away."

"No, I insist." He turned her toward the door. "There's a rather lavish bathroom down the hallway and off to your right. I think you just might enjoy what it has to offer, so mind you take your time while doing so."

The thought of a leisurely soak in a hot bathtub sounded heavenly. Especially after two days in the saddle while wearing the same clothes. "Are you sure?"

"I'm sure. Away with you now."

From inside the gorgeous bedroom, Tala gathered the things she needed for her bath. Mrs. Velica had dressed the bed and windows in soft colors of lavender and blue. They complimented the dainty floral pattern in the wallpaper and gave the room a cozy feel. Her gaze drifted back to the bed. Micah was right, it did look comfortable.

She headed for the large bathroom across the hall. A porcelain claw foot tub centered the back wall. Off to the right stood a beautiful mahogany vanity with a matching closet next to it. She found the closet filled with fluffy towels and wash cloths. Tala also noted the exotic oils, bath and hair products imported all the way from India, a most extravagant luxury for the time.

After she finished the first real bath she'd had since leaving Westbrook Manor, Tala returned to the living room. She sat down on the sofa, drew her legs up on the cushions, and gazed at her companion.

"Will either Levi or Nathaniel barge in here any

time soon and disrupt our otherwise quiet evening?" she asked.

"Not unless they have information critical to our mission. Right now their most important task is to keep a sharp eye on the insurgents and listen to every word they say. So unless they have something important to report, they'll stay put for the time being," Micah replied.

"Sounds kind of boring. I almost pity them."

He shrugged. "That kind of work can be tedious. Sometimes days will pass before anything important to a mission is discussed or discovered."

She lifted a brow as she turned her head to the side. "The voice of experience?"

"You have no idea."

The comment made her laugh.

Later that night she snuggled between the satin sheets. Despite her fatigue, sleep eluded her. The delicious recollection of Micah's kisses, the passion and emotion they invoked, wreaked havoc in her mind and heart. She couldn't stop the endless repetition of that memory. What's more, she didn't know if she'd stop it even if she could. One thing she knew for sure: What began as simple enjoyment of her guardian's company had turned into something far deeper.

Each day that passed had increased the intensity of that 'something.' Would she recognize it and name it at the end of this journey or shy away from it all together? She and Micah came from two very different worlds. No one understood that better than she did. She just didn't know if they could bridge that difference and that thought alone scared her half to death. Not that it mattered now. She couldn't change the path she followed regardless of the outcome. Dolph needed her help. She couldn't disappoint him.

****

In the early hours of the morning just before dawn, Micah stepped outside. He circled the perimeters of the property in search of anything that might threaten Tala's safety and found nothing of concern. The light wind didn't even carry so much as a hint that a shifter had roamed the area, or even a wild predatory animal for that matter. Not that he wouldn't have minded the distraction, he needed one.

He turned his gaze toward the diminishing light of the stars. Struggle as he might, he couldn't get the memory of Tala's response to his kisses out of his mind. Again, he could feel his desire chipping away at his resolve. He risked the personal code of honor he had upheld since he left that battlefield in Aughrim as well. They still had several weeks ahead of them before the night of the black moon fell. Could he hold onto the sheer power of his will for that long? He just didn't know, but by heaven, he would try. Not for his sake, but for hers.

She had asked him earlier if he had ever married or had a family. When she asked him the question, Miss Ellen Ashworth tumbled into his mind for the first time since he left his mortality behind. His father favored a match between the two of them, and encouraged his pursuit of the girl. He had no interest in her and told his father as much. Despite that lack of interest, he said that he should give her a chance before he dismissed the notion altogether. To appease the man, he had half-heartedly courted the woman. Ellen, though quite lovely and very agreeable, had never sparked so much as a shred of affection in his heart, even though she did everything society demanded for a woman in her position. He couldn't fault her efforts. Without doubt, he could lay the fault at his own doorstep. At that moment in his life, he couldn't accept marriage to a woman he merely tolerated rather than loved, regardless of looks, temperament, and pedigree. At the same time he wondered if he would ever love anyone with the depth he desired. Maybe he didn't posses the ability. Centuries of life and encounters with countless women hadn't given him an answer either.

Then Tala entered his life and resolved that question without any real effort on her part. Unlike Ellen, Tala didn't do anything to claim his heart. She simply crossed his path. Now, for the rest of his existence, he would love her. Nothing could stop or purge that now. Yet, he didn't want her returning that love, did he? How could he when he couldn't offer her any degree of forever? He couldn't steal even the smallest portion of her heart and then shatter it—

The knowledge Tala had left her bed and at this moment made her way down the hall ended his thoughts. In all likelihood, she would search the villa looking for him. Just as he headed for the house, he thought better of the decision and halted his steps. During those first four weeks he spent in her company, he discovered Tala took delight in watching the rise and set of the sun, especially those with vivid, glorious colors. This morning, the sight would be a spectacular one with all the various cloud formations that blanketed the sky. Scant minutes later, the click of the latch turned his gaze toward the door. She gave him an enchanting smile as she approached him.

He bowed low at the waist. "Good morning, Miss Westbrook."

She reciprocated with a playful curtsey. "Good morning, Mr. Berrington. So tell me, did you plan on keeping this gorgeous morning all to yourself without a thought of sharing it with your companion?"

"We have a hard day ahead of us. I didn't want to wake you before you were ready to get up."

"You wouldn't have. I usually get up at dawn; it's a habit of mine."

He nodded. "I know."

She held her silence for a few seconds as she searched his eyes. Finally, the smallest of smiles touched the corners of her lips. "I guess you would at that, wouldn't you?"

He dipped his head sideways and shrugged.

Her smile broadened. "So, do you think we can reach those castle ruins before nightfall?"

"If the weather cooperates then I think so."

She gazed up at the rising sun, which now painted the sky in vivid colors. "Most of those clouds are still pretty thick, aren't they? Still, maybe we'll get lucky and they'll pass over without drenching us."

"If lady luck deigns to accompany us today, I would rather she keep the winds at bay and the shifters from crossing our path."

Tala's hand traveled toward her neck and then toyed with her pendant. "I thought you said they had all returned to base."

"Yes, and I assume they did. Yesterday. However, the minute Beldūrq brought his troops up to date, I'm sure Cojor ordered all but a few of them to spread out and patrol what they claim as their territory today. You must keep in mind that they're now on the lookout for Dolph." He paused. "And you."

"Yes, I remember. Are the ruins included in that territory?"

"No, but their proximity will make it uncomfortable. That means we must remain on our guard." He put a hand to his chin and rubbed along its length as he looked at her. "Not long ago you told me you'd rather be prepared for all plausible situations you might face."

A trace of concern filled her eyes. "Yes, I did and I haven't changed my mind. Is something wrong?"

"Not wrong, there's just something you should know."

"What would that be?"

"I can't mask your scent, Tala. We can only hope to camouflage or delude it."

She drew her brows together as confusion beset her. "I don't know what you mean by that—"

"As I've already told you, the Gehiwans rely a great deal on their senses, most especially, their sense of smell. Even a physical connection to me won't completely shield your scent. Therefore, we must cover or alter it as best we can."

"By doing what?"

He shrugged. "I know it's a cumbersome relic and will be especially so while riding. Nevertheless, to keep you safe, I need you to wear my cloak while we're out in the open. My scent on the garment should combine with yours well enough to keep you out of harm's way if we're careful. As an added bonus, it will keep you warm. Will you do that for me?"

"Oh. When you asked Levi to get it, you wanted

him to get it just for me?"

"Yes, I did."

"Then of course I'll wear it, Micah."

He gave her a wink. "Well, I didn't expect that to be quite so easy."

A breath of laughter escaped as she placed a gentle hand against his chest. "Yes, but I wouldn't get comfortable with that notion if I were you, or you just might find yourself disappointed."

Chapter Eleven

After Tala cleared away the breakfast clutter, she went from the kitchen into the sitting room where Micah awaited her with a cloak in his hand. "Are we ready to go then?"

"Yes we are. We have all of our supplies packed. The horses are saddled and at this moment they await our arrival," he said as he walked toward her. Once he swept her braid behind her back, he settled the heavy cloak around her shoulders. He lifted the hood over her head and tucked away the loose tendrils that framed her face. Then with a critical eye, he stepped back and gazed at her in a head-to-toe sweep. "Well, the garment is a little long, but perhaps that's all for the best. We'll mask a little more of your scent that way."

Tala peeked down at the hem that all but touched her boots. As she tied the laces tight together, she took in a deep breath of the pleasant masculine odor that clung to the garment and nodded. "I'm sure you're right. This cloak definitely smells like you."

He raised a brow as he took his coat off the rack and shrugged it on. "I hope that's not a bad thing?"

She touched a hand to his cheek and gave him a smile. "Since my life is in such horrific danger, I think I can handle it without too much difficulty."

With a slight shake of his head, he offered her his hand. "I don't know if I'm supposed to be offended over that or not, but shall we?"

She placed her fingers on top of his palm. "The sooner the better."

Micah set a slow steady pace as they traveled up the mountain. All the while, he kept her close at his side. Many times along the way he reined in his mount as his gaze swept over every inch of their surroundings. Every now and again he would change their course. She could only presume they avoided the shifters when they changed their path. Despite the dangers that lurked in the forest, the luck Micah asked for had accompanied them so far on their journey. They hadn't been accosted. The winds didn't even so much as stir.

In the moment the sun peeked through the scattered clouds high above them, he turned his gaze toward her. He then took hold of her hand. "Are you getting hungry?"

"If you're suggesting we stop for lunch, then I'm all for that," she said. "I'm starving."

"I'm not at all surprised with what little you ate for breakfast."

She waved away the remark. "Well, a bowl of sticky oatmeal that early in the morning just didn't look all that appetizing once I had it in hand and yes, I know I'm the one who chose to eat it."

He nodded in response as he directed his gaze toward a small grassy clearing off to their left. "We'll stop there for awhile. The horses can get something to eat while we do the same, all right?"

"That sounds good to me."

Micah helped her dismount and then retrieved their food pack from the back of his horse. He handed it off to her and then relieved the horses of all their burdens so they could graze for a while without hindrance. Once they settled down beneath a tree, she opened the bag.

"Well, let's see. We have some cheese and crackers here," she said. "We also have some apples, pears, beef jerky, and a decent variety of granola bars—"

"Just an apple for me this time around if you don't mind."

She paused in her task as she met his gaze. "Are you only eating that so I don't complain about having to eat alone again?"

The small grin that emerged confirmed the suspicion. "I'm eating it because I enjoy the taste of apples."

"Oh, whatever," she said as she tossed the largest one she could find toward his face.

He caught it midflight without any real effort on his part. The bite he took released an aroma that smelled far more delicious than any apple she had ever eaten.

"Have you had one of these yet?" he asked.

"No, not yet," she said as she made a sandwich of sorts with the cheese and flatbread crackers.

"Well, you ought to. These apples are grown in the realm of the Bewitan Fierd. There's nothing finer, I guarantee it."

"Then I'll have one for dessert." She ate the remainder of her meal without words passing between them. Just as she went for an apple, Micah unexpectedly grabbed hold of her waist. Without any kind of warning or explanation, he yanked her onto his lap. He turned her face toward his chest while he tucked the folds of the cloak around her body and over her feet.

"Hold still Tala, don't move."

Though she couldn't see them, she could now hear the heavy thud of a large animal's paws very near the edge of the forest. The vivid picture of the wolf's body in the bedroom at Westbrook Manor stormed her mind. She gulped past the knot in her throat and shivered. "Shifters?"

"Yes."

"How many?" she whispered.

"Two, perhaps three."

"What will we do about the horses?" she asked.

"There's nothing we can do about them right now. Either they'll take them or they won't. Just hold onto me. No matter what comes, don't let go. Do you understand that? Don't. Let. Go."

Tala nodded as she wrapped her arms around his back. She held on with all of her might. In response, Micah tightened his hold and dropped his chin lightly on top of her head. Though she had the desire, she didn't look behind her as the footsteps grew ever louder. No more than a minute passed before a Gehíwan convict or convicts in their animal persona entered the clearing. The rustle of grass, coupled with the crunch of dried leaves and twigs echoed loudly in her ears. What if they stumbled on top of them? What if they detected her scent? Her heart pounded in her chest. She closed her eyes and waited.

A few minutes of sheer torture later, the animal sniffed very near where she sat. A sudden blast of hot, moist breath right next to her face followed. She found it impossible to stifle a gasp. Then before she could react or even feel the motion, Micah bounded to his feet. With an arm still wrapped about her waist, he dragged her up alongside him and grabbed hold of his gun. In a millisecond he had it cocked. He then put a bullet through the shifter that had invaded their space. The whole thing happened so fast she had difficulty taking it all in.

The yelp of the dying beast called for his companions. Just as the wolves vaulted through the trees, the sound of two more shots rang out. An almost eerie silence followed. For an incalculable amount of time Micah simply held onto her as—she assumed—he surveyed the forest for more of their kind. She fought the need to lift her head and gaze into his eyes for any telltale signs of concern.

At last the beat of her heart returned to normal. As it did, Micah relaxed his grip. He looked down into her eyes just as she tilted her chin upward. Their gazes locked and held. Time no longer existed.

He took in a breath and held onto it even as he whispered her name. His hand caressed the side of her face. He lowered his mouth onto hers and gave her the most incredible kiss he had ever given her. In that wondrous moment, nothing on this earth, in heaven, or any realm in between could've stopped that kiss.

She gripped the broad lapel of his coat and held him fast, even as her free hand traveled upward from his chest. Somewhere along the way, her arms encircled his shoulders. Her fingers brushed through the softness of his hair and she gloried in the feel of it. Micah ended the kiss just so he could give her another far deeper and more meaningful than the first. She responded with all the energy of her soul.

But then he withdrew. He took hold of her shoulders and stepped away from her. She could see anguish and the loathing he directed inward. "I'm so sorry, Tala, I didn't mean to do that. I—"

"Shh." She placed her trembling fingers against his lips and shook her head. "Don't say it."

"No, this isn't right. You don't know what you're—"

"Look," she interrupted. "I'm not asking you to give up your honor or your code of ethics here, Micah. I don't want either of us to throw caution aside. Believe it or not I know that finding ourselves in a compromising position out in the middle of the great outdoors, where shifters run rampant, is not a wise thing to do. All I want or need right now is a bit of tangible proof you feel *something* for me. The same thing in fact I feel for you. Is that too much to ask for the here and now?"

Micah turned his gaze heavenward. He drew in a deep breath and slowly let it go. She could see the war that raged deep inside him and pressed her advantage.

"Please, Micah—this is my choice if that's what's got you all in an uproar. Don't turn away from me. Don't treat me like I'm little more than a passing assignment you must be civil to while you stand guard over me. Perhaps the time for that will come, but I don't want it to come right now. Please."

Once again, he met her gaze. The very look in his eyes penetrated deep within her soul. "Are you so sure about that, Tala? Once we finish this quest, I'll be gone. Because I'm no longer part of your world, you'll never see me again. That's just the way it is—the way it has to be. Nothing I can do will change that fact. Isn't it better then, to just leave things as they are?"

She knew then and there that she had won the

battle. As far as his eventual departure? Well, she would just see about that. "I didn't ask for any kind of commitment from you, did I? I don't have the slightest desire for you to be anything but who and what you are, either. It's just that right now I don't want you to pretend you feel nothing for me. I don't want to pretend I feel nothing for you either because that would be a lie."

His eyes lit up with amusement. He cocked his head to the side as looked at her. "Is that right? A short while ago you said you weren't sure you even liked me yet."

She drew her shoulders together and gave him a sassy smile. "That was then and this is now."

Though he rolled his eyes heavenward, the action lost its effect when he chuckled. "You are the most exasperating woman I've ever met. You know that, don't you?"

"I've no doubt, but I'm sure a man with several centuries' worth of experiences under his belt can deal with one exasperating woman. After all, from the very day we met I've dealt with all of your annoying—"

He cupped her face as he cut off the remainder of her comment with a gentle, leisurely kiss that teetered on the edge of something far deeper. Yet, much to her disappointment, he found the strength and stepped away. "We should get out of here before we have any more unwanted company stumbling into the place. They're out there. I can smell them."

Tala glanced in the direction of the shifters she had all but forgotten in the passion of the moment. Before she found the resting place of the rebels, Micah put a gentle hand on her cheek. He turned her face toward him.

"You don't need the sight of that etched into your memory. Come on." He took hold of her hand and led her toward the horses. "Wait here while I pack up our supplies and get the horses ready."

She took hold of her mare's reins, slid them over her head, and gave her a gentle pat. "With all the mayhem we've just passed through, do you still think we'll arrive at the ruins by nightfall?"

He nodded. "Perhaps even as early as sunset."

Micah's instincts proved accurate. Just as the sun dipped below the horizon, her guardian reined in his horse and dismounted. Tala looked all around her. She didn't see any evidence that even hinted a castle once stood here.

"Are we here?" she asked.

"According to Dolph's map, we are here."

"Well I don't see anything that even remotely resembles the remains of a castle wall, do you?"

His gaze wandered over the landscape. "No, but that doesn't come as a surprise either. Dolph did say it took him five full years to find the ruins and that with the eyes of an eagle. I suppose we can't complain if it takes us a bit of time to uncover them ourselves."

"Time is something we don't have a lot of," she reminded him.

"Don't worry. Dolph didn't leave us completely blind. He gave us a specific marker that will serve as our guide. Nonetheless, I don't think we'll find it any before darkness sets in. As late as it is, I think we'll just find a secure place to pass the night and get you something to eat. We'll begin our search in the morning, okay?"

****

All throughout the night Micah held Tala in his arms. Yes, in so doing he kept her safe. More important, it also kept her close to his side. Though he never did before—and even condemned the decision—he finally understood the heart and mind of all the first-born sons who didn't honor the oath of their ancestor for the love of their woman. Had he met Tala while in mortality, would he have ignored his duty and chosen the same path? He didn't know. However, he did know he would take the memories of his time with Tala and forever treasure them. Perhaps at some future time, every once in a while and if he found the opportunity, he could check on her and see how she faired.

Tala's sudden deep breath alongside the gentle lift of her shoulders told him she had awakened. He gazed down on her beautiful face. Her eyelashes fluttered a bit before she opened her eyes. She then bewitched him with nothing more than a simple smile. "Good morning," she whispered.

Unable to resist, he placed a tender kiss against her lips and then drew back before she tempted him with one that expressed the far deeper emotion he longed to convey. "Good morning. Did you get enough rest?"

Her fingers traced the length of his jaw as she nodded. "For all of your concern over not putting up the tent, I slept just fine. The branches you fashioned into this makeshift hut kept me warm and you made for a very comfortable bed."

The admission prompted a grin. "I'm glad I could be of service, my lady."

A soft breath of laughter escaped as she sat up. She turned her gaze away from him and toward the opening of their shelter. "Did we have any unwanted visitors wandering about last night?"

"Not a single one. I suspect we won't run into any today either. At least I hope not."

She hid a yawn behind her hand and nodded. "I'll second that. Do you want any breakfast this morning before we get to task?"

"No, while you eat I think I'll just take a walk around the immediate area. I'll find a place for your tent and then make sure we're clear of any wild animals that call the place home."

"There are those. I've seen my fair share of brown bears, lynx, and wolves in these mountains on a photo shoot or two. Of course now I wonder whether or not they were Gehíwan rebels in their animal persona of choice."

"That's quite possible. Now, let's get you fed, shall we? After that, we'll get to work and see if we can uncover those ruins today."

Within the hour he and Tala cleared away their lean-to shelter. Together they buried all evidence of the fire that had warmed her breakfast.

Tala brushed the dirt from off her hands as her gaze swept across their lush environment. "Okay, where do we start?"

He shifted his gaze toward the east. "Though difficult to see for all the vegetation, we're standing on a rather flat plateau. The Romans built their fortification here on the high ground. The tactic gave them the advantage over any enemy seeking their wealth as well as their death."

Tala concurred with a nod. "They did a lot of that and it's probably one of the reasons they were so successful in their conquests."

"Given the limited boundaries of this particular plateau, the castle is probably not one of their larger or more opulent ones. While we conduct our search, we should keep in mind they would also build several outer buildings in the area. They would also need space to maneuver should their enemies have found a way to scale the mountain without getting butchered in the process."

"I suppose those are all reasonable assumptions. You said last night Dolph provided a marker?"

"Yes, he did. He said to look for a series of roots growing upward out of the rocks. If we follow those roots a bit deeper into the brush we'll see the foliage that has overtaken what's left of the wall he spied. That wall connects with another. He doesn't know which part of the castle those walls belong to. We'll have to figure that out ourselves before we can even begin our search for the key."

"Sounds daunting."

"I won't argue with you there."

"Do you think our search would be more productive if we split up? I could search along the north end while you take the south."

Micah shook his head even before she finished the suggestion. "No, Tala. I don't want you any farther away from me than what I can touch you if the need arises. Besides, Dolph also told me we'd find those roots on the northeast side of the plateau. We won't waste time in a fruitless search anywhere else."

Tala cast her gaze in that direction and sighed. "Still, that's a pretty good stretch of land if you ask me. Wouldn't it save time and effort if we just took a quick trip through one of your time-slip portals and take a peek at the castle? Then we'd know right where it stood. If we did that, maybe we could figure out the most likely place Chêzin hid his key."

Not that he hadn't considered and then discarded that very notion. "The problem with that solution is I don't know how far back in time we'd have to go. I don't have a clue as to what time or even the century the castle ruins were last visible to the naked eye."

"I don't see why it's necessary to see the castle at the exact period it fell into ruin," she argued. "I mean, wouldn't it be just as helpful—if not more so—if we took a look at it while it existed in all of its former glory? At least then we'd know the exact layout of the castle and the placement of all the outer buildings."

"That won't work. We'd have no idea who might be standing there as we enter such a time frame, Tala. We could walk into a whole garrison of soldiers who might not take kindly to our intrusion."

"Can't you just use your usual Jedi mind tricks and make us invisible to their eyes while we take a quick walk around the place?"

"My *what*?"

She rolled her eyes heavenward and tsked. "Jedi mind tricks—you know—*Star Wars*?"

"I'm afraid I don't know what you're talking about. However, in regards to the *invisible* thing, a shield takes a few seconds to accomplish when we step back and forth through the portals. In those few seconds, we could be seen, especially if we step right in front of a soldier with a sword in his hand. Therefore, I'll not put your safety at risk."

She stared at him for a moment. "Well, you could

just leave me here while you go. I'm sure I'll be all right during your brief absence."

"No, I'll not leave you unprotected. Ever. An unexpected breeze could carry your scent to the insurgents. You might cross paths with a wild animal, or even stumble into a deep crevice covered by vegetation. I'll not allow any of that to happen."

"What about sending Nathaniel or Levi then?"

"Their present task cannot be interrupted for any reason. Right now, gathering intelligence from the Gehíwans is vital to the success of our quest. I already told you this."

She dropped back on her heel, folded her arms, and huffed out a breath. "You're making this far more difficult than it has to be, Micah. You know that, don't you?"

"Me? You're the one that volunteered for this task and quite adamantly as I recall. I'm just here to keep you safe and assist you in finding the key."

"Fine." She gave him a curt nod. "Then let's get to it, shall we?"

Micah called up every ounce of the discipline he possessed just to keep from laughing. It had been quite a while since he had seen the fire in her eyes and he had missed it. He offered her his hand, which she ignored. She raised a disdainful brow, whirled around and stomped off in the wrong direction.

He waited a few seconds and then cleared his throat. "Tala? We need to go this way."

She took a few more steps before she stopped and whirled around toward him. Though she fought against it, the humor in the situation finally crept into her eyes and then touched the corners of her lips. Once again he extended his hand in invitation. This time she accepted it.

On the fourth day into their search, and just as he suggested they stop for lunch, Tala did a double take. She then shifted her gaze right and leaned forward for a better look. He turned in the direction of her focus. She swept passed him and approached a multitude of gnarly roots that protruded from a thick nest of vegetation.

She took hold of the largest branch, stretched it out full length, and held it up for his inspection. "Do you think this is what we're looking for?"

"Let's find out, shall we?" He took the large knife from out of his belt sheath and cut a wide, downward path, a couple of hours in the making. That path led them to a bed of broken rocks. Finally, they could see the fragmented remains of a thick stone wall that expanded no more than four feet in length. That wall then turned in a northerly direction. The remnants spanned about six feet and then abruptly ended. All the while Tala watched over his progress.

Once he had uncovered what remained of the walls, she closed her eyes. She tilted her chin toward the sun and released a dismayed sigh. "What are we supposed to do with this? I mean, we don't even know the direction we should search. Are those inner walls? Do they make up the outer walls? Are they buried beneath layers of silt—and truly, what difference would any of it make anyway?"

****

As she vented, Micah considered all of the options these small pieces of wall presented. Only one made sense. Yet not a single guardian had ever made such a choice. He didn't know how the ealdormen would react to his decision. More important, he didn't know the change in physical chemistry it would have on Tala's body, if any at all. Nonetheless, they would never find the key without far more information than what they had now and even the ealdormen agreed with the importance of their task. He rose to his feet while taking Tala along with him.

Tala drew her brows together as she gazed into his eyes. "What are you thinking?"

"That you're right. At this point finding the key is improbable, if not downright impossible. Therefore, we're leaving. Now."

She shook her head all the while he spoke. "No. We have to find that key, Micah. We can't abandon the quest now. Everyone is depending on us."

"I know that, and we won't abandon our part of this mission. We'll simply take a different path than the one we planned."

"What will you do instead?"

"Speak with Dolph. I can't help but wonder if there is more to his story than he thinks there is. Some small piece of information that might not mean anything to him, but that might make all the difference to us when it comes to the location of the key. Obviously, you can't come along with me. I can't leave you here alone, either," he said. "Therefore, I'll take you somewhere safe before I go; a place free from all danger."

She lifted a brow. "As I recall, you said there isn't any such place."

"No, I didn't say that, I just said I wouldn't leave you here unprotected."

She waved an agitated hand. "Okay, so tell me where I'm going already."

"I'll take you to my home in the realm of the Bewitan Fierd."

For a moment she stared at him as if he had quite lost his mind. "Well, if you can take me there, why can't I just go with you to see Dolph? After all, we've traveled back and forth in time countless times now."

"Though difficult for you to understand and me to explain, there's quite a bit of difference between physically transporting you great distances within your own world and stepping through time in the same location you're already in. The latter I can do, the first, I can't. Does that make any sense to you at all?"

She mulled that over for a moment. "No, but if that's true, then how do you purpose to take me into another dimension altogether?"

"Again, difficult to explain, but there is indeed, a difference. You just have to trust that I can."

"Can you do that? I mean, you said women weren't allowed."

"I don't know if I can do that or not, and I never said women weren't allowed. I just said women didn't live there." He adjusted the cloak around her shoulders. "I guess we'll find out together, won't we now. You're not afraid of the trip, are you?"

"No, not afraid, it's just that—" She bit down on her lip as a look of confusion beset her. "Well…how do we get there from here? I mean, what am I supposed to do?"

He wrapped his arms around her waist and then drew her body tight against his. In turn, she looped her arms around his neck. "I'm not sure how this will affect you. All I want you to do right now is close your eyes. Keep them closed until I tell you to open them. Should you feel any pain or discomfort of any kind, let me know right away."

"Okay—anything else?"

"You might want to hold on tight."

Chapter Twelve

With her feet planted firmly on the ground, Tala didn't say a word as the seconds slipped away. All the while she didn't feel any movement of any kind that suggested they had left the plateau. However, the upheaval deep inside her stomach put her in the mind of a roller coaster ride on a steep downhill run with no end in sight. Wooziness had overcome her and she noticed a shortness of breath. So, really, nothing all that unusual whenever she found herself in Micah's arms.

"All right, Tala, you can open your eyes now. We're here."

They were? The announcement surprised her. Although she couldn't really say what she expected, she somehow thought the journey would take far longer and feel more like someone catapulted her out of a circus cannon or something close to it. She opened her eyes and met Micah's penetrating gaze.

"Are you all right?" he asked.

She lifted her shoulders as she took in a breath of much needed air and nodded. "Couldn't be any better."

He gave her a sideways glance. "Are you sure about that? You look a bit disarrayed."

She bit down on the inside of her lip in a useless attempt to stop a smile. "Disarrayed? That's not very complimentary, you know. However, I suppose I could tell you I thought some kind of mystical whirlwind, filled with sparkling stardust, would carry me here. Yet if I said such a foolish thing, I know you'd just tell me I'm confusing a trip to your home with a journey to heaven again."

Micah chuckled as he loosened the hold he had around her waist and took a half step back. At the same time, her gaze wandered away from her overprotective guardian and around the enchanting room in which she now stood. The elegant early Baroque style furnishings he used throughout the room gave it a warm, homey feel. A vast array of interesting antiques adorned the large desk in the corner. Hurricane style lamps made of faceted crystal sat on top of the small side tables. A gorgeous beige and burgundy Persian rug accented the polished wooden floor, and a large fireplace, built with earth-colored stones, centered the wall in front of her. The ornate hand-carved, cherry wood mantel shelf and side pillars made the fireplace the defining piece of the room. Above the mantel hung a large, antique portrait of an English countryside, which the talented artist dressed in the vivid colors of autumn. The twists and the turns of the river running through the middle of the landscape sparkled in the sunlight.

She spared Micah a glance. "That's a very lovely painting. Did you choose it because you like it or does it have some significance?"

He turned his body while still holding his ground and gazed at the portrait for a time. "Both, actually. The home I grew up in is not far from the ash tree to the left of the landscape. As a boy I could see that very scene and witness the change of the seasons from my bedroom window. Of course, the area looks far different now."

The fondness in both his expression and tone made her smile. "Where in England did this delightful glade exist?"

"In the county of Herefordshire. To answer the next question I see you have, my mother gave birth to me on the 25th day of November, in the year 1661. So, in my humble opinion, somewhere between then and that battle in Aughrim, the artist took brush in hand and painted the scene."

She paused as she did the math. "So you didn't hang around long enough to see your 30th birthday then. Well, at least not here."

He shrugged off the comment. "I never put a whole lot of stock in counting the passage of time, then or now."

"Tedious thing that, isn't it?" she teased. After a moment she cleared her throat in an exaggerated manner as she gazed over every square inch of the room. "Well, I don't hear the wild ringing of bells or see flashing lights from any of your windows. So does that mean we successfully evaded the dreaded, 'Code red, the presence of a mortal woman, of all the scandalous things, has been detected inside our secret realm,' alarm?"

The sudden merriment that filled Micah's eyes accompanied his laughter. "If we have such an alarm lurking about the place, it's probably a silent one."

"Oh dear, then we still have cause for concern. Should I expect armed guards to burst through the door any minute now and carry me off to some dark, dank dungeon?"

"No, I don't think so. First of all, we don't have a dungeon—dank or otherwise—and secondly, you won't be here all that long."

"What's "not all that long" if you don't mind the question?"

"No more than a couple of hours, I should think. If my conversation with Dolph proves productive, we'll have a specific place we can begin our investigation. Regardless of what he might or might not know, I think I'll check out our Roman castle as it existed three, maybe four centuries ago anyway. Perhaps I can locate a likely area or two we can search."

Tala nodded in agreement. "That sounds like a very good plan to me."

"While I'm gone, use the kitchen if you get hungry. There's plenty of food in the pantry. You can also use my bedroom if you need a little rest. After all, it might be the last time you have access to a real bed for awhile."

"Wait. Don't I get the grand tour before you leave me to my own devices?"

In answer, he offered her the crook of his arm. Once she accepted the chivalrous gesture, he took hold of her fingers with his free hand and led her into his kitchen. The moment they stepped inside, various sizes of copper pots met her gaze. They were hung above the lovely stone archway that framed a stove, the likes of which she had never seen before. He had a plethora of small spice drawers and shelves on the left side of the sink. A beautiful cherry wood hutch sat on the right. The dining table in the center of the room complimented the colors and style of the hutch. The entire kitchen had the look and feel of the seventeenth century and it made her wonder—

"Do you have to chop wood before you can use

that thing?" she asked as she gazed pointedly at the stove that looked old-fashioned. At the same time, it looked like nothing she had ever seen before.

"I probably wouldn't eat much if I did." He turned the silver handles on the face of the stove. At once a vivid blue light heated the plates. The same blue light heated the oven. That interesting technology also cooled the refrigerator that sat against the wall next to the roomy pantry.

"What kind of power is that?" she asked.

"Nothing all that spectacular. We just have a resource native to this dimension that is different than the electricity or gas you use."

"I see."

As she puzzled over that they made their way down the hall and into his very masculine bedroom. The large four-poster bed centered the wall on her left and for the plush mattresses and quilts, looked comfortable and inviting. His bed faced a set of double doors made of glass. The oak wood that framed those doors had a unique design carved along each of the sides. The timber making up the bed frame had the same etching as well and she couldn't help but wonder if the pattern had any significance. A heraldic design used specifically by the guardians or something similar perhaps?

Her fingers traced over the design. "I love the etchings on the wood. Does it mean anything?"

"The etchings are a replica of the ancient insignia used by the original guardians. They speak of the oaths we're honored to keep."

"I see."

Beyond the doors she spied a stairway that spiraled

downward. The steps led to a lovely terrace that offered a grand view of the ocean below. She could also see an amazing variety of trees that graced the side of the mountain from the top of the hills and all the way down to the beach. A large leather chair sat in front of the fireplace. Built-in-floor-to-ceiling shelves covered the majority of the wall on her right. Most of those shelves were filled with leather-bound books in various colors and sizes. They also held a fair number of curios that looked as if they were gathered from all over the world and throughout a variety of times.

"Where did you get your fascinating assortment of collectibles?"

He shrugged away the question. "Just here and there along the way and over the years."

"Did you get them simply because they appealed to you or do they have a deeper meaning attached to them?"

His gaze wandered over his collection. "A little bit of both, I guess."

"I don't suppose you'd share the deeper meaning of the pieces that have such significance with me, would you?"

"This might not be the best time for that." He turned his gaze toward the window for a moment. "But before you get all huffy on me, I promise we'll talk about it later if you wish. With our waning time frame, I think the most important thing I can do right now is speak with Dolph."

She nodded. "You're right, of course."

"In the meantime, make yourself at home."

She gave him a bit of a smile as she lifted a brow. "So, you're saying it's okay if I snoop around the place then?"

He took hold of both of her hands and drew her a bit closer. "To your heart's content. All I ask is that you don't wander away from the house, all right? If Dolph isn't of any help, I'll be back sooner than you think."

"I'll wait right here. You have my word."

He tilted her chin upward and then gave her a toe-curling kiss she wouldn't forget anytime soon. "I'll be back before you know it."

She found she could do nothing more than nod in response. He disappeared a moment later.

Left alone, Tala wrapped her hands around her arms as she strolled out of the bedroom. As she passed by, she peeked inside his study, vowing to explore it later, and then made her way back to the sitting room. She approached the large diamond-pane window and found it very similar to the one she envisioned when Micah first mentioned his home. Far below she could see the ocean waves as they splashed up and over the large rock formations just off the beach. The sight captivated her. For a while, she stood there just gazing at it. If not for the directive to stay put, she would've gone outside and explored the sandy shore.

As she absorbed the view, a single thought overrode all others. Micah's home was everything, and at the same time nothing, she expected. More interesting than that? She could quite easily live the rest of her life, right here. If only she could find a way. Then just before she turned away, she caught a flash of movement from the corner of her eye. As she shifted her gaze toward the movement, she could see a man of average height and build, climbing the stone steps leading to Micah's doorway.

Though quite agile, he looked a bit more mature than the other guardians she had met. Perhaps the hint of gray in his sideburns and beard suggested the notion. So much for her theory all of the guardians were tall, handsome and brawny. As the man neared the door, he looked through the window and met her gaze head on. He gave her a nod alongside a pleasant smile that somehow put her at ease. She had no idea what he would say, but she knew without any doubt, he had come to speak with her and not Micah. What if he made her leave? What he if told her she couldn't stay? She took in a deep breath, made her way to the door, and opened it before he knocked.

His smile grew broader. "Hello Miss Westbrook, my name is Edward. Do you mind if I come in so we can chat for awhile?"

"Not at all." She waved him inside and then followed him into the sitting room. After he sat down, she took a seat across from the one he had chosen. Just as he opened his mouth, she lifted a hand. "You're probably going to tell me I'm not supposed to be here. I know that, really I do. It's just Micah had to—"

He interrupted her words with a shake of his head. "We know why you're here, Miss Westbrook, you needn't explain."

"Tala, please," she said as she dropped her hands into her lap and toyed with her fingers.

"Of course. Now as I just said, we know why Micah brought you here. We're also very well aware he took the best option available at the time. Had he had the opportunity to ask, we might've suggested it ourselves."

A relieved breath passed through her lips. "That's

good. But if you knew all of that and condoned the action, why did you want to talk to me?"

A quiet chuckle passed through his lips. "I didn't say I wanted to talk to *you*, Tala. Rather, I said I came so we could chat for awhile."

"I'm not sure I understand?"

He leaned forward as he pinned his gaze to hers. "If I'm not mistaken, you have something you'd like to talk to *me* about."

****

"Hello Dolph."

Dolph gasped as he whirled around and faced him. He put a hand over his heart, took in a series of deep breaths, and then gulped. "Micah."

"I'm sorry I startled you. That wasn't my intention." He stepped all the way inside the cave then and made his way toward him.

"You didn't; it's just I didn't expect company quite this soon." Dolph's expression then changed from one of surprise to one of concern. "You of all people shouldn't be here. Where's Tala? Did something happen? Is something wrong?"

"Nothing's wrong in the sense you mean. Tala and I found the wall fragments you mapped out for us. I don't know how long it's been since last you looked them over, but there isn't much left of the structure now. For the dense vegetation in the surrounding area, I believe it's impossible to find the key before the night of the black moon, if ever. At least, not without far more information and heavy equipment to dig away decades, perhaps even centuries of silt."

Dolph swallowed hard as he dropped his gaze. "Well, I guess I'm not surprised to hear you say that,

Micah. Nonetheless, I appreciate the fact you tried. I want to thank both you and Tala for your help. I'll adjust my plans accordingly. Perhaps with a bit of luck, I can locate the key without the insurgents—"

Micah held up a hand. "No, you misunderstand. We haven't given up the search nor will we. I just harbor a hope you have more information than what you think you have."

He drew his brows together. "No, I don't think so. I'm quite sure there isn't anything more I can say other than what I've already told you."

"You could be right, of course. Nonetheless, if you'll humor me, I'd like you to recall, as best you can, the entire conversation you had with Chêzin regarding his key and the circumstances surrounding it. Perhaps if you share it as it happened we'll find something new in there that will help us out."

"All right, I'll do my best." A faraway look entered Dolph's eyes as he shifted his gaze toward the cave opening. "I found Chêzin in an old barn in Bratislava I had used once before. At the time, I had every intention of using it again since the rebels had never paid much attention to it. I must say, finding Chêz there surprised me somewhat. The last time we met up, he had settled himself in the Far East."

"How long ago did this happen?"

"Well, let's see." He put a hand against his mouth and after a few moments, he dropped it. "I hadn't mastered the form of a bird as yet, so somewhere around the turn of the twentieth century I should think."

"You said you found Chêz on the brink of death?"

"Yes, after weeks of torture, the insurgents had left him for dead. Once he regained consciousness, he used his remaining strength to get to the hayloft inside the barn. He said he'd been there for a couple of days. His wounds had festered and he knew he had no hope of recovery. I didn't offer any. He took hold of my arm and told me despite the agony he had endured, the insurgents didn't break him. Despite the pain they inflicted, they couldn't make him divulge the location of the key he had hidden so long ago. I told him then he had served our nation well and he would die with his honor intact."

"He didn't happen to tell you when he did that, did he?" Micah asked.

Dolph paused for a moment as he delved deeper into the memory. A slow nod followed. "He said he moved the key only once. After that, it had safely rested in its present location since the days of Vlad the Second from the house of Drăculeşti when he ruled as Prince of Wallachia. But as to the exact spot? Nothing more than what I've already told you, I'm afraid. I'm sorry."

"You needn't be. You've given me exactly what I needed." Just as he turned toward the cave opening, Dolph put a hand on his shoulder.

"There's one more thing I now recall, Micah. I don't know if it'll help you or not, but—"

"Believe me, all information is helpful."

"Chêz told me he hid away his key under a black moon."

"Excellent. That's worth more than you know. We'll resume our search and with any amount of luck, we'll meet you at the portal as planned. However, if we don't find it in time, it doesn't mean all is lost, Dolph. I know Tala won't give up; it's not in her nature. She'll look for the key until she finds it, however long that might take. Once she does, we'll get you through the portal. You have my word."

"I appreciate that Micah, really I do. Nonetheless, I must remind you time is something we don't have a lot of, not if we have any hope of stopping the rebels in time to save this world as well as mine. At any time, they could find a key of their own. That very possibility is what haunts me most."

"I know that's your greatest worry, and I promise you we'll do our very best with the time we have left. In the meantime, we'll keep you informed."

The moment Micah left the cave he headed for the hall of records within the realm of the Bewitan Fierd. A few minutes later, he had what he needed. Vlad II ruled Wallachia from 1436 until his death in December of 1447. During those eleven years, four instances of a black moon had occurred. The last had taken place October 30, 1445. Without knowing the precise year Chêz buried his key, they should begin their search after the appearance of the final black moon during Vlad's reign. Now, he just needed a time period closest to that date where he could keep Tala safe while they looked for the key.

He didn't check on Tala. Instead, Micah made a quick trip to the plateau on the Carpathian Mountains in May of the year 1446. Upon his arrival he scouted the area for anything that might threaten Tala in any way. The shifters hadn't claimed the area nor had they passed by within recent months. The people that had once populated the plateau were long gone. He could sense the presence of wild animals in the forest, but they were not a concern. If necessary, he could protect Tala from them and even a handful of shifters should they happen across their path. Satisfied with the warmth the spring season gave them that year, he turned his attention toward the castle.

Though in a terrible state of decay, most of the Roman fortification still stood on its foundation. Only the roof that covered the northern tower and extended to the northeast hallway remained intact and in good order. A goodly portion of the walls along the south and west end of the structure looked as if they had been destroyed in battle well before time took a further toll. More than half the timber that comprised the castle doors had rotted away. The remnants of those doors hung precariously on rust-covered hinges that would soon disintegrate completely. He slipped through the arched doorway and entered the great hall, which now stood in shambles.

Various forms of vegetation protruded through what remained of the stone flooring. Boughs of the trees that had grown close to the outer walls on the first floor had entered through the glassless windows. He headed for the doorway that led to the north tower. The stairway that had once stood inside the antechamber had altogether disappeared, and thus provided additional space. With the roof overhead, the alcove would keep Tala warm and dry when she needed shelter. Good enough. He wouldn't check the upper floors. At least, not right now.

Once Micah returned to the realm of the Bewitan, he went straight to the Frithgeard in search of Edward. Then, as if the man expected him at that precise moment, Edward opened his door and waved him inside. "Come in Micah, come in." He swept a hand toward the chairs across from his desk. "Please, have a seat."

"Since you don't seem surprised to see me here, I take it you're aware of Tala's present whereabouts?" he asked as Edward rounded his desk and sat down.

"I am. We're also aware that despite the difficulty of the decision and the unknown risk Tala faced when she crossed the dimensions, bringing her here is the only sensible choice you could've made at the time."

"Well, from all appearances, she came through with her mortality still intact."

He shook his head from side to side. "We would know it if she didn't, so that's not a concern at this time. Let's hope she returns the same way, shall we? Now, did you get the information you needed from Dolph?"

Micah nodded. "Yes, I did. Somewhere between August of 1437 and October of 1445, Chêzin hid his key within or near the remains of the Roman fortification. I just did a bit of scouting there during the early days of May in the year 1446 and I found it safe enough for Tala. The timeframe also gives us a better chance of locating the key before the next black moon. At least, I hope it will."

"That's an excellent plan. Is there anything outside the norm you'll require for supplies while you're there?"

"I won't need the tent. There's an alcove inside the castle that'll suit Tala better, I think. So, just something comfortable she can sleep on alongside the warm sleeping bag if it's not too much trouble. I assume we'll need something to dig with. Also, something that can detect metal might be helpful."

"I'll have Josiah take care of those items right now.

Hopefully they'll arrive before you do. Is there anything else we can do for you before you leave?"

"Not right now, anyway," he said as he stood up. "Speaking of Josiah, how long will it be before you give him a shot at actually protecting someone? If you ask me, I think he's become a bit surly over the oversight."

"The minute someone needs his particular set of skills, he'll get his chance." Edward rose from his seat and then escorted him to the door. As he took hold of the handle, he paused briefly. He dropped his gaze toward the ground for a moment and then looked him in the eye. "I'm sorry, Micah."

Confusion beset him. "For what?"

"For the difficulty as well as the duration of this assignment. I know you hoped it would be short and sweet. Unfortunately, we can't predict these things ahead of time. You're very well aware people can and do make spontaneous choices just as Tala did once she met Dolph. I also know you've grown quite attached to her while on this assignment. I wished we could've somehow spared you the heartache that attachment brings."

"You needn't let that concern you in any way. I'll be just fine."

The directness of Edward's gaze penetrated both mind and soul. "Will you?"

"I guarantee it." Micah turned his gaze in the direction of his home. "Now with your permission, sir, I'll head home. I've been gone far longer than what Tala expected. I'm sure she's worried over the delay."

"Of course." Edward opened the door and gave him a nod. "I'll have your things packed up in the present location. We'll gather the additional supplies you need as promised, and send them straightaway. Then from time to time, I'll have someone check up on you in case you have further needs."

"Thank you. I would appreciate that."

As Micah journeyed toward his home, his thoughts centered on the conversation he had with Edward. Despite his assurances, his ealdorman didn't look the least bit convinced. Not that it mattered. Regardless of his feelings for Tala, he would return once they finished their quest. He had sworn an unalterable oath before men and God—an oath he wouldn't break, no matter how badly he wanted to.

Tala opened the door even as he climbed up the steps. Although she gifted him with a welcoming smile, he could see the worry in her eyes.

"How did it go?" she asked as she stepped aside to let him in.

He gave her a wink. "Better than I had hoped. Dolph narrowed the time Chêzin buried his key to a span of about seven years or so."

"So what does that mean in regards to our search?" she asked as he took hold of her hand and led her over to the sofa.

He sat down and then pulled her down beside him. "What it means is that we'll conduct our search within that time frame since it gives us the best shot at finding the key."

"I see, and that time frame is?"

"The fifteenth century. If all goes as planned, we'll stay there until the night of the black moon. I hope you're all right with an extended visit within the time period?"

She lifted a single shoulder. "I suppose so, since there's no other choice. We'll need to get my things first though."

"Already taken care of. On my way in I stopped by to give Edward—the ealdorman in charge of all my assignments—an update. He's already arranged for the transfer."

The comment startled her, but for the life of him, he couldn't think of a reason why it should. A warm flush stained her cheeks as she dropped her gaze for a moment and nodded. "Did Edward have anything else to say?"

The question prompted a grin. "Are you asking if the ealdormen know you're here or are you still worried about that dungeon?"

She bit down on her lip as she met his gaze. "Should I be?"

He pulled her onto his lap and then held her close to his chest. "Not in the least, Miss Westbrook. You're safe with me, at least, after a fashion." He touched his lips to hers then brushed lightly around and against them. "We have a few minutes to kill before we embark on our journey, so—"

The beat of heart accelerated even as her hand traveled up the length of his jaw. "We do?" she asked in a breathless sort of rush.

"Um-hmm, so if you don't have any objections, I thought we could just spend those few minutes right here."

Even as she whispered his name in a manner that left his heart in a muddled mess, he took full possession of her mouth. He couldn't detect a single protest in the kiss that followed or the one after that. All the while one thought repeated inside his mind. If only he could keep her here with him forever. If only.

Chapter Thirteen

"You can open your eyes now, we're here." Micah backed up a step as he examined her from the top of her head, all the way down to her toes, and back again. Heaven only knew what he searched for during these dimensional crossings of his. "Are you feeling any ill effects from the journey this time around?"

She shrugged away his concern. "Nothing to write home about so you can put that worried look away already. I'm fine."

As his gaze drifted just above her head, he released her from his arms. "Come on then, I'll show you to your home away from home for the duration of our stay."

Tala turned in the direction of his gaze and faced the three-story structure all but hidden by dense vegetation. For some reason, she didn't expect the castle to be quite this large. She didn't expect to see it on the brink of total ruin at this age in history either. How long ago did the Romans build the thing anyway?

"You had them put our things inside the castle?" she asked.

"I think you'll be more comfortable there than anywhere else. Believe it or not, the north tower is still in good repair. Good enough to keep you out of the wind and rain, anyway." He took hold of her hand and cocked his head toward the depilated doors. "Let's take a look, shall we?"

While Micah led the way, Tala took in every detail of her surroundings in search of the most probable place in which Chêzin may have stashed his key. He would want it well hidden. That meant he would've chosen a spot no one would suspect. Therefore, daunting though it might be, beneath the abundant plant life that encompassed the castle was a likely place to begin their quest. Again.

The moment they stepped through the doorway and she glimpsed the condition of both floors and walls, Tala changed her mind. Chêz wouldn't risk being caught out in the open if he had another choice, would he? The interior of the castle gave him that. The structure would keep him safe from eyes that pried and at the same time, provide a secure place to hide his key. Especially since chiseling through the dilapidated floors or walls didn't look all that difficult.

Micah stopped short of an alcove just off to the left as he turned and faced her. "May I ask what you're thinking about with such intensity?"

"That if Chêz wanted to make sure the convicts didn't catch sight of him he would've hidden his key somewhere inside the castle."

"Those were my thoughts as well once I explored the place." He gave her hand a gentle tug. "Let's get you settled first. Then we'll take a good look around, all right? Maybe something will jump out at us."

"We can only hope." As they entered the alcove a small bed with a feather mattress caught her attention. She hadn't expected more than the plush sleeping bag that now rested on top of the bed. That sight made her wonder if Micah had somehow arranged the small luxury. Though the thought pleased her, she didn't ask him. Her personal possessions were stacked in the corner. A couple of kerosene lanterns sat on top of one of the large crates probably filled with their food and supplies. Someone had also brought them a few camp chairs, a small two burner stove, cookware and—she took a second look. "Is that a metal detector?"

Micah grinned as he picked it up and turned it around for her inspection. "I thought the thing might come in handy. Therefore, I asked Edward if he could find us one."

Tala smiled her delight. "What a brilliant idea, Micah! That'll speed up our search by leaps and bounds. I could just kiss you for thinking of it, do you know that?"

Micah dropped the detector, which landed with a clatter onto the stone floor. He all but yanked her into his arms as he locked his gaze to hers. "Is that right? Well, don't let anything but fear stop you then," he said as his voice dropped to a husky whisper.

Now why did that one single look always cause such a tumultuous uproar deep inside her belly and then fill even the smallest vein with raging fire? She took in a breath and held on to it. "I just said I could—that doesn't mean I should. After all, I don't know if such a course is wise at this precise moment. We have responsibilities we shouldn't ignore right now and—"

"Then you shouldn't have offered it," he cut in as his lips played against hers.

The kiss that followed sent a delicious shiver up and down her spine. The second left her witless. She all but forgot she stood inside a castle somewhere in the fifteenth century, as well as the reason for it, during the third. The moment he gave her leave to breathe, she held up a hand. "Much more of that, Mr. Berrington, and you'll make me forget who I am and why I'm here."

He chuckled as he released her from his arms. "That might prove dangerous, so we can't have that, now can we."

"No we can't. Not, if we want to find that key, anyway," she said as she stepped away. She removed Micah's heavy cloak, and dropped it on her bed.

"Ah, the elusive key." He wiped away his grin as he looked about the chamber. "All right then, I'll let you arrange your things in the manner that suits you best. While you do that, I'll take a look around and see if I can figure out the best place to start our search come the morning."

She dropped back on her heel. As she placed a hand on her hip she lifted a brow. "Oh, I think not."

A look of confusion beset him as he turned his head to the side. "Excuse me? I don't know—"

"Well, I don't think it's fair for you to traipse through the castle. At least, not without me, anyway. We're in this together, aren't we?"

Though he fought to maintain an indifferent expression, he couldn't hide the amusement in his eyes. "Yes, we are."

"Besides, with daylight already waning, I think it makes more sense for *us* to explore the castle now."

"You have a valid point. So, what do you say *we* begin with the upper floors first—if we can get to them, that is."

"Might just as well. We'll see what's up there anyway, and there's no time like the present. I can sort out the alcove later this evening after we've had dinner."

He took hold of her hand then, led her out of the room and toward the south wing stairway. "The steps look steady enough, but stay close, just in case the stone crumbles away beneath our feet."

"Don't worry, I will," she said as they began their climb. As they arrived on the second floor landing, Micah halted and surveyed each of the extending hallways.

"Let's tackle the east passageway since we'll lose light there first."

She nodded. "All right."

As they toured the second floor, they discovered most of the individual chambers were in moderate condition all things considered. However, she couldn't say the same thing for the third floor, where time had taken its heaviest toll. Most of the roof had disintegrated along with large portions of the walls that had sectioned off the rooms. Because of the deterioration, she surmised the third floor shouldn't take more than a couple of days to search. Their most challenging areas would be in the first and second floors where most of the castle remained somewhat intact. By the time they had finished surveying the structure, the sun had set. That left the main floor all but covered in shadows.

Upon their return to the alcove Micah lit the lamps. He opened the crates and took stock of the contents. "Looks like you have a fairly decent selection of food in here."

With her sleeping bag only halfway unzipped, she stopped. She assumed her most skeptical expression and tone. "Do you really think so? I mean, you don't see any ice cream in there, do you?"

Joining in her playful banter, he once again peeked inside the crate and then tsked. "Sorry, no ice cream."

"Hmm. How about a Baby Ruth candy bar, a chocolate macadamia cookie, or a piece of fresh strawberry pie then?"

He put a hand over his heart and bowed. "Again, I must apologize for the oversight, my lady."

She lifted her chin and narrowed her eyes in mock indignation. "Decent selection, indeed. Who packs this stuff anyway?"

"I don't know what you're complaining about. I'll have you know you have quite a variety of canned goods and entire freeze-dried meals at your disposal. The cuisine is a feast meant for a king in comparison to the rot they hand out in the military."

"Allow me to remind you I have never served in the military, nor would I want to for that very reason, I'm sure. Besides, a woman needs her chocolate. Didn't you know? It's mandatory."

Micah chuckled. "Well, I'll have to see what I can do in the future to remedy the situation, now won't I?"

Tala raised a brow and smiled. "You could do that, I suppose. But how about I exchange the oversight for dinner once we've finished this quest—your treat, of course—and at the place I choose?"

She noticed a slight hesitation. In that tiny moment she recognized something in his eyes that made her heart drop into the pit of her stomach. A split second later a trace of amusement took its place.

"All right," he said. "You've got yourself a deal."

All throughout dinner, Micah kept their

conversation light. Yet, despite the levity they shared, that brief look in his eyes haunted her. Had he planned to just disappear the moment Dolph walked through the portal, with no thought of looking back? Would it be so easy for him to just walk away and forget she ever existed?

She cleared her throat as she set her plate off to the side. "So tell me, how will this whole thing work, anyway?"

He drew his brows together. "Sorry? I don't know what you mean by that."

"Once we have the key in hand, what happens next? I mean, what if we find it tomorrow? What will we do then?"

"I think the safest thing for us to do, regardless of when we find the key, is simply hang out here until the night of the black moon. We'll then meet up with Dolph just as we planned—unless directed otherwise, of course."

"We're still meeting him at the portal, right?"

Micah rubbed his thumb along his index finger as he looked at her. For a brief moment, she could see indecision in his gaze. He then replaced that indecision with resolve and it scared her half to death. "There's something you need to know, Tala."

The comment didn't erase her fear. Her heart spiraled downward as dread set in. "I'm all ears."

"If all goes well, we'll meet Dolph at the portal just as we planned. However, I don't know what we'll find when we get there."

"What do you mean?"

"The Romanians have made a decision that affects our plans. Very soon they'll begin construction on a military facility for the defense of their country—the likely location being a few miles away from the portal. They've already assigned a unit of men to assess the site. They should arrive no more than a few days to a week ahead of us. I can tell you right now the Gehíwan insurgents won't take kindly to human encroachment that close to their base. This situation might work in our favor. On the other hand, it might also have just the opposite effect."

A touch of relief replaced her earlier trepidation. "Explain that, please."

"If the rebels take their...usual confrontational measures...to the Romanian encampment with the entire force of their army, Dolph will pass through the portal safely and without notice. The black moon should ensure that. However, since they believe Dolph is in the area, their commander could very well leave a handful of men near the portal just in case he shows up. Relieving him of his key might take precedence over ridding themselves of the Romanians."

"If they make that decision, then what?"

"Well, if I had my way, we'd meet up with Dolph a day in advance. We'd give him the key and let him slip through—"

"No," she emphasized the word with a shake of her head. "We can't do that, Micah. We have to make sure he gets through that portal. If we don't see him do it ourselves, then we'll never know if he made it. On top of that, he just might need our help in getting through unscathed."

"What do you think you could possibly do to help him, Tala?"

"I don't know. Maybe we could create a diversion

or something." She nibbled at a nail and then dropped her hand to her side. "All I know is we can't leave him out there by himself. We just can't. Well, at least, *I* can't."

"I figured you'd say something like that. In light of that fact, we can only hope the commotion caused by the Romanians will work to our favor, thereby keeping the focus of all the insurgents on them rather than on the portal. Regardless of scenario, I need your promise, upon your word of honor that you'll do everything I say in the exact moment I ask you to do it. You can't allow your impulsiveness or anything else for that matter, override the directive. Not even if you think I've made an error in judgment."

She drew her brows together. "I've already promised you that and more than once."

He returned a slow nod. "I know, but I need to hear it again. I need you to really mean it. Please give me that."

Tala moved closer and took hold of his hand. "I trust you Micah, and more than you might guess. Because I trust you, I give you my absolute word I'll follow every command you make without question. I'll do it in the exact moment you give the order and I won't let my impulsiveness cloud my judgment. Is that good enough?"

"Yes, it's good enough. But do keep in mind I'll hold you to every word of your promise."

He meant to kiss her then. She could see it in his eyes. If she allowed it to happen, that would put an end to their conversation. At that moment the questions that deviled her overrode the need to be in his arms. She leaned back a bit in her chair as she briefly dropped her gaze knowing it would break the spell that held them bound. "Now that we've settled that, I'd like to know what will happen *after* Dolph walks through the portal. By that I mean what will happen to us?"

A touch of humor filled his eyes. "You already have the answer, do you not? I'll take you to dinner as promised, and then I'll take you home."

"Where's home?"

He paused as he searched her eyes. "I guess I don't know. I just assumed you'd head back to the States and visit with your father if nothing else, but if—"

"What if the danger still exists? What if the insurgents in England look for me out of vengeance? What if they track me to my father's house during one of my visits and then threaten him or worse?"

"The chances of that happening are slim to none. Once they realize Dolph has passed through the portal—and they will—their attention will be directed elsewhere. They'll know, without doubt, they'll face a Gehíwan army sooner or later. As their first priority they'll prepare for the battle that'll surely come."

"But just what if?" she pressed.

"Then I suppose that decision would be left up to the ealdormen."

"Would they keep you on as my guardian?"

"I'm not sure. They might, or they could just as easily assign someone else. You must understand, I am *not* the one who makes the decisions. I simply follow the orders I'm given."

"I see." She swallowed past the lump in her throat. "So when the time comes, and I'm no longer your concern, will you ever stop by and say hello?"

****

Micah understood her line of questioning then. For a moment he closed his eyes against the pain that knowledge caused. "Tala—"

She interrupted with a lift of her hand. "Surely the guardians who develop…unique friendships…with those they protect keep in touch with them from time to time, don't they? Or is that forbidden?"

Micah shrugged as he forced a grin. "I think I can safely say our charges forget all about us the moment we pass out of their lives."

Something mysterious flickered within her gaze. Something he couldn't quite name or even define. "What if we don't? What if we can't?"

"I guarantee you as your life returns to normal, if you think of me at all, I'll be nothing more than a distant, foggy memory. A memory I'm sure, you wouldn't want intruding into your life."

"Do you want to lay a little wager on that?"

A quiet chuckle accompanied the slight shake of his head. "We've had this conversation before. Like I said then, should I win, you wouldn't even remember you owe the debt."

"I suppose that would be true—if you're right. So let's make this a one-sided wager then. If I remember you in full and complete detail, then you must promise you'll come when I call your name. Nothing more—nothing less."

"What makes you so sure I'd hear you?"

She paused for a moment as she looked deeply into his eyes. "After having honed the ability to *feel* my presence, are you telling me that you wouldn't?"

"Ah, you remember that I said that, do you?"

"I have a very good memory, Micah."

"Yes, I can see that. Nonetheless, if I'm in the middle of an assignment, how could you possibly expect me to answer your call? As you're very well aware, I can't abandon those I protect."

"You'll find a way to work around that, I'm sure. After all, you're a man who keeps his oaths and obligations, isn't that right?"

"All right, but you can't call immediately, either. That wouldn't be a fair test of time."

"What would be a fair test of time in your opinion?"

"One year."

"No, that's much too long. Let's make it three months."

"Six and that's my final offer," he countered.

"All right, six it is. You have yourself a deal."

For a moment he said nothing. So many thoughts bombarded his mind. Of a certainty, Tala wouldn't have any recollection of the time they spent together once he erased the memory—and he would erase it. Yet, somewhere in the back of his mind, he planted a small hope she would remember anyway. If somehow she did—

"Micah?"

She looked at him and from the expression on her face it seemed she wanted an answer to a question he didn't hear. "Hmm?"

A trace of dewy liquid filled her eyes and at once she dropped her gaze to hide it. "I asked you if you would even want to…visit me, that is."

Her anguish tore at his heart. In reaction to that anguish, he rose from his chair. He tossed it aside as he wrapped an arm around her waist and drew her to her feet. With his fingers placed underneath her chin, he tilted her face upward. Her beautiful violet-blue eyes gazed into his as he battled his emotions—and lost. "That's a ridiculous question; you know that, don't you? Wager accepted and with eager anticipation of my loss."

Just as he leaned down for a kiss, the groan of rusty hinges echoed throughout the hall. Less than a second later, Josiah called out his name. Micah huffed out an irritated breath. With reluctance, he released Tala from his embrace. "Let's go see what he wants before he barges in here."

Josiah spied them just as they entered the grand hall. A smile lit up his face. "There you are."

"You say that as if you're surprised," Micah said as the man approached them. "Josiah, this is Tala Westbrook. Tala, this is Josiah Nicholson."

"Pleased to meet you, Josiah," she murmured.

"Likewise." He gave her a courteous nod alongside a smile, and then shifted his gaze toward Micah. "In answer to your observation, I didn't know for sure where you might've wandered off to. Hence the reason I called out your name."

"At this hour of the night, the safest place for Tala is inside the castle, wouldn't you agree?"

Josiah smirked as he shrugged away the question. "You never know. Perhaps a wild animal chased you out of doors or something else might've come up. Anyway, Edward sent me to deliver a message, so here I am."

"And the message is?"

"He said if there's time between the moment you find the key and your scheduled appointment with

Dolph, he wants you to take Tala to your home instead of waiting here. He has a small task he needs you to do before the black moon if at all possible."

Startled over the unexpected request, Micah turned his head and gave him a sideways glance. "Did he say what the task entailed?"

"No, he didn't, but that shouldn't surprise anyone," said Josiah.

"You're right about that," Micah murmured.

"The only thing he did say is the assignment shouldn't take you very long. Other than that? You're on your own."

"All right, tell him if luck is on our side, then we'll see him soon."

"I'll do that. In the meantime, is there anything else you might need while you're here?"

Micah turned toward Tala and gave her a conspiratorial wink. "Yes, if we're to complete this task in a timely manner and meet up with Edward as he so desires, we'll need a fair amount of Baby Ruth candy bars and chocolate macadamia cookies. That should speed things up quite a bit, shouldn't it Tala?"

She assumed a serious expression as she nodded. "Definitely."

Josiah's eyes darted toward Tala before he once again gave him his full attention. "Oh, okay. Well, I'll—uh—see what I can do then."

"We'd appreciate that, thank you. The sooner the better."

Josiah bowed his head. Without further comment, he took his leave.

For several seconds, Tala stared at the spot from which the befuddled guardian had disappeared. Her eyes filled with frivolity as she finally turned and faced him. "All this popping in and out is enough to scare the tar right out of a body. Doesn't that concern you all? I mean, what if one of your charges should drop over dead from a heart attack?"

Micah chuckled as he moved a step closer. "We haven't lost anyone yet."

"There's always a first time for everything. Now, I don't suppose you have any inkling whatsoever as to when one of your guardians is about to make a sudden appearance and can warn a person, do you?"

"Nope."

"No annoying alarms, shrieking whistles, or even a whisper carried by the wind?"

"Afraid not."

She rubbed her lips together as she nodded. "Then I suppose one should take special care as to what one says and does around here."

He staved off a grin. "Most likely."

"On top of that, one should obviously be ready to change one's well-laid plans at the drop of a hat."

"I suppose so."

"Um-hmm. Is Edward always the man responsible for such chaos?"

"No, not always."

"I see. Speaking of Edward, I've had this burning curiosity to know if he's your direct line grandfather."

"I can see where you might think that, but no, he isn't. The ealdorman I descend from is a man named Thomas."

She drew her brows together and then shrugged. "So, what's Josiah's story? He doesn't seem as "well-adjusted" as the rest of you."

"Josiah? He's a relatively new addition to the Bewitan Fierd, all things considered. During his mortality he became a doctor. Given the time period of his birth, he served in Korea following World War II as a field surgeon. The ealdorman called him into our realm just before an enemy artillery shell landed on top of his Battalion Aid Station. The explosion destroyed it and killed almost everyone inside."

"I see." Tala took in a deep breath and then slowly let it go as she regarded him. "He probably thinks you're crazy, you know—asking for cookies, candy bars, and such."

"No doubt."

"Well, just so you know, that doesn't get you out of our dinner date."

"I didn't expect it would."

She bit down on her lip to stop the smile that came anyway. "Had you added the ice-cream, specifically rocky road, I might've let you off the hook, though."

He moved closer still and all the while she held her ground. "Who said I wanted to be let off the hook?"

She took in a shallow breath as she gazed up into his eyes. "Does that also mean you wouldn't mind a visit with me in the future? If even for a short while?"

Micah brushed away her hair and then cupped the side of her face. "I'll look forward to your call."

Though he didn't intend to, he gave her the kiss then he had longed to give her. He held nothing back and she responded in kind. Never before had he experienced a kiss that turned his body and soul into a raging inferno. When at length he ended the kiss, he called up every shred of self-discipline he possessed and put some space between them, lest he cross the boundary of his honor. He gave her a nod as he fought for a sense of normalcy. "In fact, I shall look very forward to it."

An alluring smile followed the comment. Seemingly lost for words, she kissed him on the cheek and then stepped back. For several moments they did nothing more than gaze at each other. The look in her eyes stoked the fire burning within his body.

"Good night, Micah, I'll see you in the morning."

Once Tala fell into a deep enough sleep, Micah headed outside to clear his head while he inspected the castle grounds. Although he sensed the presence of a few bears not all that far from the castle, not a single shifter wandered anywhere near the place. Since he and Tala would conduct their search within the castle, the chances of the Gehíwans detecting her human scent were slim at best. Especially if he could convince her to remain indoors on windy days.

They now had just a little over three weeks before the black moon. With the aid of the metal detector they could probably locate the key in half that time. At least he hoped so. He wondered then about the duty Edward wanted him to undertake. Never once had he been called away from one assignment to take on another and it baffled him. What could possibly be so important that he would interrupt a current obligation?

Chapter Fourteen

Tala awoke to the wondrous memory of the kiss Micah gave her last night. For as long as she drew breath she would never forget the way it made her feel. Never. With every fiber of her being she knew a kiss from another man, no matter how passionate, would ever come close to his.

Ridiculous thought, she silently chided.

She couldn't imagine she would ever let another man get close enough to try. At once she altogether dismissed the notion. After all, if all went according to her hopes and dreams, such a possibility wouldn't even exist. After all, for better or worse, whether he knew it or not, Micah owned her heart.

"Well, it's nice to see such a lovely smile on your face this early in the morning," Micah said as he entered the alcove and set a bucket of fresh water down by her stove.

She sat up in her comfortable bed and wrapped her arms around her knees. "Why? Do you hope it means I'll be agreeable?"

"Not necessarily. Every now and again I enjoy that indignant fire in your eyes. Keeps things interesting." He gave her a wink.

"Does it now?" She tilted her head as she gazed at him. "Then I'll have to see what I can do for you as the day progresses."

A grin accompanied the slight shake of his head. "Would you like something out of the box for your breakfast? If so, I can get it for you if you wish."

She combed her fingers through her tangled hair as she turned her gaze toward the crate. "Actually, what I'd really like right now is a bath. Do you think it's safe enough for a quick dip in the river or should I expect a random guardian or two to make a sudden appearance just as I'm coming up out of the water?"

Micah's grin grew broader as he took hold of a bag at the foot of her bed and dropped it onto her lap. "If you're referring to Josiah, he's already come and gone."

She drew in a gasp of delighted surprise as she opened the bag. A second later, she withdrew a full-sized candy bar, and held it up. "Breakfast!"

"That looks more like dessert if you ask me."

"Nonsense. I'll have you know this little candy bar is packed with vitamins and nutrition, and no, you can't read the label." She set her hoard off to the side and climbed out of bed. "Now about that bath?"

He turned his gaze toward the small arrow slit and checked the trees for movement. "I think it's safe enough if you don't dawdle. The winds are calm now, but there's always a chance that could change."

"What difference would it make even if it did? The shifters in this century aren't looking for me."

"No, but since the place has been empty for so long, a human presence in this area might draw their curiosity nonetheless. Your scent could also attract the attention of a hungry animal looking for a quick and easy meal. I must say, you do look delicious."

Tala merely laughed in return as she dug through her pack. She picked out a fresh set of clothes, shampoo, and a bar of soap. "I'll hurry, I promise. I'm anxious to get started on our search. That being said, I don't want to smell like a field hand while doing so. Please note you can't begin without me."

"I won't. Lest you've forgotten, I'm your protector. As such I'm required to watch over you at all times, in all places and most especially, in rivers with raging currents."

Her mouth dropped a notch as heat colored her cheeks. Yet before she could sputter a word of protest he held up his hand.

"I assure you, Miss Westbrook, you're privacy will not be violated, unless of course, you need rescue. Even then I'll make sure you're covered with something, if only the shirt on my back."

A bit of mischief overtook her smile. "Now that's an interesting thought, but unfortunately, I don't think it'll be necessary. I'll be in and out before you know it."

True to her word, they began their search in less than an hour. Micah worked the metal detector. He deemed it much too heavy for her to lift for long periods of time. She could argue the point, but she wouldn't engage in a battle she couldn't win anyway. Besides, she loved his chivalrous nature. For some reason, it made her feel cherished and very feminine.

By the middle of the third day they had finished a thorough search of the entire top floor without success. Not that they had come up empty-handed. They had uncovered some huge nails, the twisted blade of a rusty sword, some old Roman coins, and a ruby gemstone ring.

She wiped the back of her hand across her brow. "So down to the second floor then?"

"Yes, but I think we'll take a lunch break first," he said.

"I'll agree to that. I am a little hungry."

He intertwined his fingers with hers and cocked his head toward the stairs. "Come on, we don't need you fainting dead away for the lack of food."

"I don't think I'm anywhere near fainting, Micah."

"Good. Then let's keep it that way, shall we?"

Just as they stepped off the stairway and turned toward the alcove, Levi entered the castle through the entry doors.

"How's the search coming?" he asked as they met him in the middle of the great hall.

"More of a process of elimination so far," Micah said.

Levi nodded. "I suspect that's a necessary part of finding the piece."

"We were just about to get some lunch," Tala said. "Would you care to join us?"

A flirtatious grin accompanied a wink. "I could take something light if you have it to offer."

"I'm sure we can find something that'll suit you. After all, I've been blessed with cuisine fit for a king in comparison to the rations served in the military, or so I'm told. Isn't that right Micah?"

In response to the jibe, Micah chuckled as he led them into the alcove.

Levi and Micah kept the conversation light all throughout the meal and it drove her crazy. Then just as she would ask Levi the reason for his visit herself since her guardian didn't bother, he leaned forward and focused his attention on Micah.

"I thought I'd let you know the military convoy

headed toward the penal colony is a little larger than we first expected."

"In what way?" asked Micah.

"They've taken one of their top engineers at his word and trust they'll find the site adequate for their needs. Since winter is not far off, they've begun the transport of some of the heavy equipment they'll need to lay the ground work. From all reports they have collected materials, tents, and supplies for everything under the sun. The government will ship this equipment by way of trucks and a transport helicopter. As I'm sure you know, all of these things will draw the attention of our mangy insurgents if it hasn't already. The reason for the change in plans is so they can have the equipment in place before the snow comes. In this way they won't postpone completion of the facility by an entire season. The Romanians figure they can also make it back down the mountain without hindrance if they deem the site impractical."

Micah scratched at the corner of his mouth. "How many additional troops have they assigned to the detail and do you have any idea when they're leaving?"

"About fifty men, give or take. They'll leave sometime within the next couple of weeks." Levi shrugged. "There's no doubt you'll run into them. I just don't know when or where."

"Well, let's hope their presence keeps the shifters busy then," Micah said. "Does Dolph know any of this yet?"

"Not yet, but I'll tell him right after I leave here."

"Do you know if the insurgents have mentioned either Dolph or Tala in their conversations?"

Levi shot a glance in her direction. "They have.

Beldūrq is a bit frustrated they haven't caught sight of either one of them. Although they didn't at first because of the bodies you left strewn around the glade, they now think that just maybe Tala is traveling with Dolph. The fact neither of them have been spotted anywhere near the penal colony makes them all the more certain they'll show up soon. With that in mind, they have spotters looking for them around the clock and in all directions."

"How many?"

"At present they have one man for each direction of the compass. Two stand guard near the portal," Levi said.

"That could change with the presence of the Romanians though," Micah mused. "Please keep us posted on that. With all of the heavy equipment, it will take the Romanians far longer to make it up the mountain. Somewhere along the way the insurgents will take notice. When they do, they might reduce the number of spotters."

"We considered that as well," Levi said as he rose from his seat. "We'll definitely keep you updated on the number as well as the position so you can avoid them if at all possible when the time comes."

She and Micah accompanied Levi all the way to the castle doors. With a gleam in his eye, Levi took her hand. He gallantly kissed the top of it before shaking hands with Micah, who looked a bit annoyed.

"Perhaps we'll see you soon and I hope when we do, we have key in hand," she said.

Levi dipped his head. "I'll look forward to it, Tala. In the meantime, don't worry about a thing. Micah's one of our best. He'll see to it you get through this adventure safe and sound. You can then put all of this behind you and get right back to life as you know it." He gave her a wink. "I bet you can't wait for that day, can you now?"

Tala returned the man's smile even though his comments had just the opposite effect. The thought of life without Micah filled her with anything but pleasure. What would she do if she failed in her quest? What if she couldn't remain at his side in the forever world of the guardians? She couldn't live without him; she just couldn't.

The second Levi took his leave; Micah turned around and faced her. As he looked at her, a touch of concern filled his eyes. "Are you all right?"

She forced another fake smile and hoped it look genuine. "Of course. What would make you think otherwise?"

"You're not worried about the Gehíwan rebel forces are you?"

"Not at all."

He turned his head and gave her a sideways glance. "Are you sure about that?"

"I've already seen you in action Micah. Many times. I'm not at all worried about the threat from a bunch of Gehíwan convicts. In fact, they have my pity. Therefore, if I have any worry at all, it's whether or not we'll find the key in time."

He offered her his arm. "Then I suppose we'd better tackle that second floor."

She turned her gaze toward the stairway as she nodded. "All right. I'll hope lady luck smiles on us, and that she'll produce the key by the end of the day."

Micah chuckled. "Dreamer—"

"Hey, it could happen."

****

Another week gone. Days wasted with nothing but a few ancient trinkets that provided proof of all their time and efforts. Very little remained of the second floor they hadn't methodically searched. Just two rooms off the main hallway remained. She had very little hope they'd find anything in them. Nonetheless, Micah insisted they finish inspecting them before they turned their attention to the first floor. Still, they should finish those rooms well before sunset. She had already faced the fact they would probably find the key outside and in the very last possible place they could search.

"Tala, will you hand me the sledgehammer, please?" Micah asked as he propped the metal detector against the corner of the wall.

"Did the detector go off?" she asked as she handed off the tool. "I didn't hear a single beep if it did."

With nothing more than a glance, Micah directed her attention toward a series of stones that rose from the floor in a square pattern of about two and a half feet in both height and width. "No, but take a look at this area right here. Do you see the difference in the color of mortar as the well as the difference in the way the stones are stacked?"

Tala stooped down for a closer look as she traced along the seams with her fingers. "Yes, I do. Do you think something's behind the wall?"

He took hold of her hand and drew her to her feet. "We'll find out here in about a minute. Stand back a bit so you don't get hit with any of the debris."

Once she complied, he swung the hammer all the way back and then hit the stones with full force. With the third swing, he had created a hole large enough for them to look through. She didn't waste any time in brushing away the fragments that blocked the opening.

Her heart raced as she peeked inside. "There's a small room in there, Micah. I wonder if Dolph could've hidden his key somewhere inside it."

He hunkered down beside her. After searching what he could see of the room himself, he nodded. "That's very possible. Although I suppose it's also possible the Romans hid some of their wealth in there."

"I think the mortar you've smashed to smithereens looks way too new for the Romans to be the ones responsible for sealing it up, don't you?"

"Or do you just hope it does?" he teased.

"Well, as you're so fond of saying, there's only one way to find out," she said as she moved out of his way.

Within minutes they crawled through the entrance he created. The small chamber they now found themselves in wouldn't take all that long to search. Micah retrieved their metal detector, turned it on, and pointed it toward the wall opposite of the opening. All the while she hoped against hope they would find the key in this small space.

The walls yielded them nothing. He then turned his attention on the far end of the floor. At once the alarms from the metal detector sounded off with a series of wild beeps that had eluded them until now. Micah continued his sweep of the floor until he zeroed in on the most promising area. He dropped down onto one knee and then brushed away the pebbles from that section of flooring.

"Hand me the hammer and chisel, please, so I don't damage anything should the key be in there," he said.

She gave him the tools he asked for as she bit down on her lip. "I think you'll find one very disappointed lady if that key's not down there."

"Well, the last thing I'd want to do is disappoint such a beautiful lady."

The compliment, alongside the look in his eyes warmed her heart and kept her company while her guardian worked with the hammer and chisel for well over an hour. Once he completed his task, he extracted a crude wooden box that could house the key with room to spare. She took in a breath and held onto it while he removed the nails that sealed the lid to the box. He then cut away several strips of rope that bound a piece of ragged leather around a square object about three inches in depth. Her heart sank. The key was round, not square.

Despite the observation, Micah swept away the wrapping. In the instant he lifted away the thin piece of square wood resting on top, delight overcame her gloom. There in all of its glory, sat the bonze disk with crescent moon and round golden circles that Chêzin once had in his possession. In her excitement she threw her arms around him and laughed.

"We found it, Micah," she murmured. "Oh, we found it!"

For a time they simply gazed at each other. The joy in Micah's eyes dimmed somewhat as the moments passed. Then, what she could only define as a touch of regret, took its place. She didn't question the reason for it. For all of a sudden the same thought dawned on her as well. Their idyllic time here at the castle would end and it would end before the sun dipped below the mountains. The night of the black moon fast approached. Once it did, he'd be gone unless she could find a way to stop it.

All of her memories from the day they arrived here and to this hour tumbled into her mind. The midnight walks, the laughter, their conversations, the breathtaking way he looked at her, and the singular way he always kissed her.

An almost imperceptible shake of his head accompanied a sigh. He took hold of her face and lowered his lips onto hers. Oh how she hated that exquisite kiss to end, but end it did.

He brushed the hair away from her face and attempted a grin. "Well, I suppose we ought to find our way back to the present."

"We're still going to your house first though, right?" she asked.

"Yes we are, but in case you've forgotten—that will also be in the present time."

"Should we take the key with us?"

"I wouldn't leave here without it. You'll need a few of your things as well. Since we don't know how long my next assignment will take, you might need something to sleep in or want a change of clothes before the ealdormen arrange the transfer of everything we leave behind."

"That sounds like a very good idea."

He took hold of her hand. "All right then, let's get to it, shall we?"

As they descended the stairs, Tala took a last good look around the place. The adventure she had shared here with Micah would forever be etched into memory. In one way or another she had found delight in every minute of her stay.

Once she had put the things she needed inside her small backpack, she turned around and faced him. "I'm ready to go if you are."

"Are you sure you didn't forget something?"

Tala looked all about the room. "No, I think I have everything I need for now."

"So you don't want your chocolate or cookies then?" he asked as he retrieved and then draped his cloak around her shoulders. "Before you answer that I think you should know I don't have anything remotely close to them in my pantry at home. If such fare is mandatory—"

She laughed as she took hold of her pack, unzipped it then and held it open. "Waste not, want not."

After he added the remainder of her stash, he took hold of the key with one hand. He then placed the other around her waist and pulled her in tight to his body. Once he held her securely in position, he gazed into her eyes. "Are you ready?"

"Yes, I think so."

"Then loop your arms around my neck. Close your eyes, and hold on tight."

She snuggled in a bit closer and waited for the now familiar signs of their journey. However for some unknown reason, this time the breathlessness and light-headedness increased ten-fold. Intense heat and nausea assaulted her. Just as she thought she might pass out, Micah loosened his grip. She opened her eyes and found him gazing at her most intently.

He drew his brows together as he placed a gentle hand against her cheek. "You're very warm. Do you feel ill?"

Tala took in a deep breath and gave it a slow

release. She shook her head as she anchored her feet against the floor and hoped he didn't notice the slight sway of her body. "No, I'm fine."

"If you don't mind my saying so, you don't look fine."

"That's a terrible thing to say to a woman, Mr. Berrington. You clearly haven't polished your social skills when it comes to dealing with the opposite sex."

A slight grin emerged. "You've just now discovered that?"

"No," she said as the dizziness finally began to dissipate somewhat. "I am, however, just now saying it out loud."

Micah chuckled as he released her from his arms and placed the key on top of his desk. As she expected, he helped her out of the cloak, which he then tossed over the back of his sofa without so much as a backward glance. "Are you hungry?"

"Yeah, a little."

"How about I make you some dinner before I go see Edward?"

"You have time for that?"

He shrugged away her worry. "I'm sure Edward won't mind. After all, he couldn't have known just how long it would take us to find the key and in likelihood, he doesn't even know we're here yet."

"True. Do you want my help?" she asked.

"No, I'd rather you just sit back and take it easy. Rest and enjoy yourself for a little while. You've earned it."

Once Micah had her seated comfortably with the book she had chosen in hand, he headed for the kitchen. He took his time making both the meal as well as the dessert, wanting them perfect. All the while he focused on his task, rather than on his waning time with Tala. Time for such thoughts would come soon enough. Once he finished, he lit the candles on top of the dining table and then made his way back into the living room. She looked up from her book and smiled.

"Whatever you're cooking smells delicious," she said. "You've had my mouth watering for quite some time now. What did you make?"

"Pan seared orange roughy with a lemon dill sauce I created myself. We also have a pasta salad to go along with it. Let's hope it tastes as good as it smells." He took hold of her hand, drew her to her feet, and then escorted her into the kitchen. Once he helped her into her chair, he took the seat opposite her.

She placed her napkin on her lap, filled her fork with the main course and then waited for him to take the first bite before she took one herself. Midway through their meal she took in a deep breath and closed her eyes. "Mmm, this is really good, Micah. Where did you learn to cook?"

"You're forgetting I've had centuries of practice. Over those centuries, the same old dishes got very boring. Therefore, I would list sheer desperation as the motivating factor for whatever skill I possess."

The revelation made her laugh. "I bet. But doesn't it ever get lonely eating here all by yourself?"

"Well, all things considered I don't eat all that often. Every now and again when I do, I'll invite a few friends over."

"And do what?"

He turned his head to the side. "I'm not sure what—"

"I mean, do you turn on the sports channel and watch a bit of football or baseball?"

He chuckled. "No, television is something we don't have here. Well, at least not yet anyway. Perhaps no one has ever suggested it."

"I see. Well, do your dinner companions ever return the favor?"

"From time to time. We either immerse ourselves in a game of cards, a board game—go outside for some sort of sport activity. Sometimes we just sit around and talk."

She picked up her napkin, dabbed at the corner of her mouth and then dropped it next to her plate. "Are Levi and Nathaniel included on your guest list?"

"I'd say they're invited more often than not, and there are a few others you haven't met."

"Is it a common thing for you, Nathaniel, and Levi, to work together?"

He'd never really thought of that one way or the other before. He took a moment to consider it. Finally he nodded. "I suppose there are some of the guardians I work with more than others. Nathaniel and Levi would definitely be included in that group."

"I thought so. You all seem to work very well together—a well oiled machine as they say." She dropped her gaze for a moment. Then with an almost imperceptible shake of her head, she finally lifted her gaze to meet with his. All the while she clenched and unclenched her fist. "I think I'm going to miss their sudden visits when they're least expected. If nothing else, it's kept life interesting."

He said nothing in return. She remained silent for a moment and in that moment, her gaze penetrated clear through to his soul.

"However, you know, don't you, that I'll miss you most of all? That's why it's so very, very important to me that you come the moment I call for you," she said as her voice dropped to a whisper. "In fact, you don't know just how important that is."

Micah took hold of her hand and twined his fingers through hers. He caressed the side of her finger with his thumb. "Earlier you said you trusted me, Tala. If that's true, then trust this. Upon my word of honor, the moment you call me I'll come to you just as quickly as I possibly can. No one or nothing will stop me, all right? All I ask is that you give me a fair amount of time to get there. After all, I can't stop while I'm in the middle of saving someone's life."

Tala gave him a wistful smile. "I can live with that."

After they finished their dinner, Micah took additional time to enjoy her company and just hold her as they watched the dance of flames in his fireplace. They had precious little time left to them before this mission ended and they parted company. He didn't want a single minute wasted and it irritated him Edward required the sacrifice of even the smallest portion of it. Unable to put off the inevitable any longer, he gave her a kiss. He told her he'd be back, and then headed for the Frithgeard.

The instant he stepped inside the hall, Edward emerged from his office. "What is so important you would have me suspend my current duty, Edward?"

"The duty isn't a matter of suspension; it's more a matter of extension," he said.

That set him back on his heels. "Extension? I'm

not sure I understand what you mean."

"Curtis Westbrook will arrive at his manor in a little less than three days. As is quite obvious, he too is a descendent of Alfred. Therefore, he will step into the same danger Tala did upon her arrival. There are a small handful of Gehíwan insurgents left in Staffordshire. Given the current circumstances, we think it would be best if they vacated the premises permanently."

"What would you have me do with them?"

The roguish gleam in his eye matched his grin. "All kinds of things have come under discussion. However, we believe the wisest course is to have you lead them somewhere back in time, rather than hunt them down one by one. Do you think you can do that without too much difficulty?"

"Not a problem. I'll just get something of Tala's that carries her scent and get them to follow it. Do you know how many of them are still in the area? I'll want them all together before I lead them through the gate."

"Yes, indeed. Beldürq left five of his men behind. They've patrolled the area in and around the manor ever since the bulk of the insurgents left for Romania. Beldürq ordered them to stay put until they either find Tala or are notified otherwise."

Micah gave him a nod as he turned to leave. "I'll take care of that little problem the minute I leave here. You can count on it."

"We already are." Edward chuckled as he gave him a pat on the back. "Imagine their utter surprise, should somewhere along the way, they happen to run into themselves. Oh, and while you're out, let Levi, Nathaniel, and maybe even Dolph know you and Tala now have the key in your possession. I think that should set their minds at ease. At present the other guardians are busy with other matters, so by necessity, you must take care of that yourself."

"I'll do that. I have something I need to discuss with Levi and Nathaniel anyway."

Chapter Fifteen

After leaving the Frithgeard, Micah headed for the glade behind his cottage, and whistled for his horse. With the sound of heavy hooves pounding against the earth, the dark bay stallion raced to his side. He then came to an abrupt halt right beside him.

"Good evening, Alcides," he said as he stroked the length of the horse's neck. "Sorry to disturb you so late in the evening, old man, but we've got a job to do. Are you up to leading a pack of wolves on a one way journey inside their own private purgatory? If all goes well, it shouldn't take us too long. What say you? Do you think you can leave the ladies unattended for awhile?"

Alcides nickered in response while giving him an affectionate shove with his nose. Micah grinned. "I see you approve of the plan. So let's get to it then, shall we? I've a lady of my own waiting at home. She shouldn't be ignored any longer than necessary, either."

He slipped a bridle over the horse's head and followed up with a lightweight saddle. Within minutes they were on their way to the London of the past and toward the lodge where Tala had set aside some of her things. Upon arrival, he left Alcides waiting just outside the door as he entered the place and looked around. Some of Tala's luggage still sat by the bedroom doorway. He strode toward the sweater she had draped

221

over the top, picked it up, and gave it a whiff. Her scent clung to the fabric in more than adequate amounts. He slung the garment over his shoulder, turned around, and headed back outside.

From the lodge he rode back through the time gate and headed for Westbrook Manor in present time. He made a couple of slow circles around the manor as well as each of its outer buildings before he turned Alcides toward the forest. All the while he whirled the sweater high above his head. Tala's scent would lure the insurgents out of their shelters easily enough. In the deepest part of the woodland, he reined in his mount and waited for them to make their appearance. The wait took far longer than he expected and it tested his patience. Beldūrq ordered a continuous patrol of the area. That meant at least one of them should be out and about at all times and more likely two. So where were they?

Just as he considered a return to the manor with a plan to be far more obvious, he finally spied the first of his targets. Minutes later, the second shifter slunk out of the thicket. All the while they sniffed both ground and air, as they sought the direction of their target. Not long thereafter, the larger of the two lifted his head toward the sky and howled.

Answering calls echoed throughout the woods. Micah waited until all five of the Gehíwan convicts had gathered together within sight of his position. In their predictable fashion, the rebels quarreled amongst themselves. They growled, nipped, and bit each other to establish dominancy and control over their companions. All the while he remained in the shadows so they would see no more than indistinct color and form when he revealed himself to their eyes. Once the shifters came to some sort of an accord, he tied the arms of Tala's sweater around his neck. He then exposed himself somewhat to their view. A split second later, he turned Alcides around and urged him into a full run.

The insurgents tore out after him in the belief that at long last, they had stumbled upon Tala. He led them back and forth through the forest. Micah kept just in sight, but never allowed them near enough to take a good look at horse and rider. As they finally tired, he led them into the middle of the sixteenth century. He found a tree with a deep hollow and stuffed Tala's sweater into the hole. Once the wolves stealthily approached their intended victim, he again shielded himself from their eyes. At that point, he turned for home, and without a backward glance, left the shifters to their fate. Dawn had just lit up the sky when he freed Alcides of his tack. He sent him back to his pasture where he could freely graze alongside his mares.

Micah turned his gaze toward his cottage. Though he had the desire, he didn't check on Tala. She was safe enough in his home and right now he deemed it more important to finish the tasks Edward had assigned him. He set off for the Ukraine first and found Dolph at the back of his cave. The man looked a bit bored as well as restless. As he entered, the Gehíwan warden rose to his feet with an anxious expression on his face.

"Dare I hope this visit means you have found the key, Micah or has something terrible happened?" he asked.

"All's well. We have the key in our possession. With the help of a metal detector, we found it fairly quickly all things considered. Rest assured we'll keep it safe until we meet you at midnight on the night of the black moon."

Dolph closed his eyes as he slowly released a breath. "You don't know how much this eases my mind. Please accept and pass along my deepest gratitude to Miss Westbrook. Let her know how very much I appreciate everything she has done for me and for what she will do. She is most kind."

"I'll tell her."

He bowed his head. "Thank you."

"So tell me, have you spoken with Levi recently?"

"If you're referring to his news surrounding the Romanian government and their plans, then yes. I told him and I'll also tell you—I'll watch for the first sign of their convoy. During the ruckus they'll surely cause, I'll get myself into position, even if that event happens a few days in advance. If necessary, I can make a nest for my key the malefactors will never notice, especially if I sit on it. With everything going on, I'm sure they won't notice me anyway. At least I hope they won't."

"I take it you've already retrieved it then?" he said as he glanced about the chamber.

Dolph pointed toward a rather large rock at the furthermost portion of the cave, all but hidden in shadows. "I have it right there where I can keep an eye on it at all times."

"Good enough. We'll see you very soon."

Dolph extended his hand. "I'll wait for your arrival in that tree, just as I promised."

"We'll look forward to seeing you there then. In the meantime, stay safe and stay out of sight," he said as they shook hands.

"Don't worry. I haven't any intention of messing

things up now. Especially not when I can all but taste the victory."

From Dolph's temporary shelter, Micah traveled to the penal colony in search of Nathaniel and Levi. He found them both inside the warden's office, and right now, they listened in on a terse conversation between Beldürq and Cojor.

A broad smile appeared on Levi's face as he entered the room. "Ah, from your expression alone I'd say you and Tala have found the key."

Micah nodded. "That we have."

Nathaniel turned around and faced him. "You did? When?"

"Yesterday afternoon."

"Where did you finally find the blasted thing?" asked Levi.

"On the second floor, behind a sealed up oratory," he said.

Levi grinned. "I bet Tala is pleased that part of the mission is over. She looked a bit worried when last we met."

"You're right on both accounts." Micah then gazed pointedly at Cojor who looked mad enough to kill his companion on the spot. "Is there anything going on here I should know about?"

Nathaniel shrugged. "No, not really. Just the same old thing—different day. Cojor and Beldürq are at odds again. They've been going at each other all day long. The truth of the matter is Beldürq wants top command over the rebel forces. He has gone behind Cojor's back and one by one, has rallied the forces loyal to him. Cojor suspects, but hasn't confronted him yet or any of the insurgents in that group. Nonetheless, so he can avoid any "unpleasantness" shall we say, he has kept Beldūrq under his thumb for the past couple of days."

"That he has," said Levi. "Beldūrq isn't the least bit happy about that either. His resentment is growing stronger by the minute. Maybe we'll get lucky and they'll kill each other. Then we can be done with this mess."

"Either that or an insurrection. An uprising would definitely give us the advantage right now," Micah mused aloud as he studied the play between the shifters. "If there's internal mistrust and fighting going on, we could slip right past them without notice."

"There are many things that *could* give us the advantage, Micah. The question is, will any of them pan out at the time we need them too," Nathaniel said.

"I guess we'll find out soon enough. I've already spoken with Dolph. He knows we have the key, so we'll keep everything moving according to plan." Micah put a hand on Levi's shoulder. "So, unless either of you have something important that needs discussion or that'll change our current strategy, I'll see you both in a few days."

"We'll hunt you down if we need to. Other than that—" Levi shrugged away the remainder of his remark.

Micah took his leave and then returned to the Frithgeard in search of Edward. He found him inside the garden, deep in his thoughts.

As their eyes met, he gave his ealdorman a respectful nod. "It's done."

Edward flashed a grin. "Good. Where did you abandon the pack of dogs, anyway?"

"In the forest since they've grown so accustomed

to it, but in the year 1558," he said.

"Perfect. Their exit from present time also provides the ideal place for Tala, once your mission ends. At that point she won't be in any danger whatsoever."

"Ideal place?"

"Yes, I'm talking about Westbrook Manor, of course. What better place for Tala to awaken than right where her trouble began? I'm sure you can fill the gap in time with something else after you've taken away her memory of what really transpired during your time together."

The blatant reminder kicked him in his gut. He swallowed past the knot in his throat. "Do you think her father will still be there?"

He shrugged. "I don't think so, but we'll follow him until he leaves the area. Once he does, we'll let you know."

"Have they begun the renovations on the house?"

"Yes they have. One of the reasons for her father's visit is to set up a bank account specific for the renovation. He's given Hiram the power of the pen as well as the authority to work with the general contractor on his behalf."

"I see."

"I'm sure Curtis left Tala a series of voice messages indicting all of that. You should listen to them before you replace the memory. He may say something in there she should know for future conversations they may have."

"Yes, I know. I won't forget."

Just as he turned to leave, Edward took hold of his arm, and then looked him in the eye. He couldn't miss his concern. "Are you sure you can handle this,

Micah?"

"I'll handle it. All I ask is that you have another assignment waiting for me when I finish this one. Preferably one that will keep me busy and will take quite some time to accomplish."

Edward took hold of his shoulder and gave it a pat. "I can't promise you anything as you know, but I'll see what I can do."

****

Tala looked out over the ocean as she strolled along the beach. She lifted her chin and took in a deep breath of the salty air. The pristine beauty of the sandy shore and ocean waves took away her breath. She turned her gaze toward the sky, and for a time she watched the gulls play beneath the bluest sky she'd ever seen. All of it together filled her with an inner peace that despite Micah's absence, she hadn't experienced in quite awhile.

Micah.

The very thought of him filled her entire body with luscious warmth. For the umpteenth time she wondered what his assignment entailed and when he'd be back. She had thought perhaps Edward might visit her while he took on his task, yet she hadn't seen him or anyone else for that matter. Should that worry her or did it mean that she—

A strong pair of arms encircled her waist and halted the thought. Micah nuzzled the side of her neck, which sent a delightful shiver down her spine. With a smile on her face, she turned around and faced him.

"What has you so deep in thought this early in the morning?" he asked.

She wrapped her arms around his neck and

snuggled a bit deeper into his embrace. "Among other things, just wondering when my handsome guardian would return from his duties."

"Wonder no longer, fair maiden," he whispered as he lowered his mouth onto hers. Never before had she experienced a kiss that expressed so much pure, passionate emotion. Never. In that single moment, he made her feel greatly treasured and deeply loved. He made her feel that no one else ever before her or anywhere in his future, could come close to the place she held in his heart. She kissed him back. All the while she hoped that through the kiss, she said those very same things to him in return. The way he looked at her right now indicated that maybe she had accomplished her goal. He kissed her twice more. Then with what seemed a struggle, he took in a deep breath and put a little space between them.

"So, what did you do to while away the time?" he asked as he brushed the wind-blown hair away from her face.

Her hands slid down the length of his arms. "Not a whole lot, really. After I had a bite to eat, I took a shower in that lovely bathroom of yours. Once I tore myself away from the shower, I lit a fire in your bedroom. I then climbed into your bed with a good book and read until I fell asleep. I woke up this morning feeling wonderfully refreshed. At that point, I thought I'd come out here and watch the sun rise. I found it so beautiful and peaceful that I just couldn't talk myself into returning to your cottage just yet."

He released her from his arms, took hold of her hand and twined his fingers through hers. "So you slept well then."

"Best I've had since I met you, actually. I have so enjoyed every minute of my stay here. As silly as it might sound, I've been thinking that maybe this is what heaven must feel like."

The comment put a smile on his face. "Think so, huh?"

She turned her gaze toward the ocean and nodded. "Yep, but I assume your return means my little bit of respite is about to end?"

He gave her hand a gentle press as they resumed her stroll. "Actually, you could have a few more days of enjoyment here. With Edward's permission, we'll stay here until the night of the black moon unless circumstances change things."

"What could possibly change?" she asked.

"Should the presence of the Romanians give us a better shot at getting Dolph through the portal undetected, then we'll seize the moment when it comes. Levi and Nathaniel will keep us updated."

Although she nodded in response, her mind had already wandered away from Romanians, shifters, and black moons. She bit down on her lip as she gazed at him in silent contemplation. The trace of amusement that filled those incredible, dark brown eyes of his puzzled her a bit. "What?"

"I've seen that look many times before, Tala. You have a question you'd like an answer to but you're not at all sure that I will, am I right?"

"No, I—well, it's just that—" She paused for a moment as she struggled for words that wouldn't sound quite as chaotic as the jumbled thoughts in her mind.

"For a while now, and more often than I care to count, I've thought about the day I met you. I've wondered if I hadn't followed the shifters into the woods that evening and hadn't collided with that tree, would you have ever shown yourself to me at any time during the course of your assignment."

His grin faded away as for a moment, he turned his gaze toward the rolling waves that splashed onto the shore. At length he took in a deep breath and gave it a slow release. "No, probably not. But, after your little mishap with the tree, it was the only option open to me at the time. You couldn't get out of the forest under your own power, and I couldn't leave you there with shifters about. If they thought for one minute they could've gotten away with it, they would've killed you on the spot. If I took you back to the manor and you awoke while I stood guard over you, you would've assumed I had broken into your home for some reprehensible purpose."

A slight smile accompanied her nod. "Most likely."

"I wouldn't have wanted that."

"Me either."

"I also knew that if I returned you to your house and you woke up thinking you were alone, you'd wonder how you got there. You'd then head back outside in an attempt to figure it out. That step would've put you in the path of the shifters once more. Therefore, I would've had to step in again. That scenario could've had more than a few chain reactions that I really didn't want to deal with in your presence either. So, that only left option number three. As you know, that's the one I chose. However, it didn't quite work out the way I thought it would."

"How did you expect it to play out, if you don't mind my asking?"

"First of all, with the danger you had just escaped, I didn't expect you to be quite so stubborn about remaining at the manor. I thought you'd get in your car and that would've put an end to our personal—"

"I'm not stubborn," she cut in as indignation beset her. "Not in the least."

He nodded as he fought so hard to suppress a grin. "Yes you are. After what you had just experienced, any other reasonable person would've found accommodations elsewhere and you know it."

"I beg to differ with you, Mr. Berrington, I'll have you know—"

"Of course after being your constant though unseen companion for the first month after your arrival, I should've known how things would turn out," he blithely interrupted. "Even as a guest of those friends of yours, you always did things your own way—never mind that someone else might've wanted some sort of compromise."

"That's not true, Micah, I—"

"Oh, but it is. I could point out several instances in validation of the claim if you'd like."

"And they'd be exaggerated beyond any kind of recognition." She held up a hand as he opened his mouth. "You needn't deny it. My father does the same thing. He takes an innocent story and spins it to suit his purposes. I can assure you, it keeps getting better, every time he tells it."

He raised a brow. "Is that right?"

"Yes it is."

"What makes you think an honorable man, such as myself, would ever deign to do such a dastardly thing?"

She stuck her nose in the air and sniffed. "Because

all men do it."

He chuckled. "Now who's exaggerating?"

Tala dismissed the subject with a slight wave of her hand as her mind wandered back to her original question and his answer to it. "Well, I'm glad then that I followed the shifters into the forest that evening. I wouldn't have wanted to miss out on this time in my life for anything, Micah. Anything," she said as she halted their journey, turned and faced him full on.

The torment reflected in his eyes ended the confession that would've ended with the "I love you" she so desperately wanted to say. In its place, she caressed the side of his face and swallowed past the lump that had formed in her throat. Along the way, she forced a smile. "We've had quite an adventure, you and I. I'll never forget it. I'll never forget it because I'm not sure anything could ever surpass it."

He held his peace for a time and then lifted a shoulder. "Oh, I don't know about that. Given the right set of circumstances, you might let it become nothing more than a distant memory." Before she could sputter a word of protest, he turned his head to the side. "Perhaps someone like your Ethan could make you forget I ever existed."

Her mouth dropped a notch as she stared. How did he—

He put his fingers underneath her chin and tilted it upward. "If not for your visit to England, you would already have spent time with him, isn't that right? As I recall, those were your plans before you plunged into this mess without as much as a second thought."

"Who told you about Ethan?"

"You did." He held up a hand. "Although I must

admit you weren't talking to me, since you didn't know of my existence at the time. You were talking to Susan."

Oh. As she worked at recalling that particular conversation, Micah cocked his head toward the cottage. "Have you had breakfast?"

She turned her gaze toward his home. "No, not yet, I—"

"Are you hungry?"

"I suppose I am, a little."

"Then let's go get you something to eat, shall we?"

As they headed homeward, Tala took in a breath and gave it a slow release. He sought a change in subject, and she knew it. Nonetheless, she couldn't let him believe that Ethan, or any other man for that matter, had a power that could make her forget him. "Whatever your conclusions are about me and Ethan, I think I can safely say they aren't anywhere near the truth of our relationship."

Micah dropped his gaze toward the ground for a moment and then once again gave her his full attention. He opened his mouth, and then closed it again without saying what he might've said.

"I met Ethan during my sophomore year in high school, Micah. High school. We steadily dated until graduation and then continued an on-and-off relationship during the first few years of college. After that, he went his way and I went mine. The split didn't break either one of our hearts, I assure you. Last year he came home for Christmas. While in Maine, he ran into my father. He asked about me during the course of their conversation. My dad happily gave him all of the information he sought. Ethan told my dad that since he moved back home where he belonged, he thought it might be nice if he got in touch with me and maybe invite me to lunch. Dad slipped him my phone number."

She paused in her story, giving Micah ample time to ask questions, but again, he held his peace. "Ethan called me just before my arrival in England. As I told Susan, he said he'd thought about me a lot over the years. He wanted us to get together so we could catch up on each other's lives and maybe see if anything we once felt for each other survived."

Micah nodded as they stopped short of his gate. "Yes, I remember the conversation well, Tala."

"I'm sure you do. However, what you don't know is that when my dad called me to tell me that he'd given Ethan my phone number, he also asked me not to turn him down. My dad always liked Ethan. He thought we'd be a good match and therefore asked me to give the man a chance." She lifted her brows. "I promised my dad that I would at least see him for lunch. I didn't promise anything beyond that because there won't be anything beyond that. I didn't say any of these things to Susan, because she already knows. The relationship I had with Ethan ended simply because we grew up and in way different directions. I don't have the slightest desire to change that now."

From all appearances Micah mulled the story over in his mind as they ascended the steps. She didn't have a clue where his thoughts had taken him. Still, the look in his eyes that went from anguish to some kind of resolution filled her with trepidation.

Then, as he opened his door, he turned toward her and gazed into her eyes. A small grin turned the corner of his mouth upward as he gently stroked the side of her face. "Well, if nothing more, it seems you've a promise to keep. Perhaps when you do, you'll discover that Ethan means more to you than you think he does."

At once heated indignation colored her cheeks. She could feel it. "You're my guardian, Micah, not my psychologist," she hissed. "Don't presume you know what I'm thinking or what I feel, because you'd obviously be wrong. Dead. Wrong."

Chapter Sixteen

Tala fluffed Micah's pillow, turned onto her side, and scrunched a little deeper into the covers. She took in a deep breath and then let it go as her dreams faded away and awareness set in. The aroma of freshly baked apple cinnamon muffins and her guardian's delicious version of caramel macchiato had wafted into the bedroom. Despite her fatigue, the combination of the two had teased her awake. So did the sound of voices deep in conversation. She strained to listen. No matter how hard she tried, she couldn't make out the identity of the visitor or hear what he and Micah said to each other. Did the visit have something to do with getting Dolph through the portal? With a sudden need to know, all desire for extra sleep disappeared. She got out of bed, grabbed a pair of blue jeans, a dark blue long-sleeved t-shirt, and dressed just as fast as she could.

The voices led her to the kitchen where Micah, Levi, and Josiah sat around the table. Levi caught sight of her a split second before the others did. He flashed a flirty smile as he rose from his chair, placed a hand over his heart and bowed. Micah and Josiah also stood as she fully entered the room. The old-fashioned gallantry of these men not only made her the center of attention, it left her feeling a little uncomfortable.

"Good morning, Tala. I hope we didn't disturb your sleep," Levi said as Micah helped her into the chair next to his.

"No, the smell of breakfast is responsible for that," she said. "Good thing too, because it looks like I've missed out on the fun you're all having in here."

"Nah, no such thing happened in your absence." Levi shook his head as he sat back down. "I mean, I don't see how we can possibly have any fun at all without you here. But now that you've arrived looking so beautiful—" He gave her a lecherous grin and winked.

As she scooted her chair forward, Tala peeked over at Micah. He looked somewhat irritated over Levi's flirtatious manner that, according to her guardian, was just part of Levi's personality, and had ever been even throughout his mortality.

"All right, Levi," she said. "The need for fun and games aside, what prompted the visit? Has something happened?"

Micah poured her a cup of macchiato and then as he sat down he slid the basket of muffins toward her. "They've come to discuss a small adjustment in our plans. That's all."

Tala's heart dropped somewhere into the pit of her stomach. She took in a shallow breath and held onto it while she met his gaze. "Like what?"

"Dolph will go through the portal tonight," he said.

The news didn't sit well at all. "Why? We still have two days before the black moon. Isn't that when the senses of the Gehíwans are at the lowest point?"

Levi nodded. "Yes, and according to the conversation they had earlier this morning, that's exactly when Beldūrq and Cojor expect Dolph will make his appearance *if* he's around and *if* he has a second key. Therefore, the portal will be well guarded at that time just in case that scenario proves correct. Since the Romanians have now invaded their territory, Dolph will use the ruckus they've caused as a diversionary tactic and sneak through the portal. He believes somewhere around the midnight hour in Romania will be his best shot. By his way of thinking that's his best chance of getting through undetected under the current circumstances."

"Well, if the Gehíwans think he's in the area, won't they watch the portal regardless of day and time?" she asked.

"Most certainly," Micah answered. "But not with the same diligence they'll use on the night of the black moon. So moving a few days early makes a great deal of sense."

"I see." Tala swallowed her disappointment. "So when do we leave?"

"Given the time difference between here and there, about six hours from now. If we do that, we should arrive fifteen, maybe twenty minutes before we're expected. That should give us plenty of time to get into place and assist Dolph with the key we have and keep you safe at the same time," Micah replied.

"How will we do that, exactly?" she asked. "The portal part, I mean."

Levi leaned forward. As he clasped his hands together, he looked her in the eye. "The portal is all but hidden in the dense vegetation that has grown around it over the centuries. We count that a good thing. Right now, Dolph awaits your arrival at the top of one of the trees behind the structure. Once you arrive, he'll swoop down beside you. The second he transforms back into his human persona, you'll both insert your keys just as close together as you can. Dolph will enter his code and the door will open. At that point, he'll collect both keys. He'll then slip through the entrance. The entire process shouldn't take more than thirty seconds, if that."

"What if the insurgents in charge of guarding the portal follow him in?" she asked.

Micah shook his head. "If they're stupid enough to try that, they'll find themselves taken into immediate custody by the Gehíwan National forces. You must keep in mind the good guys protect the other side and in numbers the rebels wouldn't fancy dealing with."

"Keep in mind also," said Levi, "if all goes well, the insurgents won't know that either one of you are there. Because of the rough terrain behind the portal, and the thick vegetation that makes maneuvering most difficult, the convicts will focus their attention in the areas in front of and off to the sides of the thing. As I said, Dolph will enter from behind where it's least expected. Should the rebels somehow catch sight of the portal lights through the surrounding foliage, he'll be long gone before they can seize him or take him down."

"If all goes well," she murmured.

Levi grinned. "Don't worry so much, Tala. Things will work out just fine; you'll see."

"This part of the mission is a piece of cake," Josiah chimed in.

"Don't worry so much, Tala," Micah said. "Levi, Josiah, and Nathaniel all have experience in battle situations."

"They do?"

"Yes, Levi during the Civil War, Nathaniel during the American revolution and you already know about

Josiah. Trust me, he was more than a field surgeon when the need arose."

She shifted her gaze back and forth between Levi and Josiah. "I suppose that makes me feel a bit better."

Levi smacked Josiah on the back as they both rose to their feet. "All right, let's get to it, shall we? We have a few details we must take care of on our end before the midnight bell sounds in Romania."

Tala stayed in the kitchen. She nibbled at her muffin without really tasting it while Micah accompanied the men to his door. All the while she worked at coming to grips with this sudden change in plans. She didn't know how badly she had wanted those last two days with Micah until they were taken away from her. Now, in just six short hours, she would say goodbye to the enchanting world of the Bewitan Fierd. She didn't know if she could do that.

"What is it that has you so lost in your thoughts?" asked Micah, all but startling her out of her wits. He turned his chair toward her. Then as he sat down, he gazed into her eyes.

She set the remainder of her muffin back on her plate and clasped her hands together. "I guess just the change in plans. I didn't expect it."

"I suppose there's wisdom in that though. The insurgents are far from stupid. I think it would be very negligent of them if they didn't consider the possibility of Dolph showing up during the black moon."

She considered that for a moment. "Micah, I know Levi doesn't think it can happen, but what if they kill Dolph before he can get through?"

He took hold of her hands and gave them a gentle press. "We won't let that occur, so you needn't worry

241

about that."

"But you said you couldn't protect him—"

"That's true, but I'll be protecting you at that portal. That being the case, the insurgents won't get past me, in order to get to him."

The comment made her smile. "Then I guess I'll cross that concern off my list."

He chuckled. "You have a list of concerns?"

"Yes, but it's not really all that long."

"What else is on it?"

"Nothing important."

"Oh, come on. You can tell me, can't you?"

A flirty grin emerged as he asked the question. The look in his eyes filled every particle of her body with sumptuous, molten warmth and it made her want to give him everything he asked for whether or not she desired it. Nonetheless, she just didn't want the heart of the matter discovered, at least not if she could help it.

"We haven't discussed how I'll get down the mountain once Dolph is gone," she said.

He lifted a brow. "How you're getting down the mountain?"

"Well, you told me you can't physically transport me from one place to another within my own dimension. I'm pretty sure Edward will tell you that you can't bring me back here, if he hasn't already. At least you've hinted at that fact more than once. So, how will we get back down the mountain and eventually to the airport while we're right in the middle of shifter territory?" She held up a hand. "And before you tell me they won't come after me, let me remind you they might, if for nothing more than a thirst for revenge for helping Dolph get home."

"We've already worked that out. Once your task is finished, we'll slip through a time portal where we'll have a couple of horses awaiting our arrival. At a specific place about four, maybe five hours into our journey, we'll return to the present. There, off to the side of a dirt road, we'll find a four-wheel drive pickup truck. The vehicle can get us the rest of the way down the mountain and to the airport without any difficulty."

"Once we're at the airport, then what?" she asked.

"You'll board a plane to whatever destination you might choose."

"You'll come with me, won't you? To see me safely all the way home, I mean?"

"I wouldn't think of leaving you any earlier than that. You already know this."

"What about the dinner you promised me?"

"I haven't forgotten our date. I certainly wouldn't leave you before that happens either. Does that set your mind at ease?"

"Yes, I suppose it does."

"Good." He gave her a nod. "Is there anything else on your list?"

She fell silent for several seconds as she struggled to put her thoughts and feelings into words. "Just one. I looked forward to having two more days with you, Micah. Now I must deal with the loss of those days. If that isn't bad enough, I find I must also say goodbye far sooner than I thought I would have to. I don't like it. Now, I know that sounds petty, but—"

"No, it doesn't, at least not to me," he whispered just as he leaned forward and joined his lips to hers.

The enthralling kiss he gave in response to the admission released a flood of emotion. Though she couldn't describe the raging storm taking place in heart, body, and soul, she didn't have any problem feeling the ferocity of it. Without conscious thought, her hand touched the side of his face, and then traveled upward where her fingers weaved through his hair. She held onto him and all of the emotions that engulfed her, for all she was worth. Would that she could stay right here, just like this, and feel this way forever.

She could feel Micah's reluctance as he ended the kiss that so obviously affected him too. A wistful smile emerged as he caressed the top of her hand with his thumb. "Then let's not waste a moment of the time we have left."

"I'm all for that," she said in a breathless sort of rush.

"Okay, so what would you like to do first?"

Somehow she suppressed a smile. Barely. "Are you really leaving that decision up to me?"

The delight that filled his eyes matched his grin. "I don't know. I'd like to say whatever you want. For the look in your eyes, I'm not at all sure that would be wise, though."

"So then what are my options?"

"Options." He cleared his throat. "Well, let's see. I think you should finish your breakfast first. After that we could take a walk along the beach. Maybe we could explore the mountains. There's also a waterfall not far from here that splashes into a clear blue lake. We could take along some food and a blanket and spend what's left of our day out there if you wish."

"How about we start with breakfast and just go from there," she said.

"Your every wish is my command, *princess*."

She laughed. "Careful, I might take advantage of that."

Somewhere between the washing of the breakfast dishes and their romantic walk along the sandy shore, determination to enjoy her final hours in the realm of the Bewitan Fierd conquered her disappointment over having to leave earlier than she expected—and she did enjoy every single minute. The cherished memories she and Micah created here would remain forever in her heart. Still, if all went according to the way she believed it would, she would return just months from now. Together they would make many, many more such memories. Right?

"Are you ready to go then?" Micah asked as he approached her with cloak in hand.

Her gaze drifted one last time around the room. She took in a deep breath and nodded. "As ready as I'll ever be I suppose. Do you have the key?"

"I have it tucked safely inside my coat." He settled his cloak around her shoulders, drew the hood up over her head, and then tied the laces tight together. "Levi said we might encounter some wind. So make sure you keep wrapped up tight once we get there, all right? We don't need the shifters catching a whiff of your scent."

"I promise I'll take every precaution. Besides, from what Josiah says, this little job is a thirty-second piece of cake."

Micah tilted her chin upward until their gazes met. "Don't let the supposed ease of the task make you careless, Tala. Any number of things could go wrong and at the worst possible moment. You must remain on your guard at all times. Do you understand that?"

Tala breathed out a sigh and then gave him a

playful salute. "Aye, aye, captain."

He drew her into his arms and held her close to his heart. She clung to him in return. "Hang on tight and don't let go, not even for a second."

She squeezed her eyes shut while she stifled the tears that threatened. "I won't let go, Micah, not even for a second." *Not ever*, she silently added.

"All right then, let's get this done, shall we?"

****

Tala leaned her head against his chest. In the very moment of their arrival, Micah could see the wave of dizziness and the flush in her cheeks had escalated even more since her last dimensional crossing. So did the heat that radiated from her body. Just as she suspected, Edward told him not to bring her back to the Bewitan realm again. Right now, he could see the wisdom in that decision. He held her close while she steadied her feet and the beat of her heart returned to its normal pace. Only then did he speak.

He loosened his hold and put a bit of space between them. "Okay, you can open your eyes now, we're here."

Once she opened her eyes, her gaze wandered away from his and she took in what she could see of the area. She drew her brows together as a look of confusion beset her. "Which way is the portal?"

He pointed off to the left while he maintained possession of her waist. "Through those trees right there."

"Really? How can you tell? The foliage is so thick that not even starlight is making its way through," she whispered.

"I know, but that little fact will work well for us."

Just as the words left his mouth, Levi, Nathaniel, and Josiah stepped out of the inky shadows with weapons in hand. Micah gave them a nod as the guardians approached them.

Nathaniel aimed a thumb skyward as his eyes drilled into his. "Dolph said he's ready whenever you are. Keep in mind we have both shifters and Romanians in the vicinity. Just so you know, the shifters have made their presence known in more than one grisly way throughout the day. Right now, the sheer number of wolves they've seen has caused the Romanians quite a bit of concern. They're hunting them down even as we speak, futile as that might be."

Micah understood Nathaniel's underlying message. The shifters had already attacked the Romanians. Perhaps even killed one or two of them. They would have to be on their guard. "Give Tala a moment to adjust to the darkness. I don't want her to lose her footing, coming or going."

Levi cocked, and then handed him his rifle. All the while he gazed at Tala. "You're right about that. Take all the time you need, Tala. We've got your back."

Tala waved away their concern. "We can go. I can see well enough now."

Micah turned and faced her. "Are you sure you're ready? There will be no second chances."

She took in a deep breath and then released it as she nodded. "I'm sure. Just give me the key."

Micah retrieved the disk from inside his coat and placed it in her hand. "There are two indentations midway of the portal, one on each side. You can't miss them. Dolph will take the one on the left. You'll insert yours on the right."

"Sounds easy enough," she said. She then wrapped the disk within the folds of her cloak and then clung to it with a single hand.

Micah eased his arm from around her waist. As he took hold of her free hand, he turned his gaze toward Levi. "The guards?"

"Right now we have six of them in close proximity. Two on each side and two that guard the front of the gate. All of them are within forty to fifty yards of the portal itself, but their attention is faced outward. If you take care as you slip around from the back of it, they'll never know you're there."

"I'll give you all a few seconds to get into position. Then we'll follow," Micah said.

After the men melted into the shadows, Micah leaned his rifle against the tree. He looked Tala over and then pulled the hood of the cloak a little more forward so he could cover as much of her face as possible.

"Stay alert," he said as he again took hold of his weapon.

"Don't worry, I will."

"All right then, let's go. Remember I'm right here beside you."

"I know."

"Mind where you place your feet, and don't do anything foolish."

"I don't plan to."

"No matter what happens in the next few minutes, don't break your physical contact with me—not for any reason even if it means dropping the key."

She huffed out a breath. "I won't let go of you, Micah. Now come on. Let's get this over with and get out of here. This place gives me the creeps."

"The creeps?"

"Yes, I feel like there are a multitude of eyes out there watching every move I make."

"Probably nothing more than the nocturnal creatures that live in this forest."

"Yes, that's what I'm afraid of and I'm sure not all of them are natives to this earth."

He firmed the grip he had on her hand and led her through the dense forest, one careful step at a time. The journey took several minutes. All the while he could feel her impatience. Nonetheless, he would not grow careless at this stage of the game. As they approached the back of the gate, now covered in a thick blanket of moss and vegetation, he could hear the flap of wings as Dolph took flight. He could also feel the presence of numerous shifters in the area just as Nathaniel reported. Tala drew in a deep breath and held on to it. They rounded the corner and faced the portal. In that same instant Dolph transformed into his human persona.

Dolph and Tala gazed at each other. The warden smiled his gratitude even as he gave her a nod. She withdrew her key from underneath her cloak. Almost in unison, they inserted their keys. At once the gate lights flickered in varying shades of blue, purple, and white. Dolph's fingers raced as he entered his code. In return, the portal emitted a harsh, grating reverberation that grew louder as each second passed.

The sound would surely alert the keen ears of the insurgents. He raised his rifle to the height of his chest as he searched the forest for any sign of the Gehíwan convicts.

Just then, Levi and Nathaniel hollered out a

warning. The door that should already have opened remained shut while a mass of voices echoed all around them. So did the howling of wolves. A multitude of gunshots rang out in close succession. The activation of the portal had drawn the attention of the rebels away from the Romanians that hunted them. They now shifted their focus solely onto Dolph. In a chain reaction, the overwhelming number of wolves that raced in from all directions and toward the gate caused sheer pandemonium among the Romanian forces. They fired their high-powered machine guns and AK-47's at the shifters without hesitation or a shred of caution.

Micah thrust Tala behind him just as the doorway finally opened. Dolph snatched the keys. At once he slipped through as two large wolves bounded toward them. In keeping with her promise to maintain contact, Tala slipped her arms around his waist and clasped her hands together. She buried her face into his back in the same moment he dispatched the shifter closest to their position. Nathaniel, Josiah, and Levi took out targets of their own. So did the Romanians who pursued the wolves with an apparent need to avenge their fallen comrades.

"Go on ahead Micah, get Tala out of here! We can handle this until you're gone," Levi shouted out.

The words no more than left Levi's mouth when a stray bullet slammed into the right side of Micah's lower torso. He could feel the projectile from the AK-47 passing through his body. Tala sucked in a breath even as her hand slid away from his waist. Dread consumed him. He turned around just in time to catch her before she fell all the way to the ground. As he gathered her into his arms he could feel the warmth of her blood oozing out of her body. Within seconds the shifters would smell it and then attack.

"Josiah!" he yelled out. "Follow me."

He raced toward the time gate with Josiah at his heels. Nathaniel and Levi dispatched the wolves that nipped at their heels. The moment he stepped through the time portal, he dropped to a knee. He flung the folds of the cloak she wore off to the side. Blood soaked the entire front of Tala's t-shirt. She looked up at him then and though weak, she smiled.

"Don't...don't look so...worried, Micah, I'm...I'm all right."

He clenched his teeth together as he shook his head. "No. No, you're not all right. Now just—"

Tala lost consciousness before he could tell her to lie still and not talk. Before he could tell her that she should conserve her strength. Before he could tell her that he loved her.

"Hang on tight, my love," he whispered. "Stay with me now and don't let go—please, don't leave me."

A firm hand squeezed his shoulder. He turned his head and looked up as Josiah knelt beside him. The doctor inside the guardian emerged. He lifted Tala's shirt and assessed the damage caused by the bullet that had passed through him and slammed into her ribs.

"She's lost a lot of blood, Micah. We need to get her to the nearest hospital just as quickly as we can," he said.

"Can't you do something for her here, Josiah? We have no way of getting her there in time to save her life. Even if somehow we could, every hospital in Romania could be crawling with insurgents. They could be acting as staff, orderlies, nurses, even the doctors. We can't mask her scent. They would know who she is the moment she arrives. You and I both know they'd want her dead and they'd seek out the first opportunity to accomplish that."

Josiah rubbed a hand against his mouth. "We can't leave her out in the open either. I need to get that bullet out of her. If I don't have the proper tools, medications, and environment, she could develop some serious complications and that wouldn't be good."

"How about this instead," said Levi as he and Nathaniel thundered through the gate and strode toward them. "Let's get her to Velica's house. There's plenty of room there. In addition, it's the closest place we have available with running water and the modern amenities we'll want. Josiah can gather everything he'll need from the nearest hospital and we'll bring it all to her."

"In case you haven't noticed, we're several hours away from Velica's villa, Levi," Micah ground out. "We have no way of getting her there without physically crossing the miles.

"By horseback, yes, but not by way of helicopter. I'm sure the Romanians wouldn't mind if I borrowed theirs for a few minutes. In fact, with everything going on out there right now, they won't even know it's gone." Levi turned his gaze toward the north. "I can have it in the air by the time you get Tala to that little glade just over the hill."

Josiah considered the notion for a moment and then nodded. "That's doable, Micah. I have operated in conditions far worse than that. You and Levi get Tala to the house. Nathaniel and I will go get the supplies I need. We'll meet you as soon as we can. In the meantime, don't press anything at all into the wound because you can't stop the flow of blood internally. You'll just make everything worse if you try. All I want you to do is lay her down flat with her legs elevated. You can put a towel or something on top of her body that will absorb the blood. Keep her covered. If she wakes up, see if you can get some water into her. She'll need all she can get."

Micah scooped Tala up into his arms. With the greatest of care, he cuddled her into his chest. He gazed down upon her beautiful face that looked far too pale. "Please hurry. I'm sure I needn't remind any of you that every second counts."

Chapter Seventeen

Within the hour Micah had settled Tala into the same bedroom she had used before. Josiah busied himself with setting up all of the equipment and instruments he had borrowed from the hospital. All the while he, Nathaniel, and Levi, watched, hovered, and waited. Each minute that passed was an eternity of torment. He just wanted Josiah to get that bullet out of her. Now. Before the loss of blood drained the life right out of her.

"This isn't your fault, Micah. So get that look out of your eyes right now," Nathaniel chided. "There's nothing you could've done to prevent this from happening the way it did. To blame yourself for something you had no control over is a foolish thing for you to do."

"She's still alive," Levi added. "That counts for something too."

Micah swallowed past the lump in his throat. "No, I shouldn't have let her go out there. If she hadn't gone, she wouldn't have gotten hurt."

"You couldn't have stopped her and you know it," Levi countered. "As I recall, you already tried that avenue once. You and I both know it didn't work. Tala is just as stubborn as any woman I've ever met. Believe me; I've known my fair share of them. Come hell or high water, she would've met Dolph at that portal with or without your help."

Josiah glanced up from his task. "If it makes you feel any better, you probably saved Tala's life when you first absorbed and then slowed down that projectile. From the look of things, the bullet could've done far more damage than it did. Now, if you can spare the time away from your self-recriminations, I need your help as I get her out of her clothes. In the meantime, Levi and Nathaniel can go boil some water."

Levi drew his brows together. "I thought you said the instruments you collected were already sterile."

"They are. I just thought I'd give you something else to do, hmm? If you don't want to boil water, then go out into the other room and pace, or chop some wood or something. Your choice."

"Oh. Got it. The lady needs her privacy. Come on Nathaniel, let's go boil some water. Tala may want some tea when she awakens. Right now, it doesn't sound half-bad to me either."

The moment the men left the room, Josiah picked up a pair of scissors from off the nightstand he now used as his instrument table. "I'll cut her clothes all the way down the front so we can remove them easier. Once I have that done, we'll roll her as gently as we can onto her side. We'll then slip them out from underneath her, all right?"

Micah rose from his chair and approached the bed. Josiah turned down the blankets and gasped at the sight that met his gaze. Tala's blood had soaked the towel clear through and dripped onto the sheet.

Alarm filled Josiah's eyes as he looked from the towel to Tala's face and back to the towel again. He grabbed a cotton ball and some alcohol. With a sense of urgency, he rubbed it over the top of her hand. He then inserted a needle underneath her skin.

"What are you doing, man?" Micah ground out. "Shouldn't you get that bullet out of her and staunch the flow of blood before she bleeds to death?"

Josiah glared at him as he clenched his teeth. "You want her to survive this surgery, don't you?"

"That isn't even worthy of an answer," he spat.

He huffed out a breath. "Look, I've got to get some fluids into her before I go digging around inside her ribcage. You've got to trust that I know what I'm doing. Now stand back and let me do my job."

Micah backed away as Josiah hooked her up to an IV bag. He also connected her to a machine that monitored her heart, oxygen levels, and blood pressure. The step-by-step explanations Josiah gave him kept his mind occupied despite the impatience that gnawed at him. Once they removed Tala's clothes, the man picked up his scalpel and got to work.

No more than ten minutes into the surgery, a series of beeps interrupted the surgery. Josiah paused, looked at the monitor and then cursed underneath his breath.

"What's wrong?" Micah asked.

"Her blood pressure is dropping and dropping fast. If I don't get her bleeding under control we'll lose her. I just don't know if I'll have the time I need," he muttered.

Micah's heart dived into a raging fire that burned deep within his gut. Never before, in all of his years as a guardian, had he experienced this sense of helplessness. He didn't know what to do or how to overcome this obstacle. Yet, one thing he did know, and he knew it with absolute certainty. He wouldn't just sit here and watch her die.

With the greatest of care, he took Tala's hand within his own. "This will not end this way, Tala. Not today. You keep that beautiful heart of yours beating, do you hear me? You can't just give up because it's the easy thing to do. Besides, as I recall we have a dinner date that you cannot cancel out on. I won't let you. There's also a matter of a little wager. You do remember that wager, don't you? I'm sure it's one you'll win if nothing more than to prove me wrong. Isn't that right?"

While he spoke, the beeps slowed down. A few minutes later, they diminished altogether. Once again, Josiah glanced at the monitor. A ragged sigh escaped his lips as he nodded. "Keep talking to her Micah. She's responding well to your voice. Right now, I need that response. We're not out of the woods yet. In fact, we're far from it."

The entire process from beginning to end took almost two hours. Micah could see the concern in Josiah's eyes as he worked over Tala. Yet all the while, the man never uttered a word. He wouldn't break his concentration by asking questions that could wait for a better time. After Josiah had removed the round, and repaired the internal damage, he gently stitched up and then bandaged the wound.

"Do you think she'll be all right now?" Micah asked.

Josiah lifted his brows as he took in a breath. "I hope so. But I would be less than honest if I said we didn't have any concerns. All we can do is wait and watch. However, since she's my only patient, I can respond to any emergency in the very moment it happens. If we're lucky, I'll have nothing to do but change her dressings and make sure she has the medication she needs."

For twenty-four full hours, Micah remained at Tala's side. All the while he held her hand. From time to time, he talked about some of the things they had shared. He reminded her of their rocky start that had grown into a grudging friendship. A friendship that had turned into something far more than that. In explicit detail, he recalled the morning she had first kissed him. He then told her how that kiss had affected him and led to the relationship they enjoyed now. Finally, he told her that he had never met anyone quite like her, and knew he never would again. Certain in her unconscious state she wouldn't remember, he told her again that he loved her. He would have her know nothing could take that away from him. Nothing.

Nathaniel and Levi popped in every once in a while so they could check on her progress. Josiah stepped into the room only to take her vital readings or administer her medication. That gave him more time than he wanted—or needed—to think. During that time, he toyed with the idea of taking Tala's memories away from her before she awoke, but then he thought better of it. After all, he still had a promise to keep. He had never once gone back on his word and he wouldn't start now.

In addition, he wouldn't have her wake up and feel vulnerable in a strange house with a couple of men she didn't recognize. Not even if the story he concocted wherein he found her wounded and unconscious in the forest with a damaged camera at her side, seemed a good one. No, the time for erasing memories would come soon enough. He would not hasten that day. Indeed, if he were honest, he would admit that if he could extend the time they had left, he would take it in a heartbeat.

Levi's entrance into the room ended Micah's troubled thoughts. The man gave him a casual salute and then shifted his gaze toward Tala. "How's our patient this afternoon?"

"Her eyes have opened a couple of times in the last hour or so, but after a few seconds they close again. Josiah says that's a good thing. He says it means she'll wake up before too long."

Levi nodded and for a moment he held his peace. He then took in a deep breath and faced him head on. "And then what, Micah?"

"I'm not sure what you mean by that?"

"Come on now, the question isn't all that difficult. What comes next?"

"That seems obvious. Even after she wakes up, she must heal before we can move her out of here and get her the rest of the way down the mountain."

"That's not what I meant. What are you going to do about Tala once this assignment ends?"

"I'll do what I've always done. Once I take her home, she'll go on with her life as she sees fit. I'll move on to my next assignment. Isn't that the way this has always worked?"

"For the most part, yes. But in this case, I'd say it's quite different."

"How so?"

A gleam entered his eyes. "Because you love her."

Micah opened his mouth to deny it, but found that he couldn't. "Is it that obvious?"

"Only to those closest to you, my friend," he said as he gave his shoulder a squeeze and then settled himself into the chair across from him.

"Well, at this point in our existence and under the circumstances in which we find ourselves that doesn't mean a thing, Levi."

"Oh yes it does, Micah; it means that should you choose, you don't have to give her up once your duty ends."

"No, I'll not condemn her to that kind of a life. Tala deserves a man that's there for her all of the time, not just an evening here and an evening there when he can find the time. The memories of which will be taken away every time she arises. She should have a husband that loves her and a house filled with children that adore her. She should experience all the joys of life that—"

"You never experienced during your own mortality?" Levi finished for him. "Well in case it has somehow escaped your notice, Tala has fallen in love with *you*. Despite what you might think, she will never want anyone else."

Micah raised a dubious brow. "That's an interesting observation coming from you, Levi."

Levi smirked. "Well, we're a bit different, aren't we? While I love all of the ladies out there equally well, you've fallen in love with just one. Still, you must trust that I'm right about this. Believe me; I've seen it time and again."

"At the end of the day, Tala won't even remember who I am. Have you forgotten that? She can't possibly remain in love with someone she doesn't know."

"Are you so sure that somewhere, deep inside her heart and soul she won't remember what she *feels* for you? Should that be the case, and I believe it will be, she'll compare that feeling to every other man who courts her. He'll come up short and then she'll move on. She'll always seek and never find." He shrugged. "Can't see where that's much of a life either. She might as well have some happiness, even if during her waking hours she doesn't remember the reason for it."

"You don't know that, Levi."

"No, I don't. At least not with any degree of certainty. All I'm saying is you should make sure I'm wrong before you drop her off without so much as a backward glance. Don't leave her heart shattered beyond all repair and for reasons she can't quite put her finger on. That, in my opinion, would not only be tragic, but wrong."

A soft sigh from Tala interrupted any response he might've made. He shifted his gaze toward her lovely face in the same moment she opened her eyes and then kept them open. She blinked a few times, turned her head toward him, and then met his gaze even as her hand drifted toward her wound. Her brows knit themselves together as she explored the area with gentle fingers.

"What happened? Where am I? No, wait—did Dolph get through the portal?"

Micah swept a few wayward locks away from her face. "Dolph made it safely through just as we planned. You didn't do as well though. You see, as he slipped through the gate, a stray Romanian bullet made its way from me and into you. Hence the reason you feel the way you do. As to where you are, we're back at Velica's villa in the same moment of time we were before. Under the circumstances we thought it the best place available where Josiah could get that bullet out of you and let you heal. At the same time, we also needn't worry that a bunch of cutthroat insurgents would show up at your door."

"Oh." Tala mulled that over for a minute. "I don't remember anything after we inserted the keys and the lights turned on. After that? Nothing."

"Perhaps that's a good thing," Micah said. "I'd rather you didn't have any recollection of the pain."

"Why? Did Josiah dig the bullet out of me without using some form of anesthesia or something?"

"No, the doctor didn't resort to such torturous practices," said Josiah as he entered the room. "We might've stepped back a bit in history to keep you safe, but we had all of the modern conveniences necessary when it came to your surgery and recovery, well, almost all of them. So tell me, how are you feeling, Miss Westbrook?"

"A little sore. Other than that, I'm all right."

"Mind if I take a peek and change the dressing?"

"You're the doctor."

Josiah gazed pointedly at Levi. "Would you excuse us for a minute please?"

"Yeah, I'll go make some more tea." Just before he stepped through the doorway, Levi put a hand on the doorjamb. After a pause, he turned and faced him. "You might want to think on what I said, Micah."

Not that Micah could forget. Throughout the days of Tala's recovery, Levi's words echoed inside his mind more times than he could count. Could he be right? Deep inside her subconscious, would Tala somehow remember him? The part of him that wanted and needed her in his life hoped it would be so. The other part damned him for his selfishness. Finally, Josiah's announcement that Tala's wound had healed and she could go home put an end to the conflict if not the torment.

The journey down the mountain didn't take nearly as long as he might've liked. Fate must've had a hand in the flight scheduled for departure within a couple of hours after their arrival in Bucharest as well. Now, he sat next to Tala in a small, out of the way restaurant near her home in Portland, Maine. In a few hours he would say goodbye. Once she fell into a deep enough sleep, he would take away her memories of the time they had together. The very thought cut far deeper than he had ever imagined it would.

"Micah?"

He looked up from his plate and met her gaze. "Hmm?"

A small breath of laughter accompanied the slight shake of her head. "Nothing important."

"Whatever it is, it's important to me."

"Really? Even if I just wanted to know if you were going to have dessert?"

"Is there something on the menu that should I neglect to taste, I'll live to regret it for the rest of my existence?" he countered.

The impish look in her eyes faded away as a touch of sorrow took its place. "No, not really. I suppose I just didn't want the evening to end just yet."

"If you look at the clock, you'll see the evening ended long ago. We are now solidly into the wee hours of the morning. If you're not careful, you'll fall asleep where you sit."

"You're probably right, but wanting your company

a little while longer is overriding my need for sleep."

Micah let go of a heavy breath as he took hold of her hand and twined his fingers through hers. "Tala, we both knew this day would come. I've tarried here far longer than I should have. I have another assignment already waiting for me and you can't stay in this limbo. You've done what you set out to do. Now you must go on with your life."

Tala gazed at her glass of lemonade for a moment and then nodded. "Do you have any idea when we can expect the return of Dolph and his army?"

"No, not with any degree of certainty. As I've already said, the time clock of the Gehíwan world moves far slower than your own. However, by now I'm sure the officials are aware of the state of affairs in this dimension. They'll take time and care in planning their strategy. They'll come when they feel certain they can win the battle."

"Do you think we'll know it when that time comes?"

"Are you speaking of you and me, or the world in general?"

"I suppose I should include the world, but right now I'm talking about you and me. You see, I have this irrational hope that if they return, I'll need your protection once more. That way I wouldn't have to see you just every now and again." A sudden look of confusion mingled with pain, filled her eyes. She leaned back against her chair. All the while her hand fought for release. He didn't allow its escape.

"What is it? What's wrong?"

"Nothing."

That *nothing* seemed far worse in tone and

meaning than her "whatever" or "fine" ever did. "No, it's something. If you don't want to be here all night, you'll tell me what it is."

She bobbed her head. "All right. Now that your guardianship of me has ended, it appears from the look in your eyes that you either have no recollection of or intention to keep your promise."

"What promise?"

She gritted her teeth. "See? That's exactly what I mean."

"No, I don't know what you mean unless you tell me, Tala."

She rolled her eyes heavenward and tsked. "Your promise to come when I call—after your ridiculous six-month wait, of course."

He suppressed a grin. "Oh. That."

"Yes, *that*," she hissed.

The grin finally won out. "Well, I recall that more as a bet than a promise. So you can understand my confusion. Just so you know? I have never once broken a promise or failed to fulfill my end of a bargain."

She lifted a brow. "So then, you don't think I'll win?"

He put his curled fingers underneath her chin and gazed into her beautiful eyes that drilled into his with such indignant fire. "I hope you do, Tala, I truly hope you do."

The transcendent kiss that followed his remark—one that somehow had the power to thrust him into the depths of despair while at the same time infusing his soul with more elation than he thought possible—lingered on his lips all the way to her door. Despair, because he'd never get another. The joy because he had experienced it with the woman who had claimed his heart and soul when he never believed he'd have such an experience. After one final kiss, he stepped back.

"I must say it's been a pleasure, Tala. More so than you'll ever know." He gave her a wink as he swallowed past the pain in his throat. "See you in six months then?"

Dread filled her eyes. "You're not coming in?"

He looked away. "I have another duty I have to attend to and it's one I must prepare myself for."

She dropped her gaze and nodded as she rubbed her lips together. He could see that she fought for some kind of composure and that intensified his own anguish. "Then I won't keep you from it any longer."

Just as he turned away she called his name. He stopped and looked back. She met his gaze and attempted a smile. "I just wanted you to know that I... that I'll miss you... and that... I'll definitely see you in six months."

"I'll look forward to it."

****

Micah disappeared from her view before his resolve crumbled altogether and he tossed his oaths and every shred of honor he possessed to the wind. However, he didn't wander far. Once Tala fell into a deep enough sleep, he returned to her house and slipped quietly into her bedroom. He sat down in the chair beside her bed, took hold of her hand, and drew it to his lips. Once he had himself under a sufficient amount of control, he gazed down on her beautiful face one last time.

"When you awake in the morning you'll feel a sense of joy and anticipation for having returned home to your family and friends. All of the memories of your time with me, your knowledge of the Bewitan Fierd, the Gehíwan world and anything connected to it in any way will have vanished from your mind. You'll recall with clarity your visit with Susan, the reason for it, and all that transpired while you were her guest. In regards to Westbrook Manor, you won't remember anything more than taking pictures and speaking with your father about the needed repairs and the contractors who submitted their bids.

"You'll recall the visit to the home of Hiram, your grandfather's cousin, at the request of the elderly gentleman who appeared at your doorstep. This man, Theodore Crosby, told you he once lived at the manor. He hoped you could help him find a family heirloom he had left behind after a family emergency called him away. Your father put you in touch with this cousin who had stored all of the items abandoned by past tenants. Theodore accompanied you and together you found the cane he sought.

"Once you completed the task you headed for the airport. You mulled over your options. Your father wanted you to give your relationship with Ethan another chance, but you didn't know if you were ready for that step. So, to give yourself a little additional time and think that decision through, you bought a ticket to Cambridge, Tasmania instead. You thought it would be a good time to get some photographs of the spotted-tail quoll you and Susan talked about while you were in England. However, you didn't count on all of the rain. You were wet, miserable, and knee deep in mud almost the entire time. For several weeks you toughed it out. After a while, you took all of the photographs you needed. You couldn't put it off any longer. The time had come for you to go home.

"On the way back to civilization, you met with an accident. The torrential rains had soaked the ground. While on the trail, the ground gave way. You tumbled down the steep incline. As fate would have it, you landed in the bramble, and severely injured yourself, the scar of which is still fresh. That unfortunate incident also damaged your camera. Consequently, you lost all of your photographs. One of your guides took great care of you. You only have a vague recollection of this event because for the most part you remained unconscious. Once you were sufficiently healed, you went home. You didn't tell your family about your return flight because you wanted a few days to relax and unwind before you greeted them. You landed at the airport yesterday afternoon, and hailed the taxi that took you to your door. After you settled in, you ordered dinner, had a lovely soak in a hot bathtub and then went off to your bed. Oh, and by the way? You decided you would give Ethan one more chance as your father asked. Perhaps he could win your heart once again."

For a time, Micah did nothing more than caress the top of her hand. Although he had now completed his assignment, he found it difficult to leave her. Yet, staying here didn't do either of them any good. Despite his reluctance, he rose from the chair. All the while he retained possession of her hand.

"I don't know, Tala," he whispered. "But if Levi is right, and there's some place deep down inside your heart or soul that remembers me and the time we had together, then remember this—the love I feel for you runs deep and strong. No matter what comes or what might lie ahead, I'll always love you. No power that exists in this great universe can change it or lessen it. Stay safe my love. For my sake, be happy. A beautiful life awaits you."

He leaned down, gently kissed her lips, and then disappeared.

Chapter Eighteen

Tala stared down at the blood-stained towel wrapped around her hand as she sat at her kitchen table. She didn't know if she should feel alarm, panic, or simply add this bizarre occurrence to the growing list of things that had mystified and plagued her since she returned home from Tasmania. Things for which she had no explanation. Things that had left her feeling unsettled and things she couldn't talk about with anyone. If she did, whomever she chose as her confidant would probably think she had gone quite insane. He or she probably wouldn't be far wrong.

Take for instance, this unfounded feeling of emptiness and sadness she had carried with her every minute of every day since she stepped off that plane. She couldn't find a reason for it. Not even the loss of all of the photographs she had taken of the spotted-tail quoll should make her feel this way. After all, she'd lost pictures a time or two before. She had taken those losses in stride, as did most every other wildlife photographer who had ever lived. Those in her profession expected the loss of photographs every now and again.

If nothing else, the visits with family and friends should've lifted her spirits, but they hadn't. The family gathering on Christmas day didn't drive away her inexplicable sorrow either. Shouldn't the joy of that day have had some positive effect? Why didn't it?

Why did she even entertain the notion of more than one meal with Ethan after her arrival? The whole lunch thing set her teeth on edge. She couldn't wait for that little chore to be over with. Even though her father expressed his disappointment when she told him she wouldn't see Ethan again, he said he understood. The dates she had accepted with other men simply intensified her distress. Why? They were all pleasant enough. But they just didn't—didn't have something she couldn't quite explain.

Perhaps she could blame her disinterest on the dreams she had every night. Although they were always different, they centered on a man she could never quite see in the misty shadows that cloaked him. Nonetheless, his mere presence filled her with a sense of joy that all but overwhelmed her. Yet, she could never hold on to that joy once she awoke. Quite the contrary. Those dreams did nothing but increase her sense of agitation, longing, and loss. Did that mean something?

Her passport baffled her as well. Not a single thing had been recorded in it since her arrival in England. No matter how hard she tried, she couldn't remember going through customs in or out of Tasmania or after she arrived home. The loss of those memories and explanations, as well as so many others during her recent journey, scared her half to death. There were holes in her days she just couldn't fill. Why couldn't she recall the face of her Tasmanian guide? The man took care of her after her injury for goodness sake. Did she even thank him for that? What about everyone else that surely accompanied them on that photo shoot? She and her guide couldn't have been the only ones on that trip. No matter how hard she tried, she couldn't recall a single name, face, specific event, or conversation.

Tala closed her eyes and drew in a deep breath meant to sweep away the clutter inside her mind. Once she let it go, she again looked at her hand wrapped snugly in the towel. She bit down on her lip. With slow deliberation, she peeled away the layers of cloth that had sopped up the blood. Again she stared. While she stared at this newest change, a change that defied all explanation, a strange mix of disbelief, horror, and curiosity sent a chill through her body. She turned her gaze toward the water glass that had broken while she washed it and the jagged shards that had sliced through her hand before she even knew it happened. The blood on the towel also testified the event had taken place. So then, why now, didn't her hand show any signs of that injury at all?

Except—except she had seen something like this once before, hadn't she? But not in herself. She struggled for more of the memory that beckoned from the darkest corners of her mind. Yet, the harder she struggled, the more the memory eluded her. For the umpteenth time, she called her sanity into question.

"Come on, Tala," she berated herself aloud. "You're not crazy…you're not! There's an explanation for all of this. Somewhere buried deep inside your brain, you know what it is. For the love of Pete, just find it."

Her eyes wandered toward the broken glass on top of the counter, to the towel soaked with her blood, and then down to her hand. She traveled that same path two more times before vague flashes of memory moved a little closer to the forefront of her mind. Tala battled for more and then with a sudden barrage, the haze gave way. She could now see a tattered arm—a very muscular arm at that. That arm looked as if some wild animal had gotten firm hold of it with its teeth or its claws. Did she see that in Tasmania?

No. Wait.

For whatever the reason, she accepted responsibility for his injury. She had wanted to tend it and…and the man said he didn't need her help…that if he did, he'd ask. She didn't care what he wanted, though. With determination or maybe even stubbornness, she slid the sleeve of his shirt up to his elbow so she could see the wound and take care of it. But the injury had disappeared—just like the one on her hand.

At that moment, a flood of disjointed memories pelted her mind with an intensity she had never experienced before. She didn't know how to stop them or even make sense of them. Is this what people experienced when they lost their mind? As she bolted to her feet, she flung her hands against her temples. She squeezed her eyes shut, and opened her mouth to scream.

"Micah!"

The unexpected name she gasped out without any forethought whatsoever surprised her beyond measure. Yet at the same time, all of the fears and doubts she had carried disappeared. A sense of peace and calm replaced them. The disjointed bits and pieces of memory stitched themselves together into their full and proper order. She didn't even have to work for it.

She had never gone to Tasmania, though someone convinced her she had. No, shortly after she arrived at

Westbrook Manor, she had spent every minute of her time with Micah—her beloved guardian of the Bewitan Fierd. They had embarked on an unbelievable journey to recover a key. They helped get a sweet Gehíwan warden through a portal into another dimension. His dimension, in fact, and she even knew why. During that time, she fell so deeply and hopelessly in love with Micah that her emptiness and despair now made perfect sense. She well understood the reason for the sorrow she had endured every minute of every single day during the past four and a half months. She also knew that Micah could take full responsibility for stealing away her memories on the final day they were together.

That sudden knowledge made her angrier than she could ever remember being in her life.

How dare he take her memories away from her! How dare he! Is that why he seemed so sure she would forget him? Did he accept her bet only because he believed he had some kind of power that could make her forget he ever existed? How, with any sense of decency or the honor he held so dear, could that be fair? Then again, maybe fairness had never been a consideration. Perhaps Micah made the bet simply to appease her because he never had any intention of seeing her again. Not ever.

Tala's throat tightened. She had difficulty swallowing past the pain as she wandered into her living room and over to the large picture window. Through her tears, her gaze settled on the picturesque view the window offered. She didn't really see it. Instead, she recalled the details of every memory she and Micah shared. For the preservation of her heart and soul, she didn't have any other choice. They were important because somewhere in there she could swear he said—

"By my way of reckoning, you're about a month and a half early, are you not?"

Tala whirled around to face the man who had captured her heart. Immense joy wrapped itself around her as she gazed into his deep brown eyes. He looked so happy to see her. "Oh, Micah, you came," she whispered. "You actually came."

"Why do you sound so surprised? I promised you I'd come if you called me, didn't I?" He folded her into his arms and she reveled in the joy of it. .

He brushed away the tear that had trickled down her cheek. His lips then joined with hers in a kiss that made her forget everything but this moment. That kiss led to another and then another still before a sense of time and place returned. Once it did, her indignation also returned, and in full force. She stiffened and then pushed against his chest with all of her might, but he held her fast. The amusement that filled his eyes didn't appease her anger. In fact, it had quite the opposite effect.

"Let me go, Micah," she sternly commanded.

The grin he so obviously fought broke through its barrier. "No, I don't think so. At least not until you've calmed down a bit."

"What makes you think such a need exists?" she asked.

He traced the side of her cheek with his finger. In so doing, he produced a delightful shiver that raced all the way down her spine. "Because that captivating fire in your eyes still rages. Since you have a number of fragile objects inside this house you might throw at me,

I think I'm quite happy holding you in my arms."

"Do I have just cause in throwing any number of my things at you?" she asked.

"None that I think can of," he blithely replied. "But apparently you think you have at least one."

Her eyes narrowed as she turned her head to the side. "How can you, in all honesty, say that?"

"I'm not sure I understand what you mean, Miss Westbrook."

"Ah, but your annoying smirk tells me you do. Therefore, I am not about to let you—"

He interrupted the remainder of her comment with another soul-shattering kiss that diffused her anger. Somehow, it also made her forget the reason for it in the first place. Besides, she shouldn't bicker with him, should she? Not when he held her so close and kissed her like he kissed her now.

Micah tightened his hold as he broke away from the kiss and nuzzled the side of her face. "I've missed you, Tala, you have no idea how much," he murmured.

She drew back just enough to gaze into his eyes. "I missed you, though I must confess I didn't understand just whom or what I missed—and mourned—until a few minutes ago."

"Believe me; I didn't think when I left that you that you'd have even the smallest memory of our past together or that you'd suffer in any way. I'm so sorry that despite my best efforts, you did. I didn't mean for that to happen. In truth, I don't know how it could have happened."

"So, you do have some kind of power that can erase memories then."

He nodded. "I do."

"As do all of the guardians?" she asked.

"Yes, and I'm sure you can understand the reason as well as the necessity for that."

"Why didn't you just ask me if I wanted those memories taken away from me? Shouldn't that have been my choice?"

Micah released a heavy breath and then turned his gaze toward her sofa. "Come on. Let's sit down, shall we? We might as well be comfortable while I answer your questions. Knowing you, we'll be here for quite a while."

He led over to the sofa, sat down and then cuddled her into arms. "All right, fire away."

"Why couldn't you just have trusted me? Do you really think I would've exposed your world to anyone else? I mean even if I had, not a soul would've believed me. They'd have me locked up for sure and that's not something I would've risked."

"Trust has nothing to do with it."

"Then what else?"

"I think you already know the answer to the question."

She shrugged. "Because mere mortals are not allowed even the smallest shred of knowledge that you exist? After all, that would cause complete and utter chaos. Everyone on this planet who is not a direct descendent of good ol' Alfred would scream bloody murder at the top of his or her lungs over the unfairness of it all. They and all of their lawyers would then drag all of you into court, and demand equal treatment. Right?"

"I'd say you went a little overboard, but you're on the right track." He paused for a moment. "Let me put it this way. In all of my centuries as a guardian, I have never once taken away the memory of what I am, or who I am, from anyone else. As I told you after we first met, very few of the men I've protected over the centuries ever glanced at my face. Those who did had no idea that I had come from a different realm or that by assignment, I protected them. They believed I was just like everyone else."

"Is that the case with the other guardians as well?" she asked.

"I can't answer that with any degree of certainty. I'm sure some of them have used that power a time or two though."

"So the memory wiping thing is something you don't normally use then." She waited for him to answer far longer than she thought necessary.

Finally, he cleared his throat. "Well, I can't speak for all of my colleagues, but like I just said, I've only used it on you. Just so you know, if I had any other choice at the time, I wouldn't have used that power. In truth, Tala, because of my own selfishness, I didn't want you to forget what we shared. I don't know. Maybe that part of me somehow withheld a portion of the power and allowed you to remember."

The beat of heart picked up its pace for the look in his eyes right now. That look scared her. "If you had another choice? Does that mean you didn't have a choice?"

"No, I didn't. I'm bound to keep the oaths I take, Tala. All of them. We can't pick and choose whatever pleases us at the time.

She stared at him as her mouth dropped. "You're not planning on making me forget that you're here right now, are you?"

He shifted his position so he could look at her more directly. "Tala—"

She placed a trembling hand against his lips. "No, you can't do that, Micah, you can't! You'll ruin everything."

He took hold of her hand and held onto it. "Wait a minute, let me fully explain how this works and then you can decide if you want me—"

"No, you don't understand. Decisions aren't necessary. Not now," she cut in. "I've already made them. I made them the moment I fell deeply in love with you, and I haven't changed my mind. Edward knows this already, and he said that I—"

"Wait just a minute." Micah searched her eyes. "You met Edward? You spoke with him?"

"Yes."

"When?"

She dropped her gaze to her lap and shrugged. "During my first visit to your world."

"Why didn't you tell me?" he asked.

"Well, you didn't ask. I didn't want to tell you if I didn't have to because—" she stopped short. She shouldn't have said that. Dear heaven, she shouldn't have said that.

Confusion filled his eyes. "Because what?"

Tala bit down on her lip. She couldn't have this conversation with him. Not now. At least not yet. She sought a way out of her dilemma and settled on the first thing that popped into her mind. "I'll tell you, I promise I will. But the answer needs a bit of an explanation. Can you bear with me while I give it even if you don't think it's relative? Please?"

"You know I can do that."

"Okay. I know this will sound strange and you'll probably think I'm just changing the subject, but I'm not—"

"Just tell me, Tala. I'll listen to everything you have to say. Don't be afraid."

She nodded. "All right, here goes. I remembered something the moment all of my memories returned, and it isn't something I remembered before. So it has to be something my subconscious spewed out along with everything else. At least, I hope so."

He cocked his head to the side as he gazed at her. "What did you remember?"

"I recalled, in complete and total detail, what happened at the portal before Dolph went through it— the chaos, the sound of voices, wolves howling, and all of the gunshots. I also remember what it felt like when that bullet slammed into my body."

Guilt marred his features. "I'm so sorry, Tala. That should never have happened, I should have—"

"You couldn't have stopped it, Micah," she interrupted. "The bullet went through you before it hit me. So, please don't blame yourself for something you couldn't have prevented. The only reason I'm telling you this part is so you understand what happened next."

"All right, please, go on."

"As you took me into your arms, I began to feel very light-headed. More so than I ever have before. The spinning that enveloped me seemed slow and gentle, like a slow moving whirlpool of ocean waves, if that makes sense. Pleasurable warmth filled every portion of my body. Then all at once a sensation of floating overcome me. That sensation filled me with pure delight. I wanted nothing more than to continue the journey wherever it led me. At the same time, I had the distinct impression that if I continued that journey, I wouldn't return from it. At that moment, I didn't care. I didn't want to return."

Micah swallowed hard as he gazed into her eyes. "You were dying."

"I think maybe I might've been, except…you talked to me then and the sound of your voice called me back. You asked me to stay with you, and not let go. You called a second time as well—at Velica's villa."

He confirmed her memories with a single nod, but said nothing.

"What I want to know, what I *have* to know, is why you did that? Wouldn't it have been so much easier for nature to take her course during either one of those moments? Your duty would have ended. You wouldn't have had to erase anything at all from my memory. Surely you must've considered that choice."

He swallowed hard. "No, I didn't. In fact, that option didn't even cross my mind. I couldn't let you die. I couldn't have lived with that. Not even for a day."

"Why? Is it because you would've believed you failed in your duty to protect me and you didn't want that failure to blemish your perfect record?" she prodded.

He huffed out a breath. "Don't be ridiculous. My duty didn't have anything to do with the need—"

"Then tell me what did, please. It's very important that I know."

"I asked you to stay with me because I love you, Tala. Do you understand that? I love you so much it hurts. I didn't think I could exist without seeing your beautiful face every once in awhile, even if you thought me nothing more than a stranger at such times in return."

Though she tried, she couldn't stop the smile that followed his declaration. Those were precisely the words she needed him to say. "Well, just so you know, from this moment forward, whenever I see your handsome face I'll know exactly who you are and I'll know just how very much I love you."

He drew his brows together. "No, Tala, you won't. Not in the way you mean, anyway. I'd like nothing better, you know this, but there are rules. There are some things you must understand before I—"

She shook her head. "No, Edward promised and if a guardian from the Bewitan Fierd won't ever go back on his word, then surely an ealdorman wouldn't either."

"Tala, I have no idea what you're talking about."

"I know you don't, in fact you couldn't, so I'll just tell you. During my first visit to your realm, Edward stopped by your home right after you left. I thought maybe he would kick me out or put me in jail or something. But he didn't. He said he came so that I could chat with him."

"And chat she did," said Edward as he suddenly appeared inside the room. He had a smile on his face and a twinkle in his eye. All the while his gaze darted back and forth between her and Micah.

At once Micah rose to his feet. "Edward—"

"Oh, sit back down, Micah," Edward said as he settled into the chair opposite the sofa. "For the time being you're not going anywhere. Therefore, you might as well make yourself comfortable while I provide a little enlightenment as to this interesting situation we find ourselves in, if that's all right with you, Tala?"

"Yes, please. I'm sure you can do a better job of it than I can."

"All right then. Let me tell you that during our visit Tala let me have it with both barrels blazing, as the saying goes. Since she didn't as much as pause long enough for a body to get a word in edgewise, I simply listened. I found her words had merit. Alongside her worthy list of arguments as to why I should allow the two of you to stay together within our realm, and how she could contribute, she had an additional advantage she didn't even know she had at the time. But that advantage is not important right now.

"What is important is our agreement. I told her that she had two obstacles she must overcome after you had her safely home. I must admit she didn't fully understand what that meant at the time since I didn't give her full disclosure. One, she had to call your name. Nothing more, nothing less. Two, after your arrival, you had to tell her that you loved her, without her point-blank asking you if you did. If she managed to complete those two conditions, then she would become the first female resident of the Bewitan realm, with duties of her own."

Tala turned her gaze toward Micah. The broad smile on his face surely matched hers. He took hold of her hand and all but squeezed the life out of it. "So, since the two conditions have been met, I get to stay with Micah forever, then. Right?"

"Indeed, you do. A promise is a promise. However, there is one truly fascinating thing in all of this. The bargain became completely unnecessary the moment the bullet passed from Micah and entered into you my dear, although none of us knew it at the time."

"Why?" Micah asked. "What difference could that possibly make?"

"That unfortunate incident made Tala immortal," Edward replied.

Tala gasped. "How?"

Edward dipped his head from side to side and shrugged. "We're not quite sure, since it's never happened before. However, we now believe it has something to do with the bullet that carried a small portion of Micah's blood into you. From everything we can determine, that small drop or two of immortal blood eventually overcame the mortal properties of your blood. The accident you had today confirmed as much."

"What accident?" Micah asked.

Tala glanced at Micah before she gave the ealdorman her full attention. "Are you speaking about my hand?" she asked.

"I am."

Micah's gaze darted back and forth between them. "What are you two talking about?"

"While I washed the dishes this morning, the glass I held shattered in my hand. As a result, I got a pretty deep cut. So deep, in fact, I thought I would need stitches, but I didn't. The wound healed all by itself and in a very short amount of time. That's when I remembered the damage the shifters did to your arm the day we met. After that, all of my memories returned."

"I see." Micah gazed at Edward. "Is that the advantage you just referred to?"

"No, that particular advantage has everything to do with bloodline and in something she said."

"What did I say and what do you mean by

bloodline?" she asked.

"You might recall that you once asked Micah if we had enough guardians to take care of all Alfred's descendents should the Gehíwan insurgents take their war to the human populace of this world. You made a valid point and it's one all of the ealdormen discussed at length. Such a thing is possible, you see. Now, the short answer is no, we probably don't. One way we can increase the number of our guardians is to invite the first-born *child* of each descending guardian into our realm, *if* the first-born son failed to have a son. The latter applies to you since you are the only child Curtis has ever produced."

Tala placed her hand over her heart. "Me? I don't understand."

"Your father carries the distinction that very few guardians ever do. He's not only a direct descendent of Alfred through his mother's line; he's also the first-born son of a first-born son bound by oath to protect Alfred's progeny. Your grandfather is a guardian within our realm right now. When the proper time comes, we'll invite your father to join us as well. Though we are muddling the order of things, these unique circumstances give us no other choice in the matter. Now, do either of you have any further questions before I go?"

"Just one," Micah said. "I only think it proper that if Tala is going to live with me, that she does so as my wife. There won't be any problem with that, will there?"

"None that I can see and I would expect no less from you. Since we don't have any clergymen among us, I suppose you'll have to take care of that here. Oh, and uh, I suggest you don't dawdle in this realm overly long. Sooner rather than later I'm sure, someone will pop up with news of another assignment at the most inopportune time and the most inopportune place, if you understand my meaning."

Edward rose from his seat as did they. Tala took a step toward the ealdorman and gave him a kiss on the cheek. "Thank you, Edward, thank you for everything."

Micah held out a hand which Edward readily grasped. "I can't thank you enough either."

"Well, if any of our guardians deserve this concession, it's you, Micah. Now, let's just hope this decision doesn't open the proverbial can of worms we'll soon regret, shall we?"

As Edward disappeared from the room, Micah tugged her into his arms. For several moments, he did nothing more than gaze into her eyes. "I suppose I shouldn't assume what I ought not. It never even occurred to me that I'd have the opportunity to do this, so I'm not as prepared as I'd like to be. Had I had known the outcome of this day in advance, I would've provided you a most romantic evening, maybe brought you some flowers and that chocolate you love so much."

"Micah, you don't—"

"Shh, just let me finish. I love you, Tala, with a powerful love that is infinite in its very nature. The depth and strength of that love is something no words can describe. Just know that it exists. Know that it will grow stronger with the rising of each sun. I waited my whole life for you. When I finally found you, I didn't think I had a snowball's chance in the flaming pit of hell in making you mine. Now I find that's not so. You just don't know how grateful I am you had such an amazing influence on Edward. So, having said that, would you, Tala Westbrook, marry me and remain at my side for no less than forever and a day? I promise you, the flowers and chocolate will come later."

Tala threw her arms around his neck. Since she couldn't speak past the lump in her throat, she simply nodded and then cried like a baby until the tears ran dry.

Micah kissed her then, and that sweet, gentle kiss somehow not only conveyed his love, but also declared the deep passion stirring in him as well.

He cleared his throat. "Would you think me unreasonable if I asked you to marry me right now? I mean, I think we've waited long enough, don't you?"

That statement, and the look in his eyes, turned her insides into a churning puddle of mush that her swarm of butterflies had trouble mucking through.

"I'd love to marry you right now, this very minute. I just don't how we can. You might not know this, but we must have a marriage license before a judge or a clergyman will marry us. That requires some sort of photo identification on both our parts. Can you somehow conjure a driver's license or use your Jedi mind tricks to make them believe you have one?"

He flashed a devilish grin. "Everything is possible. So is getting married in a time where a marriage license, or Jedi mind tricks, isn't required."

Tala's smile grew ever broader. "If that isn't just the most wondrous idea I've ever heard, then I don't know what is! You couldn't have come up with a better solution than that, Micah. Now that you've brought the obvious to my attention, I wouldn't marry you anywhere else."

He shrugged away the compliment. "I do have my moments from time to time."

"So, what do you suggest for the when and the where?"

"Oh, no. I came up with the idea. You come up with the time and place. Just, uh, don't take more than fifteen minutes to plan this out."

Chapter Nineteen

For a moment, Micah simply watched his beautiful wife as she sat on the rock and gazed out over the ocean. Finding her here didn't surprise him in the least. Tala never missed an opportunity to see a sunrise. Today, the billowy clouds in their varying shades of gold, red, and gray, not only colored the sky for as far as the eye could see, but cast a shimmering reflection on the rollicking ocean waves as well. He tucked away the memory and then stepped toward her, because right now he wanted her in his arms more than he wanted anything else.

"Good morning, Mrs. Berrington," he said as he approached her.

With a beautiful smile on her face, she rose to her feet, whirled around and faced him full on. "Oh, Micah! You're back!"

At once he drew her into his arms and held her just as close as he could get her while still allowing her breath. He then indulged his overwhelming need and kissed her as he had never kissed her before. She kissed him back and with a burning passion that equaled his own. He should've expected as much, given the length of his first absence away from her. Yet, before he took advantage of their rising passion, he had something he just had to share with her. He loosened his hold and gazed into her beautiful violet-blue eyes, the sight of which had never strayed far from his mind all the while he had attended his latest duty. "I've missed you, Tala."

The declaration broadened her smile. "I've missed you too, more so than you'll ever know."

He grinned. "Is that right? I would've thought with all of the rigorous training, you wouldn't have had the time to give me more than a passing thought."

She shrugged away the notion. "Not so. Didn't you know? There's no amount of training, rigorous or otherwise, that can silence the voice of the heart."

"I whole-heartedly concur with that, my love." He gave her a wink. "So in speaking of that training, I must tell you Edward is very pleased with your progress."

"He is? When did you talk to him?"

"Just now. After I reported in, he said you had far exceeded all of his highest expectations. Furthermore, he said if the rising generations of Alfred's female descendents were anything like you, then they'd be quite an asset to our realm."

"You don't know just how happy that makes me. I've been working very hard."

"So I've heard."

"Well to be honest, there have been a few things that have been a little more difficult than others."

"Oh? Like what?"

"From all appearances, it seems that some of the guardians are less than pleased with a woman disrupting their well-ordered structure."

"Edward told me about that as well. You needn't worry though; you'll win them all over before long."

"Do you really think so?"

"I know so." He cocked his head toward the rock she had just occupied. "So all that aside, what had you so lost in thought this morning?"

A winsome smile touched her lips. "You. Always you."

The simple answer warmed his heart and prompted a grin. "What about me?"

"An assortment of things, I guess. I don't really recall what got it all started, but the memory of our wedding day flooded into my mind as I walked along the beach. That led to the ceremony when we stood before that minister in his little white church, in the middle of the nineteenth century. I'll never forget it, Micah, not ever."

"Neither will I, but now that you bring it up, I must confess I had a little concern at that very moment. The vicar stared at us so long and so hard I wondered if he'd marry us at all. I thought we might have to find another church or local judge or maybe something even more drastic."

A soft breath of laughter accompanied her nod. "Me too. I thought maybe we weren't properly dressed for the time period and that gave him pause for concern."

"Either that or he simply couldn't believe how such a beautiful woman would consent to marry the likes of me. I think he just wanted to make sure you were sure."

She turned her head to the side and sniffed. "Don't be ridiculous. If anything, his hesitation came out of fear over your intimidating height and form, especially in comparison to his. You probably scared him half to death. Maybe he wondered if he had cause to fear for his life."

Micah chuckled. "Whatever his reason, I'm grateful he finally performed the ceremony. I remember my patience wearing quite thin."

"I know." She blessed him then with an enchanting smile. "Of course, I can't ever think of our wedding without thinking of the wondrous days that followed, nestled inside Velica's villa. They are among my most treasured memories you know that, don't you?"

"As they are mine. Now for my sake, you must hold onto that very thought for a little while longer. Because right now I have some news I must share with you before I forget and then get myself in trouble for it."

"Well, we can't have that, now can we—and especially not upon your return," she teased.

"No we can't, so here goes. Edward has just given me another assignment, and this time—"

"No, that's not fair, Micah," she cut in. "You just got home. Can't they send someone else, please?"

"I'm afraid not. You know they match the guardian with the person in need of protection." Even as she lowered her gaze and sighed, he gently tilted her chin upward. "You didn't let me finish."

"I'm sorry, please continue."

"That's just it. There's no need for any kind of sorrow at all. You see this time you'll be coming with me."

She drew in a shallow breath and held on to it. "I will?"

"You will. Edward thinks we have the potential of working very well together. With this assignment, he'll see if he's correct in his assumption. Without any doubt I know we'll prove him right."

"Yes, we will!" She threw her arms around his neck and as he lifted her off of her feet she laughed.

"Oh, Micah! Let's go thank him."

He lowered her to the ground and gave her a wink. "Absolutely not. That's not at all necessary I assure you. Besides, I don't want to take what little private time we have together, and spend it at the Frithgeard if you don't mind."

"I don't mind at all. So where are we going, and did Edward say anything else in regards to our assignment?"

He took hold of her hand and as they began their stroll toward the cottage, he gazed into her eyes. "Not all that much, really. He just said he found it extraordinary your talents and skills complemented mine. Therefore, from his very astute observation, I think we can assume he'll assign us to work together quite often."

"I couldn't ask for anything better than that."

"Neither could I, my love; neither could I. As far as our destination goes? We'll be in Austria by day's end. I'll fill you in on all of the details later, but as things stand right now, we shouldn't be gone more than a couple of weeks."

Tala dipped her head from side to side. "Yes, well, if you recall, that's what you thought when Edward assigned you to me."

"True, but the lad we'll protect in the days ahead isn't the troublesome sort as were you. So, probably just a week or two should do it and that suits me fine."

She halted in her tracks as delightful indignation flashed from her eyes. "Why would you say such a thing? I am not, nor was I ever, the troublesome sort."

"Oh, but you were and still are, my love. Look at it this way. If not for your reckless, impulsive nature, and your knack for getting yourself into trouble, we wouldn't be where we are right now."

She mulled that over and then nodded. "All right, I'll give you that one. So hurrah then for my reckless, impulsive nature."

"I'll second that."

Tala slipped into her thoughts and for a short while they walked in silence. Finally, she turned her gaze toward him. "How many people have you protected over the centuries Micah?"

"I really don't know. I stopped counting a long time ago."

"Do you ever get tired of it?" she asked.

"Not so far. At least to this point, I have always enjoyed what I do. Why do you ask, are you afraid you'll get tired of it after awhile?"

"No, I don't think I ever will. I just wondered—that's all."

"Well, I suppose in all fairness I should tell you such a thing isn't unheard of in this realm. There were a few of our guardians, mostly the older ones, who did grow tired of the oath they had taken and—in a manner of speaking—retired from duty."

She drew her brows together. "Oh. How does one retire?"

"Please keep in mind it has only happened a handful of times. But, as I told you once before, it all comes down to a matter of choice. Hence, there are those who choose not to become guardians at all, and others who decide they want to move on after having honorably served."

"I understand that, but where do they go?" she asked as they climbed the steps leading to their cottage.

"By all accounts, they go to Heaven."

"Really? How exactly do they get there from here? I mean, I've always thought the entrance to Heaven followed one's death and then by invitation only. A guardian can't die. He's already immortal, for goodness sake."

"That's true. But Heaven is just a place Tala, and as such, a guardian can step into that realm just as easily as they can anywhere else."

"I see."

Micah put a hand on the door handle but didn't open the door. He turned and gazed into her eyes. "I'm not going to regret telling you all of this, am I?"

"Why would you regret it? I would probably have found out eventually anyway. So—"

"True enough, but I'm the one who just planted the seed. Therefore, I'll be the one responsible if someday you leave me behind."

Tala lifted her hand to his face and as she caressed the length of his jaw, an undeniable look of love and passion filled her eyes. Specifically, the love and passion she had for him. He responded to it just as he had every time before. With a gentle tug, she urged his lips to meet with hers. He didn't waste any time at all in accepting the invitation that left them both very short of breath.

"I would never leave you behind, Micah, not ever," she whispered. "You are my heart and my soul. Just so you know? I *am* in Heaven whenever I'm with you. I'll never have the need or the desire to go anywhere but where you are."

"That's a compliment I can return in full." Micah grinned as he opened the door. "Now if you just accompany me inside, I believe we can find a little bit of Heaven right here at home before we head for Austria in about six hours from now."

Far sooner than he might've liked, a persistent knock sounded at the door. Micah dropped a heavy sigh and shook his head. One would think the guardians would allow him and Tala their last few private moments together without interruption.

"We're in the courtyard," he hollered out. Seconds later Nathaniel and Levi made their appearance.

"There you are, even if you are a bit surly," Levi said. "I thought maybe the two of you had already taken off."

Micah wrapped his arms a little tighter around Tala as she stood in front of him. "Nope, as you can see, Tala and I are simply enjoying the view with what little time we have left."

"Yes, I can see that."

"So what brings you here?" he asked.

"Edward sent me with a message. He says your assignment has changed a little bit from when he last spoke with you. That change might complicate things beyond what he first thought," Levi replied.

"In what way?"

Nathaniel shrugged. "He said just before your foreign correspondent boarded the plane bound for Austria, his boss called and told him they were sending him to Kosovo instead. Edward said that'll give you a couple of extra hours at home if you want them. He also wants you to stop in on the way out. He'll fill you in on all of the additional details once you get there."

"All right, we'll do that." The kiss Micah dropped against Tala's cheek put a radiant smile on her face.

"Whoa now," Levi said as his eyes darted back and forth between them. "Any more of that and I'll feel like I'm intruding."

"You are intruding," Micah replied.

"Okay then, I can take a hint. Come on Nathaniel; let's leave Micah to his marital bliss."

"Try not to be jealous, Levi," Micah countered.

Levi chuckled. "I don't see any reason for that, my friend. No disrespect to you Tala, but the way I look at it, why settle for one beautiful woman, when I can enjoy the company of so many of them in the eons ahead?"

Micah rolled his eyes as he huffed out a breath. "You know your way out, right?"

"Yeah, yeah, we're going. We do have other things to do after all."

Tala's gaze remained fixed on the glass doors long after the men had gone. Finally, she broke free of his embrace, turned around and gazed into his eyes. "What did he mean by that?"

"By what?" he asked, feigning ignorance.

"The many women comment. I know you hinted about that before, but I don't think I understood what it all meant."

"That's really not all that important right now." He paused. "Have you gotten everything you need for this assignment together?"

"You already know I have. Now answer the question please—or are you trying to evade it?"

"Not evade really, just put it off. The way I look at it, that particular discussion can wait for a far better time." Without meeting any resistance whatsoever, he cuddled her into his arms and lowered his lips onto hers. After all, right now they had more desirable things to do than discuss things better left unsaid.

Like spending a little more time in Paradise.

A word about the author...

Debbie is an author of paranormal and fantasy romance. She has a soft spot for fairy tales, the joy of falling in love, making an impossible love possible, and happily ever after endings. She loves music, art, beautiful sunrises, sunsets, the smell of rain, and thunderstorms.

When she is not busy conjuring her latest novel, Debbie spends time with the members of her very large family within the lovely, arid deserts of southern Nevada. She also pursues her interests in family history, which she also teaches, mythology, and history.

Debbie is the author of *Court of the Hawk, Spirit of the Knight, Spirit of the Revolution,* and *Spirit of the Rebellion*, all published by The Wild Rose Press.

www.dk-peterson.com

Thank you for purchasing
this publication of The Wild Rose Press, Inc.

If you enjoyed the story, we would appreciate your
letting others know by leaving a review.

For other wonderful stories,
please visit our on-line bookstore at
www.thewildrosepress.com.

For questions or more information
contact us at
info@thewildrosepress.com.

The Wild Rose Press, Inc.
www.thewildrosepress.com

Stay current with The Wild Rose Press, Inc.

Like us on Facebook

https://www.facebook.com/TheWildRosePress

And Follow us on Twitter
https://twitter.com/WildRosePress

www.ingramcontent.com/pod-product-compliance
Lightning Source LLC
Chambersburg PA
CBHW051520260626
47170CB00003B/711